'The late Ruth Rende
on crime fiction with 6
suspense' *The*

'Rendell was a prolific and hugely popular writer of intricately plotted mystery novels that combined psychological insight, social conscience and, not infrequently, teeth-chattering terror'
New York Times

'[Rendell is] wonderful at exploring the dark corners of the human mind, and the way private fantasies can clash and explode into terrifying violence'
Daily Mail

'Ms Rendell exercises a grip as relentless as an anaconda's' *Guardian*

'Ruth Rendell was unquestionably the most important British crime novelist of the past 50 years'
Mail on Sunday

'Rendell is a great storyteller who knows how to make sure that the reader has to turn the pages out of a desperate need to find out what is going to happen next' *Sunday Times*

"She is the peer of Kingsley Amis and Muriel Spark"
Evening Standard

'The most astonishing imagination in British crime fiction' *Daily Telegraph*

'There are few writers who can create characters of such convincing creepiness as Ruth Rendell . . . chilling in the extreme' *Times Literary Supplement*

Also available by Ruth Rendell

Omnibuses
Collected Short Stories
Collected Short Stories 2
Wexford: An Omnibus
The Second Wexford Omnibus
The Third Wexford Omnibus
The Fourth Wexford Omnibus
The Fifth Wexford Omnibus
Three Cases for Chief Inspector Wexford
The Ruth Rendell Omnibus
The Second Ruth Rendell Omnibus
The Third Ruth Rendell Omnibus

Chief Inspector Wexford Novels
From Doon with Death
A New Lease of Death
Wolf to the Slaughter
The Best Man to Die
A Guilty Thing Surprised
No More Dying Then
Murder Being Once Done
Some Lie and Some Die
Shake Hands For Ever
A Sleeping Life
Put on by Cunning
The Speaker of Mandarin
An Unkindness of Ravens
The Veiled One
Kissing the Gunner's Daughter
Simisola
Road Rage
Harm Done
The Babes in the Wood
End in Tears
Not in the Flesh
The Monster in the Box
The Vault
No Man's Nightingale

Short Stories
The Fallen Curtain
Means of Evil
The Fever Tree
The New Girlfriend
The Copper Peacock
Blood Lines
Piranha to Scurfy

Novellas
Heartstones
The Thief

Non-Fiction
Ruth Rendell's Suffolk
The Reason Why: An Anthology of the Murderous Mind

Novels
To Fear a Painted Devil
Vanity Dies Hard
The Secret House of Death
One Across, Two Down
The Face of Trespass
A Demon in My View
A Judgement in Stone
Make Death Love Me
The Lake of Darkness
Master of the Moor
The Killing Doll
The Tree of Hands
Live Flesh
Talking to Strange Men
The Bridesmaid
Going Wrong
The Crocodile Bird
A Sight for Sore Eyes
Adam and Eve and Pinch Me
The Rottweiler
Thirteen Steps Down
The Water's Lovely
Portobello
Tigerlily's Orchids
The Saint Zita Society
The Girl Next Door
Dark Corners

ruth rendell

PUT ON BY CUNNING

arrow books

8

Arrow Books
20 Vauxhall Bridge Road
London SW1V 2SA

Arrow Books is part of the Penguin Random House group of companies
whose addresses can be found at global.penguinrandomhouse.com

First published in Great Britain by Hutchinson in 1981
This edition first published in paperback by Arrow Books in 1982
Reissued by Arrow Books in 2010

www.penguin.co.uk

A CIP catalogue record for this book is available from the British Library.

ISBN 9780099534938

Typeset by Replika Press Pvt Ltd, India

Penguin Random House is committed to a sustainable future for
our business, our readers and our planet. This book is made from
Forest Stewardship Council® certified paper.

Printed and bound in Great Britain by Clays Ltd, St Ives plc

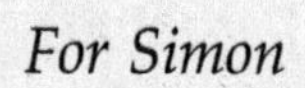

For Simon

So shall you hear . . .
Of deaths put on by cunning and forc'd cause;
And, in this upshot, purposes mistook
Fall'n on th'inventors' heads – all this can I
Truly deliver.

Hamlet

Part One

1

Against the angels and apostles in the windows the snow fluttered like plucked down. A big soft flake struck one of the Pre-Raphaelite haloes and clung there, cotton wool on gold tinsel. It was something for an apathetic congregation to watch from the not much warmer interior as the rector of St Peter's, Kingsmarkham, came to the end of the second lesson. St Matthew, chapter fifteen, for 27 January.

'For out of the heart proceed evil thoughts, murders, adulteries, fornications, thefts, false witness, blasphemies. These are the things which defile a man . . .'

Two of his listeners turned their eyes from the pattern the snow was making on a red and blue and yellow and purple 'Annunciation' and waited expectantly. The rector closed the heavy Bible with its dangling marker and opened an altogether more mundane-looking, small black book of the exercise variety. He cleared his throat.

'I publish the banns of marriage between Sheila Katherine Wexford, spinster, of this parish, and Andrew Paul Thorverton, bachelor, of the parish of St John, Hampstead. This is the first time of asking. And between Manuel Camargue, widower, of this parish, and Dinah Baxter Sternhold, widow, of the parish of St Mary, Forby. This is the third time of asking. If any of you know cause or just impediment why these persons should not be joined together in holy matrimony, ye are to declare it.'

He closed the book. Manuel Camargue resigned himself, for the third week in succession, to the sermon. As the congregation settled itself, he looked about him. The same crowd of old faithfuls came each week. He saw only one newcomer, a beautiful fair-haired girl whom he instantly recognized without being able to put a name to her. He worried about this a good deal for the next half-hour, trying to place her, annoyed with himself because his memory had become so hopeless and glasses no longer did much for his eyes.

The name came to him just as everyone was getting up to leave. Sheila Wexford. Sheila Wexford, the actress. That was who it was. He and Dinah had seen her last autumn in that Somerset Maugham revival, though what the name of the play had been escaped him. She had been at school with Dinah, they still knew each other slightly. Her banns had been called before his but her name hadn't registered because of that insertion of Katherine. It was odd that two people as famous as they should have had their banns called simultaneously in this country parish church.

He looked at her again. She was dressed in a coat of sleek pale fur over a black wool dress. Her eye caught his and he saw that she also recognized him. She gave him a quick faint smile, a smile that was conspiratorial, rueful, gay, ever so slightly embarrassed, all those things expressed as only an actress of her calibre could express them. Camargue countered with a smile of his own, the best he could do.

It was still snowing. Sheila Wexford put an umbrella up and made an elegant dash towards the lychgate. Should he offer her a lift to wherever she lived? Camargue decided that his legs were inadequate to running after her, especially through six-inch deep snow. When he reached the gate he saw her getting into a car driven by a man at least old enough to be her father. He felt a pang for her. Was this the bridegroom? And then the absurdity of such a thought, coming from him, struck him forcefully and with a sense which he often had of the folly of human beings and their blindness to their own selves.

Ted was waiting in the Mercedes. Reading the *News of the World*, hands in woollen gloves. He had the engine running to work the heater and the wipers and the demisters. When he saw Camargue he jumped out and opened the rear door.

'There you are, Sir Manuel. I put a rug in seeing it's got so perishing.'

'What a kind chap you are,' said Camargue. 'It was jolly cold in church. Let's hope it'll warm up for the wedding.'

Ted said he hoped so but the long range weather forecast was as gloomy as per usual. If he hadn't held his employer in such honour and respect he would have said he'd have his love to keep him warm. Camargue knew this and smiled to himself. He pulled the rug over his knees. Dinah, he thought, my Dinah. Towards her he felt a desire as passionate, as youthful, as intense, as any he had known as a boy. But he would never touch her, he knew better than that, and his mouth curled with distaste at the idea of it, of him and her together. It would be enough for him that she should be his dear companion – for a little while.

They had entered the gates and were mounting the long curving drive that led up to the house. Ted drove in the two channels, now filling once more with snow, which he had dug out that morning. From the smooth, pure and radiant whiteness, flung like a soft and spotless cloth over the hillocks and little valleys of Camargue's garden, rose denuded silver birches, poplars and willows, and the spikes of conifers, dark green and slate-blue and golden-yellow, as snugly clothed as gnomes.

The jam factory came into view quite suddenly. Camargue called it the jam factory, or sometimes the shoebox, because it was unlike any of the houses around. Not mock or real Tudor, not fake or genuine

Georgian, but a long box with lots of glass, and at one end, dividing the original building from the newer wing, a tower with a peaked roof like an oast house. Perched on the weathervane, a facsimile of a treble clef in wrought iron, was a seagull, driven inland in its quest for food. It looked as white as the snow itself against the cinder-dark sky.

Ted's wife, Muriel, opened the front door. You entered the house at the lower level, where it was built into the hillside. There was a wide hall here which led through an arch into the dining room.

'It's so cold, sir,' said Muriel, 'that I'm cooking you a proper lunch since you said you wouldn't be going to Mrs Sternhold's.'

'Jolly thoughtful of you,' said Camargue, who no longer much cared what he ate. Muriel took his coat away to dry it. She and Ted lived in a house in the grounds, a period piece and as much unlike the jam factory as could be. Camargue liked her to have her afternoons off and all of her Sundays, but he couldn't be always checking her generous impulses. When he was half-way up the stairs the dog Nancy came down to meet him, wide smiling mouth and eager pink tongue and young strong paws capable of sending him flying. She was his fifth Alsatian, a rich roan colour, just two years old.

The drawing room, two of its walls entirely glass, shone with the curious light that is uniquely reflected off snow. The phone began to ring as he stepped off the top stair.

'Were they well and truly called?'

'Yes, darling, the third time of asking. And at St Peter's?'

'Yes. My word, it was cold, Dinah. Is it snowing in Forby?'

'Well, it is but not all that heavily. Won't you change your mind and come? The main roads are all right and you know Ted won't mind. I do wish you'd come.'

'No. You'll have your parents. They've met me. Let them get over the shock a bit before Saturday.' Camargue laughed at her exclamation of protest. 'No, my dear, I won't come today. Muriel's cooking lunch for me. Just think, after Saturday you'll have to have all your meals with me, no excuses allowed.'

'Manuel, shall I come over this evening?'

He laughed. 'No, please.' It was strange how his accent became more marked when he talked to her. Must be emotion, he supposed. 'The villages will be cut off from Kingsmarkham by tonight, mark my words.'

He went into the music room, the dog following him. Up inside the cone-shaped roof of the tower it was dark like twilight. He looked at the flute which lay in its open case on the table, and then reflectively, no longer with pain, at his clawed hands. The flute had been exposed like that to show to Dinah's mother and Muriel would have been too much in awe of it to put it away. Camargue closed the lid of the case and sat down at the piano. He had never been much of a pianist, a second-class concert average, so it brought him no frustration or sadness to strum away occasionally with those (as he called them) silly old hands of his. He played *Für Elise* while Nancy, who adored piano music, thumped her tail on the marble floor.

Muriel called him to lunch. He went downstairs for it. She liked to lay the big mahogany table with lace and silver and glass just for him, and to wait on him. Far more than he had ever been or could ever be, she was aware of what was due to Sir Manuel Camargue. Ted came in as he was having coffee and said he would take Nancy out now, a good long hike in the snow, he said, she loved snow. And he'd break the ice at the edge of the lake. Hearing the chain on her lead rattle, Nancy nearly fell downstairs in her haste to be out.

Camargue sometimes tried to stop himself sleeping the afternoons away. He was rarely successful. He had a suite of rooms in the wing beyond the tower; bedroom, bathroom, small sitting room where Nancy's basket was, and he would sit determinedly in his armchair, reading or playing records – he was mad about James Galway at the moment. Galway, he thought, was heaps better than he had ever been – but he would always nod off. Often he slept till five or six. He put on the Flute Concerto, Köchel 313, and as the sweet, bright, liquid notes poured out, looked at himself in the long glass. He was still, at any rate, tall. He was thin. Thin like a ramshackle scarecrow, he thought, like an old junk-shop skeleton, with hands that looked as if every joint had been broken and put together again awry. *Tout casse, tout lasse, tout passe.* Now that he was so old he often thought in one or other of the two languages of his infancy. He sat down in the armchair and listened to the music Mozart wrote for a cantankerous Dutchman, and by the time the second movement had begun he was asleep.

Nancy woke him, laying her head in his lap. She had been back from her walk a long time, it was nearly five. Ted wouldn't come back to take her out again. Camargue would let her out himself and perhaps walk with her as far as the lake. It had stopped snowing, and the last of the daylight, a curious shade of yellow, gilded the whiteness and threw long blue shadows. Camargue took James Galway off the turntable and put him back in the sleeve. He walked along the passage and through the music room, pausing to straighten a crooked picture, a photograph of the building which housed the Camargue School of Music at Wellridge, and passed on into the drawing room. As he approached the tea tray Muriel had left for him, the phone rang. Dinah again.

'I phoned before, darling. Were you asleep?'

'What else?'

'I'll come over in the morning, shall I, and bring the rest of the presents? Mother and Dad had brought us silver pastry forks from my uncle, my godfather.'

'I must say, people are jolly generous, the second time round for both of us. I'll have the drive specially cleared for you. Ted shall be up to do it by the crack of dawn.'

'Poor Ted.' He was sensitive to the slight change in her tone and he braced himself. 'Manuel, you haven't heard any more from – Natalie?'

'From that woman,' said Camargue evenly, 'no.'

'I shall have another go at you in the morning, you know, to make you see reason. You're quite wrong about her, I'm sure you are. And to take a step like changing your will without . . .'

His accent was strong as he interrupted her. 'I saw her, Dinah, not you, and I know. Let's not speak of it again, eh?'

She said simply, 'Whatever you wish. I only want what's best for you.'

'I know that,' he said. He talked to her a little longer and then he went downstairs to make his tea. The tranquillity of the day had been marred by Dinah's raising the subject of Natalie. It forced him to think of that business again when he had begun to shut it out.

He carried the teapot upstairs and lifted the folded napkin from the plate of cucumber sandwiches. That woman, whoever she was, had made the tea and brought the pot up, and it was after that that she had looked at Cazzini's golden gift on the wall and he had known. As is true of all honest and guileless people, Camargue resented attempts to practise deceit on him far more than do those who are themselves deceitful. It had been a hateful affront, and all the worse because it had taken advantage of an old man's weakness and a father's affection. Dinah's plea did not at all alter his feelings. It only made him think he should have told the police or his solicitors, after all. But no. He had told the woman that he had seen through her and he had told her what he meant to do, and now he must do his best to forget it. Dinah was what future he had, Dinah would be his daughter and more than daughter.

He sat by the window with the curtains undrawn, watching the snow turn blue, then glow dully white again as the darkness closed in. The moon was coming up, a full, cold, midwinter's moon, a glowing greenish-white orb. At seven he took the tea things down and fed Nancy a large can of dog meat.

By the light of the moon he could see the lake quite clearly from the drawing-room window. To call it a lake was to flatter it, it was just a big pond really. It lay on the other side of the drive, down a shallow slope and ringed with willow trees and hawthorn bushes. Camargue could see that Ted, as good as his word, had been down to the pond that afternoon and broken the ice for air to get in to the fish. There were carp in the pond, some of them very large and very old. Ted's footprints led down to the water's edge and back up again to the drive. He had cast the ice on to the bank in great grey blocks. The moon showed it all up as well as any arc lamp. Nancy's pawprints were everywhere, and in places in the drifts there were signs of where she had plunged and rolled. He stroked her smooth brown head, drawing her against him, gently pushing her to settle down and sleep at his feet. The moon sailed in a black and shining sky from which all the heavy cloud had gone. He opened his book, the biography of an obscure Romanian composer who had once written an étude especially for him, and read for an hour or so.

When it got to half-past eight he could feel himself nodding off again, so he got up and stretched and stood in the window. To his surprise he saw it was snowing once more, snow falling out of the wrack which was drifting slowly over the clear sky and towards where the moon was. The conifers were powdered again, all but one. Then he saw the tree move. He had often thought that by night and in the half-light and through his failing eyes those trees looked like men. Now he had actually mistaken a man for a tree. Or a woman for a tree. He couldn't tell whether it had been Ted or Muriel that he had seen, a trousered figure in a heavy coat moving up now where the path must be towards the birch copse. It must have been one of them. Camargue decided to postpone letting Nancy out for ten minutes. If Ted saw him he would take over and fuss and probably insist on giving the dog a proper walk which she didn't need after all the exercise she had had. If Muriel saw him she would very likely want to come in and make him cocoa.

The figure in the garden had disappeared. Now the moon was no longer so bright. He couldn't remember that he had ever before seen such snow in all the years he had lived in Sussex. In his youth, in the Pyrenees, the snows had come like this with an even more bitter cold. It was remembering those days that had made him plant in this garden all the little fir trees and yews and junipers . . .

He could have sworn he saw another tree move. How grotesque was old age when the faculties one took for granted like trusted friends began to play on one malicious practical jokes. He called out:

'Nancy! Time to go out.'

She was there at the head of the stairs long before he was. If he had gone first she would have knocked him over. He walked down behind her, propelling her with his toe when she looked anxiously back and up at him. At the foot of the stairs he switched on the outside light to illuminate the wide court into which the drive led. The snowflakes danced like sparks in the yellow light but when he opened the door the sharp cold of the night rushed in to meet him. Nancy bounded out into the whirling snow. Camargue took his sheepskin coat and gloves and a walking-stick from the cloaks cupboard and followed her out.

She was nowhere to be seen, though her paws had ploughed a path down the slope towards the lake. He fastened his coat and pulled the woollen scarf up around his throat. Nancy, though well aware this outing was no regular walk but merely for the purpose of stimulating and answering a call of nature, nevertheless would sometimes go off. If the weather conditions were right, damp and muggy, for instance, or like this, she had been known to go off for half an hour. It would be a nuisance were she to do that tonight when he felt so tired that even on his feet, even with this icy air stinging his face, he could feel drowsiness closing in on him.

'Nancy! Nancy, where are you?'

He could easily go back into the house and phone Ted and ask him to come over and await the dog's return. Ted wouldn't mind. On the other hand, wasn't that yielding to the very helplessness he was always striving against? What business had he to be getting married, to be setting up house again, even recommencing a social life, if he couldn't do such a little thing for himself as letting a dog out before he went to bed? What he would do was return to the house and sit in the chair in the hall and wait for Nancy to come back. If he fell asleep her scraping at the front door would awaken him.

Even as he decided this he did the very opposite. He followed the track she had made down the slope to the lake, calling her, irritably now, as he went.

The marks Ted had made when he broke the ice at the water's edge were already obliterated by snow, while Nancy's fresh tracks were fast becoming covered. Only the stacked ice showed where Ted had been. The area he had cleared was again iced over with a thin grey crust. The lake was a sombre sheet of ice with a faint sheen on it that the clouded moon made, and the willows, which by daylight looked like so many crouched spiders or daddy-long-legs, were laden with snow that clung to them and changed their shape. Camargue called the dog again. Only last week she had done this to him and then had suddenly appeared out of nowhere and come skittering across the ice towards him.

He began breaking the new ice with his stick. Then he heard the dog behind him, a faint crunching on the snow. But when he turned round, ready to seize her collar in the hook of the walking-stick, there was no dog there, there was nothing there but the gnome conifers and the light shining down on the white sheet of the circular courtyard. He would break up the rest of the thin ice, clear an area a yard long and a foot wide as Ted had done, and then he would go back into the house and wait for Nancy indoors.

Again the foot crunched behind him, the tree walked. He stood up and turned and, raising his stick as if to defend himself, looked into the face of the tree that moved.

2

The music met Chief Inspector Wexford as he let himself into his house. A flute playing with an orchestra. This was one of Sheila's dramatic gestures, he supposed, contrived to time with his homecoming. It was beautiful music, slow, measured, secular, yet with a religious sound.

His wife was knitting, on her face the amused, dry, very slightly exasperated expression it often wore while Sheila was around. And Sheila would be very much around for the next three weeks, having unaccountably decided to be married from home, in her own parish church, and to establish the proper period of residence beforehand in her father's house. She sat on the floor, between the log fire and the record player, her cheek resting on one round white arm that trailed with grace upon a sofa cushion, her pale gold water-straight hair half covering her face. When she lifted her head and shook her hair back he saw that she had been crying.

'Oh, Pop, darling, isn't it sad? They've had this tremendous obituary programme for him on the box. Even Mother shed a tear. And then we thought we'd mourn him with his own music.'

Wexford doubted very much if Dora, a placid and eminently sensible woman, had expressed these extravagant sentiments. He picked up the record sleeve. Mozart, Concerto for Flute and Harp, K 229; the English Chamber Orchestra, conductor, Raymond Leppard; flute, Manuel Camargue; harp, Marisa Roblès.

'We actually heard him once,' said Dora. 'Do you remember? At the Wigmore Hall it was, all of thirty years ago.'

'Yes.'

But he could scarcely remember. The pictured face on the sleeve, too sensitive, too mobile to be handsome, the eyes alight with a kind of joyous humour, evoked no image from the past. The movement came to an end and now the music became bright, liquid, a singable tune, and Camargue, who was dead, alive again in his flute. Sheila wiped her eyes and got up to kiss her father. It was all of eight years since he and she had lived under the same roof. She had become a swan since then, a famous lady, a tele-face. But she still kissed him when he came and went, putting her arms around his neck like a nervous child. Wryly, he liked it.

He sat down, listening to the last movement while Dora finished her row in the Fair Isle and went to get his supper. Andrew's regular evening phone call prevented Sheila from getting full dramatic value out of her memorial to Camargue, and by the time she came back into the room the record was over and her father was eating his steak-and-kidney pie.

'You didn't actually know him, did you, Sheila?'

She thought he was reproaching her for her tears. 'I'm sorry, Pop, I cry so easily. It's a matter of having to learn how, you know, and then not being able to unlearn.'

He grinned at her. 'Thus on the fatal bank of Nile weeps the deceitful crocodile? I didn't mean that, anyway. Let me put it more directly. Did you know him personally?'

She shook her head. 'I think he recognized me in church. He must have known I come from round here.' It was nothing that she should be recognized. She was recognized wherever she went. For five years the serial in which she played the most beautiful of the air hostesses had been on television twice a week at a peak-viewing time. Everybody watched *Runway*, even though a good many said shamefacedly that they 'only saw the tail-end before the news' or 'the kids have it on'. Stewardess Curtis was famous for her smile. Sheila smiled it now, her head tilted reflectively. 'I know his wife-that-was-to-be personally,' she said. 'Or I used to. We were at school together.'

'A young girl?'

'Thank you kindly, father dear. Let's say young to be marrying Sir Manuel. Mid-twenties. She brought him to see me in *The Letter* last autumn but I didn't talk to them, he was too tired to come round afterwards.'

It was Dora who brought them back from gossip to grandeur. 'In his day he was said to be the world's greatest flautist. I remember when he founded that school at Wellridge and Princess Margaret came down to open it.'

'D'you know what its pupils call it? Windyridge.' Sheila mimed the blowing of a woodwind, fingers dancing. Then, suddenly, the tears had started once more to her eyes. 'Oh, to die like that!'

Who's Who is not a volume to be found in many private houses. Wexford had a copy because Sheila was in it. He took it down from the shelf, turned to the C's and read aloud:

'Camargue, Sir Manuel, Knight. Companion of Honour, Order of the British Empire, Chevalier of the Legion of Honour. British fluteplayer. Born Pamplona, Spain, 3 June, 1902, son of Aristide Camargue and Ana Parral. Educated privately with father, then at Barcelona Conservatoire. Studied under Louis Fleury.

'Professor of Flute, Madrid Conservatoire, 1924 to 1932. Fought on Republican side Spanish Civil War, escaped to England 1938. Married 1942 Kathleen Lister. One daughter. Naturalized British subject 1946. Concert flautist, has toured Europe, America, Australia, New Zealand and South Africa. Founded 1964 at Wellridge, Sussex, the Kathleen

Camargue School of Music in memory of his wife, and in 1968 the Kathleen Camargue Youth Orchestra. Recreations apart from music: walking, reading, dogs. Address: Sterries, Ploughman's Lane, Kingsmarkham, Sussex.'

'They say it's a dream of a house,' said Sheila. 'I wonder if she'll sell, that one daughter? Because if she does Andrew and I might really consider . . . Wouldn't you like me living just up the road, Pop?'

'He may have left it to your friend,' said Wexford.

'So he may. Well, I do hope so. Poor Dinah, losing her first husband that she *adored* and then her second that never was. She deserves some compensation. I shall write her a letter of sympathy. No, I won't. I'll go and see her. I'll phone her first thing in the morning and I'll . . .'

'I'd leave it a day or two if I were you,' said her father. 'First thing in the morning is going to be the inquest.'

'Inquest?' Sheila uttered the word in the loaded, aghast tone of Lady Bracknell. 'Inquest? But surely he died a perfectly natural death?'

Dora, conjuring intricately with three different shades of wool, looked up from her pattern. 'Of course he didn't. Drowning, or whatever happened to him, freezing to death, you can't call that natural.'

'I mean, he didn't do it on purpose and no one did it to him.'

It was impossible for Wexford to keep from laughing at these ingenuous definitions of suicide and homicide. 'In most cases of sudden death,' he said, 'and in all cases of violent death there must be an inquest. It goes without saying the verdict is going to be that it was an accident.'

Misadventure.

This verdict, which can sound so grotesque when applied to the death of a baby in a cot or a patient under anaesthetic, appropriately described Camargue's fate. An old man, ankle-deep in snow, had lost his foothold in the dark, slipping over, sliding into water to be trapped under a lid of ice. If he had not drowned he would within minutes have been dead from hypothermia. The snow had continued to fall, obliterating his footprints. And the frost, ten degrees of it, had silently sealed up the space into which the body had slipped. Only a glove – it was of thick black leather and it had fallen from his left hand – remained to point to where he lay, one curled finger rising up out of the drifts. Misadventure.

Wexford attended the inquest for no better reason than to keep warm, the police station central heating having unaccountably broken down the night before. The venue of the inquest (Kingsmarkham Magistrates' Court, Court Two, Upstairs) enjoyed a reputation for being kept in winter at a temperature of eighty degrees. To this it lived up. Having left his rubber boots just inside the door downstairs, he sat at the back of the court, basking in warmth, surreptitiously peeling off various disreputable layers, a khaki green plastic mac of muddy translucency, an aged black-and-grey herringbone-tweed overcoat, a stole-sized scarf of matted fawnish wool.

Apart from the *Kingsmarkham Courier* girl in one of the press seats, there were only two women present, and these two sat so far apart as to give the impression of choosing each to ostracize the other. One would be the daughter, he supposed, one the bride. Both were dressed darkly, shabbily and without distinction. But the woman in the front row had the eyes and profile of a Callas, her glossy black hair piled in the fashion of a Floating World geisha, while the other, seated a yard or two from him, was a little mouse, headscarfed, huddled, hands folded. Neither, as far as he could see, bore the remotest resemblance to the face on the record sleeve with its awareness and its spirituality. But when, as the verdict came, the geisha woman turned her head and her eyes, dark and brilliant, for a moment met his, he saw that she was far older than Sheila, perhaps ten years older. This, then, must be the daughter. And as the conviction came to him, the coroner turned his gaze upon her and said he would like to express his sympathy with Sir Manuel's daughter in her loss and a grief which was no less a personal one because it was shared by the tens of thousands who had loved, admired and been inspired by his music. He did not think he would be exceeding his duty were he to quote Samuel Johnson and say that it matters not how a man dies but how he has lived.

Presumably no one had told him of the dead man's

intended re-marriage. The little mouse got up and crept away. Now it was all over, the beauty with the black eyes got up too – to be enclosed immediately in a circle of men. This of course was chance, Wexford told himself, they were the escort who had brought her, her father's doctor, his servant, a friend or two. Yet he felt inescapably that this woman would always wherever she was be in a circle of men, watched, admired, desired. He got back into his coverings and ventured out into the bitter cold of Kingsmarkham High Street.

Here the old snow lay heaped at the pavement edges in long, low mountain ranges and the new snow, gritty and sparkling, dusted it with fresh whiteness. A yellowish-leaden sky looked full of snow. It was only a step from the court to the police station, but a long enough step in this weather to get chilled to the bone.

On the forecourt, between a panda car and the chief constable's Rover, the heating engineer's van was still parked. Wexford went tentatively through the swing doors. Inside it was as cold as ever and Sergeant Camb, sitting behind his counter, warmed mittened hands on a mug of steaming tea. Burden, Wexford reflected, if he had any sense, would have taken himself off somewhere warm for lunch. Very likely to the Carousel Café, or what used to be the Carousel before it was taken over by Mr Haq and became the Pearl of Africa.

This was a title or sobriquet given (according to Mr Haq) to Uganda, his native land. Mr Haq claimed to serve authentic Ugandan cuisine, what he called 'real' Ugandan food, but since no one knew what this was, whether he meant food consumed by the tribes before colonization or food introduced by Asian immigrants or food eaten today by westernized Ugandans, or what these would be anyway, it was difficult to query any dish. Fried potatoes and rice accompanied almost everything, but for all Wexford knew this might be a feature of Ugandan cooking. He rather liked the place, it fascinated him, especially the plastic jungle vegetation.

Today this hung and trembled in the steamy heat and seemed to sweat droplets on its leathery leaves. The windows had become opaque, entirely misted over with condensation. It was like a tropical oasis in the Arctic. Inspector Burden sat at a table eating Nubian chicken with rice Ruwenzori, anxiously keeping in view his new sheepskin jacket, a Christmas present from his wife, which Mr Haq had hung up on the palm tree hatstand. He remarked darkly as Wexford walked in that anyone might make off with it, you never could tell these days.

'Round here they might cook it,' said Wexford. He also ordered the chicken with the request that for once potatoes might not come with it. 'I've just come from the inquest on Camargue.'

'What on earth did you go to that for?'

'I hadn't anything much else on. I reckoned it would be warm too and it was.'

'All right for some,' Burden grumbled. 'I could have found a job for you.' Since their friendship had deepened, some of his old deference to his chief, though none of his respect, had departed. 'Thieving and break-ins, we've never had so much of it. That kid old Atkinson let out on bail, he's done three more jobs in the meantime. And he's not seventeen yet, a real little villain.' Sarcasm made his tone withering. 'Or that's what I call him. The psychiatrist says he's a pathological kleptomaniac with personality-scarring caused by traumata broadly classifiable as paranoid.' He snorted, was silent, then said on an altered note, 'Look, do you think you were wise to do that?'

'Do what?'

'Go to that inquest. People will think . . . I mean, it's possible they might think . . .'

'People will think!' Wexford scoffed. 'You sound like a dowager lecturing a debutante. What will they think?'

'I only meant they might think there was something fishy about the death. Some hanky-panky. I mean, they see you there and know who you are and they say to themselves, he wouldn't have been there if it had all been as straightforward as the coroner . . .'

He was saved from an outburst of Wexford's temper by an intervention from outside. Mr Haq had glided up to beam upon them. He was small, smiling, very black yet very Caucasian, with a mouthful of startlingly white, madly uneven, large teeth.

'Everything to your liking, I hope, my dear?' Mr Haq called all his customers 'my dear', irrespective of sex, perhaps supposing it to be a genderless term of extreme respect such as 'excellency.' 'I see you are having the rice Ruwenzori.' He bowed a little. 'A flavourful and scrumptious recipe from the peoples who live in the Mountains of the Moon.' Talking like a television commercial for junk food was habitual with him.

'Very nice, thank you,' said Wexford.

'You are welcome, my dear.' Mr Haq smiled so broadly that it seemed some of his teeth must spill out. He moved off among the tables, ducking his head under the polythene fronds which trailed from polyethylene pots in polystyrene plant-holders.

'Are you going to have any pudding?'

'Shouldn't think so,' said Wexford, and he read from the menu with gusto, 'Cake Kampala or ice cream eau-de-Nil – does he mean the colour or what it's made of? Anyway, there's enough ice about without eating it.' He hesitated. 'Mike, I don't see that it matters what people think in this instance. Camargue met his death by misadventure, there's no doubt about that. Surely, though interest in the man will endure for years, the manner of his death can only be a nine days' wonder. As a matter of fact, the coroner said something like that.'

Burden ordered coffee from the small, shiny, damson-eyed boy, heir to Mr Haq, who waited at their table. 'I suppose I was thinking of Hicks.'

'The manservant or whoever he was?'

'He found that glove and then he found the body. It wasn't really strange but it might look strange the way he found the dog outside his back door and took her back to Sterries and put her inside without checking to see where Camargue was.'

'Hicks's reputation won't suffer from my presence in court,' said Wexford. 'I doubt if there was a soul there, bar the coroner, who recognized me.' He chuckled. 'Or if they did it'd only be as Stewardess Curtis's dad.'

They went back to the police station. The afternoon wore away into an icy twilight, an evening of hard frost. The heating came on with a pop just as it was time to go home. Entering his living room, Wexford was greeted by a large, bronze-coloured Alsatian, baring her teeth and swinging her tail. On the sofa, next to his daughter, sat the girl who had crept away from the inquest, Camargue's pale bride.

3

He had noticed the Volkswagen parked in the ruts of ice outside but had thought little of it. Sheila got up and introduced the visitor.

'Dinah, this is my father. Pop, I'd like you to meet Dinah Sternhold. She was engaged to Sir Manuel, you know.'

It was immediately apparent to Wexford that she had not noticed him at the inquest. She held out her small hand and looked at him without a flicker of recognition. The dog had backed against her legs and now sat down heavily at her feet, glaring at Wexford in a sullen way.

'Do forgive me for bringing Nancy.' She had a soft low unaffected voice. 'But I daren't leave her alone, she howls all the time. My neighbours complained when I had to leave her this morning.'

'She was Sir Manuel's dog,' Sheila explained.

A master-leaver and a fugitive, Wexford reflected, eyeing the Alsatian who had abandoned Camargue to his fate. Or gone to fetch help? That, of course, was a possible explanation of the curious behaviour of the dog in the night.

Dinah Sternhold said, 'It's Manuel she howls for, you see. I can only hope she won't take too long to – to forget him. I hope she'll get over it.'

Was she speaking of the dog or of herself? His answer could have applied to either. 'She will. She's young.'

'He often said he wanted me to have her if – if anything happened to him. I think he was afraid of her going to someone who might not be kind to her.'

Presumably she meant the daughter. Wexford sought about in his mind for some suitable words of condolence, but finding none that sounded neither mawkish nor pompous, he kept quiet. Sheila, anyway, could always be relied on to make conversation. While she was telling some rather inapposite Alsatian anecdote, he studied Dinah Sternhold. Her little round sallow face was pinched with a kind of bewildered woe. One might almost believe she had loved the old man and not merely been in it for the money. But that was a little too much to swallow, distinguished and reputedly kind and charming as he had been. The facts were that he had been seventy-eight and she was certainly fifty years less than that.

Gold-digger, however, she was not. She appeared

to have extorted little in the way of pre-marital largesse out of Camargue. Her brown tweed coat had seen better days, she wore no jewellery but an engagement ring, in which the ruby was small and the diamonds pinheads.

He wondered how long she intended to sit there, her hand grasping the dog's collar, her head bowed as if she were struggling to conquer tears or at least conceal them. But suddenly she jumped up.

'I must go.' Her voice became intense, ragged, charged with a sincerity that was almost fierce. 'It was so *kind* of you to come to me, Sheila. You don't know how grateful I am.'

'No need,' Sheila said lightly. 'I wanted to come. It was kind of *you* to drive me home. I had a hire car, Pop, because I was scared to drive in the snow but Dinah wasn't a bit scared to bring me back in the snow and the dark.'

They saw Dinah Sternhold out to her car. Ice was already forming on the windscreen. She pushed the dog on to the back seat and got to work competently on the windows with a de-icing spray. Wexford was rather surprised that he felt no compunction about letting her drive away, but her confidence seemed absolute, you could trust her somehow to look after herself and perhaps others too. Was it this quality about her that Camargue had needed and had loved? He closed the gate, rubbed his hands. Sheila, shivering, ran back into the house.

'Where's your mother?'

'Round at Syl's. She ought to be back any minute. Isn't Dinah nice? I felt so sorry for her, I went straight over to Forby as soon as the inquest was over. We talked and talked. I think maybe I did her a bit of good.'

'Hmm,' said Wexford.

The phone started to ring. Andrew, punctual to the minute. 'Oh, darling,' Wexford heard Sheila say, 'do you remember my telling you about someone I know who was going to marry . . .' He began picking Alsatian hairs off the upholstery.

Father and daughter is not the perfect relationship. According to Freud, that distinction belongs to mother and son. But Wexford, looking back, could have said that he had been happy with his daughters and they with him, he had never actually quarrelled with either of them, there had never been any sort of breach. And if Sheila was his favourite he hoped this was so close a secret that no one but himself, not even Dora, could know it.

Any father of daughters, even today, must look ahead when they are children and anticipate an outlay of money on their wedding celebrations. Wexford realized this and had begun saving for it out of his detective inspector's salary, but Sylvia had married so young as almost to catch him napping. For Sheila he had been determined to be well prepared, then gradually, with wonder and a kind of dismay, he had watched her rise out of that income bracket and society in which she had grown up, graduate into a sparkling, lavish jet set whose members had wedding receptions in country mansions or else the Dorchester.

For a long time it had looked as if she would not

marry at all. Then Andrew Thorverton had appeared, a young businessman, immensely wealthy, it seemed to Wexford, with a house in Hampstead, a cottage in the country somewhere that his future father-in-law suspected was a sizeable house, a boat and an amazing car of so esoteric a manufacture that Wexford had never before heard of it. Sheila, made old-fashioned and sentimental by love, announced she would be married from home and, almost in the same breath, that she and Andrew would be paying for the entertainment of two hundred people to luncheon in the banquet room of the Olive and Dove. Yes, she insisted, it must be so and Pop must lump it or else she'd go and get married in a register office and have lunch at the Pearl of Africa.

He was slightly humiliated. Somehow he felt she ought to cut garment according to cloth, and his cloth would cover a buffet table for fifty. That was absurd, of course. Andrew wouldn't even notice the few thousand it would cost, and the bride's father would give her away, make a speech and hang on to his savings. He heard her telling Andrew she would be coming up to spend the weekend with him, and then Dora walked in.

'She won't be supporting her friend at the cremation then?'

Sheila had put the phone down. She was sometimes a little flushed and breathless when she had been talking to Andrew. But it was not now of him that she spoke. 'Dinah's not going to it. How could she bear it? Two days after what would have been their wedding day?'

'At least it's not the day itself,' said Wexford.

'Frankly, I'm surprised Sir Manuel's daughter didn't fix it on the day itself. She's capable of it. There's going to be a memorial service at St Peter's on Tuesday and everyone will be there. Solti is coming and probably Menuhin. Dinah says there are sure to be crowds, he was so much loved.'

Wexford said, 'Does she know if he left her much?'

Sheila delivered her reply slowly and with an actress's perfect timing.

'He has not left her anything. He has not left her a single penny.' She sank to the floor, close up by the fire, and stretched out her long legs. 'Her engagement ring and that dog, that's all she's got.'

'How did that come about? Did you ask her?'

'Oh, Pop darling, of course I did. Wasn't I with her for hours and hours? I got the whole thing out of her.'

'You're as insatiably inquisitive as your father!' cried Dora, revolted. 'I thought you went to comfort the poor girl. I agree it's not like losing a young fiancé, but just the same . . .'

'Curiosity,' quoted Wexford, 'is one of the permanent and certain characteristics of a vigorous intellect.' He chuckled. 'The daughter gets it all, does she?'

'Sir Manuel saw his daughter a week before he died and that was the first time he'd seen her for nineteen years. There'd been a family quarrel. She was at the Royal Academy of Music but she left and went off with an American student. The first

Camargue and his wife knew of it was a letter from San Francisco. Mrs Camargue – he wasn't a Sir then – got ill and died but the daughter didn't come back. She didn't come back at all till last November. Doesn't it seem frightfully unfair that she gets everything?'

'Camargue should have made a new will.'

'He was going to as soon as they were married. Marriage invalidates a will. Did you know that, Pop?'

He nodded.

'I can understand divorce would but I can't see why marriage.' She turned her legs, toasting them.

'You'll get scorch marks,' said Dora. 'That won't look very nice on the beach in Bermuda.'

Sheila took no notice. 'And what's more, he was going to cut the daughter out altogether. Apparently, that one sight of her was enough.'

Dora, won uneasily on to the side of the gossips, said, 'I wish you wouldn't keep calling her the daughter. Doesn't she have a name?'

'Natalie Arno. Mrs Arno, she's a widow. The American student died some time during those nineteen years. Dinah was awfully reticent about her, but she did say Camargue intended to make a new will, and since he said this just after he'd seen Natalie I put two and two together. And there's another thing, Natalie only got in touch with her father after his engagement to Dinah was announced. The engagement was in the *Telegraph* on 10 December, and on the 12th he got a letter from Natalie telling him she was back and could she come and see him? She wanted a reconciliation. It was obvious she was scared stiff of the marriage and wanted to stop it.'

'And your reticent friend told you all this?'

'She got it out of her, Dora. I can understand. She's a chip off the old block, as you so indignantly pointed out.' He turned once more to Sheila. 'Did she try to stop it?'

'Dinah wouldn't say. I think she hates discussing Natalie. She talked much more about Camargue. She really loved him. In a funny sort of daughterly, worshipping, protective sort of way, but she did love him. She likes to talk about how wonderful he was and how they met and all that. She's a teacher at the Kathleen Camargue School and he came over last Founder's Day and they met and they just loved each other, she said, from that moment.'

The somewhat cynical expressions on the two middle-aged faces made her give an embarrassed laugh. She seemed to take her mother's warning to heart at last, for she got up and moved away from the fire to sit on the sofa where she scrutinized her smooth, pale golden legs. 'At any rate, Pop darling, it's an ill wind, as you might say, because now the house is bound to be sold. I'd love to get a look at it, wouldn't you? Why wasn't I at school with Natalie?'

'You were born too late,' said her father. 'And there must be simpler ways of getting into Sterries.'

There were.

'You?' said Burden first thing the next morning.

'What do *you* want to go up there for? It's only a common-or-garden burglary, one of our everyday occurrences, I'm sorry to say. Martin can handle it.'

Wexford hadn't taken his overcoat off. 'I want to see the place. Don't you feel any curiosity to see the home of our former most distinguished citizen?'

Burden seemed more concerned with dignity and protocol. 'It's beneath you *and* me, I should think.' He sniffed. 'And when you hear the details you'll feel the same. The facts are that a Mrs Arno – she's the late Sir Manuel's daughter – phoned up about half an hour ago to say the house had been broken into during the night. There's a pane of glass been cut out of a window downstairs and a bit of a mess made and some silver taken. Cutlery, nothing special, and some money from Mrs Arno's handbag. She thinks she saw the car the burglar used and she's got the registration number.'

'I like these open-and-shut cases,' said Wexford. 'I find them restful.'

The fingerprint man (Detective Constable Morgan) had already left for Sterries. Wexford's car only just managed to get up Ploughman's Lane, which was glacier-like in spite of gritting. He had been a determined burglar, Burden remarked, to get his car up and down there in the night.

The top of the hill presented an alpine scene, with dark-green and gold and grey conifers rising sturdily from the snow blanket. The house itself, shaped like a number of cuboid boxes pushed irregularly together and with a tower in the midst of them, looked not so much white as dun-coloured beside the dazzling field of snow. A sharp wind had set the treble-clef weathervane spinning like a top against a sky that was now a clear cerulean blue.

Morgan's van was parked on the forecourt outside the front door which was on the side of the house furthest from the lane. Some attempt had been made to keep this area free of snow. Wexford, getting out of the car, saw a solidly built man in jeans and anorak at work sweeping the path which seemed to lead to a much smaller house that stood in a dip in the grounds. He looked in the other direction, noting in a shallow tree-fringed basin the ornamental water newspapers had euphemistically called a lake. There Camargue had met his death. It was once more iced over and the ice laden with a fleecy coat of snow.

The front door had been opened by a woman of about forty in trousers and bulky sweater whom Wexford took to be Muriel Hicks. He and Burden stepped into the warmth and on to thick soft carpet. The vestibule with its cloaks cupboard was rather small but it opened, through an arch, into a hall which had been used to some extent as a picture gallery. The paintings almost made him whistle. If these were originals . . .

The dining-room was open, revealing pale wood panelling and dark red wood furnishing, and in the far corner Morgan could be seen at his task. A flight of stairs, with risers of mosaic tile and treads that seemed to be of oak, led upwards. However deferential and attentive Mrs Hicks may have been towards Sir Manuel – and according to Sheila he had been adored by his servants – she had no courtesy to spare for policemen. That 'she' was upstairs somewhere was the only introduction they got. Wexford went upstairs while Burden joined Morgan in the dining room.

The house had been built on various different levels of land so that the drawing room where he found himself was really another ground floor. It was a large, airy and gracious room, two sides of which were made entirely of glass. At the farther end of it steps led down into what must surely be the tower. Here the floor was covered by a pale yellow Chinese carpet on which stood two groups of silk-covered settees and chairs, one suite lemon, one very pale jade. There was some fine *famille jaune* porcelain of that marvellous yellow that is both tender and piercing, and suspended from the ceiling a chandelier of startlingly modern design that resembled a torrent of water poured from a tilted vase.

But there was no sign of human occupation. Wexford stepped down under the arch where staghorn ferns grew in troughs at ground level and a *Cissus antarctica* climbed the columns, and entered a music room. It was larger than had appeared from outside and it was dodecagonal. The floor was of very smooth, polished, pale grey slate on which lay three Kashmiri rugs. A Broadwood grand piano stood between him and the other arched entrance. On each of eight of the twelve sides of the room was a picture or bust in an alcove, Mozart and Beethoven among the latter, among the former

Cocteau's cartoon of Picasso and Stravinsky, Rothenstein's drawing of Parry, and a photograph of the Georgian manor house in which the music school was housed at Wellridge. But on one of the remaining sides Camargue had placed on a glass shelf a cast of Chopin's hands and on the last hung in a glass case a wind instrument of the side-blown type which looked to Wexford to be made of solid gold. Under it was the inscription: 'Presented to Manuel Camargue by Aldo Cazzini, 1949'. Was it a flute and could it be of gold? He lifted the lid of a case which lay on a low table and saw inside a similar instrument but made of humbler metal, perhaps silver.

He was resolving to go downstairs again and send Muriel Hicks to find Mrs Arno, when he was aware of a movement in the air behind him and of a presence that was not wholly welcoming. He turned round. Natalie Arno stood framed in the embrasure of the further arch, watching him with an unfathomable expression in her eyes.

4

Wexford was the first to speak.

'Good morning, Mrs Arno.'

She was absolutely still, one hand up to her cheek, the other resting against one of the columns which supported the arch. She was silent.

He introduced himself and said pleasantly, 'I hear you've had some sort of break-in. Is that right?'

Why did he feel so strongly that she was liberated by relief? Her face did not change and it was a second or two before she moved. Then, slowly, she came forward.

'It's good of you to come so quickly.' Her voice was as unlike Dinah Sternhold's as it was reasonably possible for one woman's voice to differ from another's. She had a faint American accent and in her tone there was an underlying hint of amusement. He was always to be aware of that in his dealings with her. 'I'm afraid I may be making a fuss about nothing. He only took a few spoons.' She made a comic grimace, pursing her lips as she drew out the long vowel sound. 'Let's go into the drawing room and I'll tell you about it.'

The cast of her countenance was that which one would immediately categorize as Spanish, full-fleshed yet strong, the nose straight if a fraction too long, the mouth full and flamboyantly curved, the eyes splendid, as near to midnight black as a white woman's eyes can ever be. Her black hair was strained tightly back from her face and knotted high on the back of her head, a style which most women's faces could scarcely take but which suited hers, exposing its fine bones. And her figure was no less arresting than her face. She was very slim but for a too-full bosom, and this was not at all disguised by her straight skirt and thin sweater. Such an appearance, the ideal of men's fantasies, gives a woman a slightly indecent look, particularly if she carries herself with a certain provocative air. Natalie Arno did not quite do this but when she moved as she now did, mounting the steps to the higher level, she walked very sinuously with a stressing of her narrow waist.

During his absence two people had come into the drawing room, a man and a woman. They were behaving in the rather aimless fashion of house guests who have perhaps just got up or at least just put in an appearance, and who are wondering where to find breakfast, newspapers and an occupation. It occurred to Wexford for the first time that it was rather odd, not to say presumptuous, of Natalie Arno to have taken possession of Sterries so immediately after her father's death, to have moved in and to have invited people to stay. Did his solicitors approve? Did they know?

'This is Chief Inspector Wexford who has come to catch our burglar,' she said. 'My friends, Mr and Mrs Zoffany.'

The man was one of those who had been in the circle round her after the inquest. He seemed about forty. His fair hair was thick and wavy and he had a Viking's fine golden beard, but his body had grown soft and podgy and a flap of belly hung over the belt of his too-tight and too-juvenile fawn cord jeans. His wife, in the kind of clothes which unmistakably mark the superannuated hippie, was as thin as he was stout. She was young still, younger probably than Camargue's daughter, but her face was worn and there were coarse, bright threads of grey in her dark curly hair.

Natalie Arno sat down in one of the jade armchairs. She sat with elegant slim legs crossed at the calves, her feet arched in their high-heeled shoes. Mrs Zoffany, on the other hand, flopped on the floor and sat cross-legged, tucking her long patchwork skirt around her knees. The costume she wore, and which like so many of her contemporaries she pathetically refused to relinquish, would date her more ruthlessly than might any perm or pair of stockings on another woman. Yet not so long ago it had been the badge of an élite who hoped to alter the world. Sitting there, she looked as if she might be at one of the pop concerts of her youth, waiting for the entertainment to begin. Her head was lifted expectantly, her eyes on Natalie's face.

'I'll tell you what there is to tell,' Natalie began, 'and I'm afraid that's not much. It must have been around five this morning I thought I heard the sound of glass breaking. I've been sleeping in Papa's room. Jane and Ivan are in one of the spare rooms in the other wing. You didn't hear anything, did you, Jane?'

Jane Zoffany shook her head vehemently. 'I only wish I had. I might have been able to *help*.'

'I didn't go down. To tell you the truth I was just a little scared.' Natalie smiled deprecatingly. She didn't look as if she had ever been scared in her life. Wexford wondered why he had at first felt her presence as hostile. She was entirely charming. 'But I did look out of the window. And just outside the window – on that side all the rooms are more or less on the ground floor, you know – there was a van parked. I put the light on and took a note of the registration number. I've got it here somewhere. What did I do with it?'

Jane Zoffany jumped up. 'I'll look for it, shall I? You put it down somewhere in here. I remember, I was still in my dressing gown . . .' She began hunting about the room, her scarves and the fringe of her shawl catching on ornaments.

Natalie smiled, and in that smile Wexford thought he detected patronage. 'I didn't quite know what to do,' she said. 'Papa didn't have a phone extension put in his room. Just as I was wondering I heard the van start up and move off. I felt brave enough to go down to the dining room then, and sure enough there was a pane gone from one of the casements.'

'A pity you didn't phone us then. We might have got him.'

'I know.' She said it ruefully, amusedly, with a soft sigh of a laugh. 'But there were only those half-dozen silver spoons missing and two five-pound notes out of my purse. I'd left my purse on the sideboard.'

'But would *you* know exactly what was missing, Mrs Arno?'

'Right. I wouldn't really. But Mrs Hicks has been round with me this morning and she can't find anything else gone.'

'It's rather curious, isn't it? This house seems to me full of very valuable objects. There's a Kandinsky downstairs and a Boudin, I think.' He pointed. 'And those are signed Hockney prints. That yellow porcelain . . .'

She looked surprised at his knowledge. 'Yes, but . . .' Her cheeks had slightly flushed. 'Would you think me very forward if I said I had a theory?'

'Not at all. I'd like to hear it.'

'Well, first, I think he knew Papa used to sleep in that room and now poor Papa is gone he figured no one would be in there. And, secondly, I think he saw my light go on before he'd done any more than filch the spoons. He was just too scared to stop any longer. How does that sound?'

'Quite a possibility,' said Wexford. Was it his

imagination that she had expected a more enthusiastic or flattering response? Jane Zoffany came up with the van registration number on a piece of paper torn from an exercise book. Natalie Arno didn't thank her for her pains. She rose, tensing her shoulders and throwing back her head to show off that amazing shape. Her waist could easily have been spanned by a pair of hands.

'Do you want to see the rest of the house?' she said. 'I'm sure he didn't come up to this level.'

Wexford would have loved to, but for what reason? 'We usually ask the householder to make a list of missing valuables in a case like this. It might be wise for me to go round with Mrs Hicks . . .'

'Of *course*.'

Throughout these exchanges Ivan Zoffany had not spoken. Wexford, without looking at him, had sensed a brooding concentration, the aggrieved attitude perhaps of a man not called on to participate in what might seem to be men's business. But now, as he turned his eyes in Zoffany's direction, he got a shock. The man was gazing at Natalie Arno, had probably been doing so for the past ten minutes, and his expression, hypnotic and fixed, was impenetrable. It might indicate contempt or envy or desire or simple hatred. Wexford was unable to analyse it but he felt a pang of pity for Zoffany's wife, for anyone who had to live with so much smouldering emotion.

Passing through the music room, Muriel Hicks took him first into the wing which had been private to Camargue. Here all was rather more austere than what he had so far seen. The bedroom, study-cum-sitting-room and bathroom were all carpeted in Camargue's favourite yellow – wasn't it in the Luscher Test that you were judged the best-adjusted if you gave your favourite colour as yellow? – but the furnishings were sparse and there were blinds at the windows instead of curtains. A dress of Natalie's lay on the bed.

Muriel Hicks had not so far spoken beyond asking him to follow her. She was not an attractive woman. She had the bright pink complexion that sometimes goes with red-gold hair and piglet features. Wexford who, by initially marrying one, had surrounded himself with handsome women, wondered at Camargue who had a beautiful daughter yet had picked an ugly housekeeper and a nonentity for a second wife. Immediately he had thought that he regretted it with shame. For, turning round, he saw that Mrs Hicks was crying. She was standing with her hand on an armchair, on the seat of which lay a folded rug, and the tears were rolling down her round, red cheeks.

She was one of the few people he had ever come across who did not apologize for crying. She wiped her face, scrubbing at her eyes. 'I've lost the best employer,' she said, 'and the best friend anyone could have. And I've taken it hard, I can tell you.'

'Yes, it was a sad business.'

'If you'll look out of that window you'll see a house over to the left. That's ours. Really ours, I mean – he *gave* it to us. God knows what it's worth now. D'you know what he said? I'm not having you and Ted living in a tied cottage, he said. If you're good enough to come and work for me you deserve to have a house of your own to live in.'

It was a largish Victorian cottage and it had its own narrow driveway out into Ploughman's Lane. Sheila wouldn't have wanted it, he supposed, its not going with Sterries would make no difference to her. He put up a show for Mrs Hicks's benefit of scrutinizing the spot where Natalie Arno said the van had been.

'There weren't many like him,' said Muriel Hicks, closing the door behind Wexford as they left. It was a fitting epitaph, perhaps the best and surely the simplest Camargue would have.

Along the corridor, back through the music room, across the drawing room, now deserted, and into the other wing. Here was a large room full of books, a study or a library, and three bedrooms, all with bathrooms *en suite*. Their doors were all open but in one of them, standing in front of a long glass and studying the effect of various ways of fastening the collar of a very old Persian lamb coat, was Jane Zoffany. She rushed, at the sight of Wexford, into a spate of apologies – very nearly saying sorry for existing at all – and scuttled from the room. Muriel Hicks's glassy stare followed her out.

'There's nothing missing from here,' she said in a depressed tone. 'Anyway, those people would have heard something.' There was a chance, he thought, that she might lose another kind of control and break into a tirade against Camargue's daughter and her friends. But she didn't. She took him silently into the second room and the third.

Why had Natalie Arno chosen to occupy her father's bedroom, austere, utilitarian and moreover the room of a lately dead man and a parent, rather than one of these luxurious rooms with fur rugs on the carpets and duck-down duvets on the beds? Was it to be removed from the Zoffanys? But they were her friends whom she had presumably invited. To revel in the triumph of possessing the place and all that went with it at last? To appreciate this to the full by sleeping in the inner sanctum, the very holy of holies? It occurred to him that by so doing she must have caused great pain to Mrs Hicks, and then he reminded himself that this sort of speculation was pointless, he wasn't investigating any crime more serious than petty larceny. And his true reason for being here was to make a preliminary survey for a possible buyer.

'Is anything much kept in that chest?' he asked Mrs Hicks. It was a big teak affair with brass handles, standing in the passage.

'Only blankets.'

'And that cupboard?'

She opened it. 'There's nothing missing.'

He went downstairs. Morgan and his van had gone. In the hall were Burden, Natalie Arno and the Zoffanys, the man who had been sweeping the path, and a woman in a dark brown fox fur who had evidently just arrived.

Everyone was dressed for the outdoors and for bitterly cold weather. It struck Wexford forcefully, as he descended the stairs towards them, that Natalie and her friends looked thoroughly disreputable compared with the other three. Burden was always well turned-out and in his new sheepskin he was more than that. The newcomer was smart, even elegant, creamy cashmere showing above the neckline of the fur, her hands in sleek gloves, and even Ted Hicks, in aran and anorak, had the look of a gentleman farmer. Beside them Natalie and the Zoffanys were a rag-bag crew, Zoffany's old overcoat as shabby as Wexford's own, his wife with layers of dipping skirts hanging out beneath the hem of the Persian lamb. Nothing could make Natalie less than striking. In a coat that appeared to be made from an old blanket and platform-soled boots so out of date and so worn that Wexford guessed she must have bought them in a secondhand shop, she looked raffish and down on her luck. They were hardly the kind of people, he said to himself with an inward chuckle, that one (or the neighbours) would expect to see issuing from a house in Ploughman's Lane.

That the woman in the fur was one of these neighbours Burden immediately explained. Mrs Murray-Burgess. She had seen the police cars and then she had encountered Mr Hicks in the lane. Yes, she lived next door, if next door it could be called when something like an acre separated Kingsfield House from Sterries, and she thought she might have some useful information.

They all trooped into the dining room where Hicks resumed his task of boarding up the broken window. Wexford asked Mrs Murray-Burgess the nature of her information.

She had seen a man in the Sterries grounds. No,

not last night, a few days before. In fact, she had mentioned it to Mrs Hicks, not being acquainted with Mrs Arno. She gave Natalie a brief glance that seemed to indicate her desire for a continuation of this state of affairs. No, she couldn't recall precisely when it had been. Last night she had happened to be awake at five-thirty – she always awoke early – and had seen the lights of a vehicle turning out from Sterries into the lane. Wexford nodded. Could she identify this man were she to see him again?

'I'm sure I could,' said Mrs Murray-Burgess emphatically. 'And what's more, I *would*. All this sort of thing has got to be stopped before the country goes completely to the dogs. If I've got to get up in court and say that's the man! – well, I've got to and no two ways about it. It's time someone gave a lead.'

Natalie's face was impassive but in the depths of her eyes Wexford saw a spark of laughter. Almost anyone else in her position would now have addressed this wealthy and majestic neighbour, thanking her perhaps for her concern and public spirit. Most people would have suggested a meeting on more social terms, on do-bring-your-husband-in-for-a-drink lines. Many would have spoken of the dead and have mentioned the coming memorial service. Natalie behaved exactly as if Mrs Murray-Burgess were not there. She shook hands with Wexford, thanking him warmly while increasing the pressure of her fingers. Burden was as prettily thanked and given an alluring smile. They were ushered to the door, the Zoffanys following, everyone coming out into the crisp cold air and the bright sunlight. Mrs Murray-Burgess, left stranded in the dining room with Ted Hicks, emerged in offended bewilderment a moment or two later.

Wexford, no doubt impressing everyone with his frown and preoccupied air, was observing the extent of the double glazing and making rough calculations as to the size of the grounds. Getting at last into their car, he remarked to Burden – apropos of what the inspector had no idea – that sometimes these cogitations still amazed the troubled midnight and the noon's repose.

5

The owner of the van was quickly traced through its registration number. He was a television engineer called Robert Clifford who said he had lent the van to a fellow-tenant of his in Finsbury Park, north London, a man of thirty-six called John Cooper. Cooper, who was unemployed, admitted the break-in after the spoons had been found in his possession. He said he had read in the papers about the death of Camargue and accounts of the arrangements at Sterries.

'It was an invite to do the place,' he said impudently. 'All that stuff about valuable paintings and china, and then that the housekeeper didn't sleep in the house. She didn't either, the first time I went.'

When had that been?

'Tuesday night,' said Cooper. He meant Tuesday the 29th, two days after Camargue's death. When he returned to break in. 'I didn't know which was the old man's room,' he said. 'How would I? The papers don't give you a plan of the bloody place.' He had parked the van outside that window simply because it seemed the most convenient spot and couldn't be seen from the road. 'It gave me a shock when the light came on.' He sounded aggrieved, as if he had been wantonly interrupted while about some legitimate task. His was a middle-class accent. Perhaps, like Burden's little villain, he was a pathological kleptomaniac with personality-scarring. Cooper appeared before the Kingsmarkham magistrates and was remanded in custody until the case could be heard at Myringham Crown Court.

Wexford was able to give Sheila a favourable report on Camargue's house, but she seemed to have lost interest in the place. (One's children had a way of behaving like this, he had noticed.) Andrew's house in Keats Grove was really very nice, and he did have the cottage in Dorset. If they lived in Sussex they would have to keep a flat in town as well. She couldn't go all the way back to Kingsmarkham after an evening performance, could she? The estate agents had found a buyer for her own flat in St John's Wood and they were getting an amazing price for it. Had Mother been to hear her banns called for the second time? Mother had.

The day of the memorial service was bright and sunny. Alpine weather, Wexford called it, the frozen snow sparkling, melting a little in the sun, only to freeze glass-hard again when the sun went down. Returning from his visit to Sewingbury Comprehensive School – where there was an alarming incidence of glue-sniffing among fourteen-year-olds – he passed St Peter's church as the mourners were leaving. The uniform men wear disguises them. Inside black overcoat and black Homburg might breathe equally Sir Manuel's accompanist or Sir Manuel's wine merchant. But he was pretty sure he had spotted James Galway, and he stood to gaze like any lion-hunting sightseer.

Sheila, making her escape with Dinah Sternhold to a hire car, was attracting as much attention as anyone – a warning, her father thought, of what they might expect in a fortnight's time. The Zoffanys were nowhere to be seen but Natalie Arno, holding the arm of an elderly wisp of a man, a man so frail-looking that it seemed wonderful the wind did not blow him about like a feather, was standing on the steps shaking hands with departing visitors. She wore a black coat and a large black hat, new clothes they appeared to be and suited to the occasion, and she stood erectly, her thin ankles pressed together. By the time Wexford was driven away by the cold, though several dozen people had shaken hands with her and passed on, four or five of the men as well as the elderly wisp remained with her. He smiled to himself, amused to see his prediction fulfilled.

By the end of the week Sheila had received confirmation from the estate agents that her flat was sold, or that negotiations to buy it had begun. This threw her into a dilemma. Should she sign the contract and then go merrily off on her Bermuda honeymoon, leaving the flat full of furniture? Or should she arrange to have the flat cleared and the furniture stored before she left? Persuaded by her prudent mother, she fixed on the Wednesday before her wedding for the removal and Wexford, who had the day off, promised to go with her to St John's Wood.

'We could go to Bermuda too,' said Dora to her husband. 'I know it was the custom for Victorian brides to take a friend with them on their honeymoon,' said Wexford, 'but surely even they didn't take their parents.'

'Darling, I don't mean at the same time. I mean we could go to Bermuda later on. When you get your holiday. We can afford it now we aren't paying for this wedding.'

'How about my new car? How about the new hall carpet? And I thought you'd decided life was insupportable without a freezer.'

'We couldn't have all those things anyway.'

'That's for sure,' said Wexford.

A wonderful holiday or a new car? A thousand pounds' worth of sunshine and warmth took priority now, he reflected as he was driven over to Myringham and the crown court. The snow was still lying and the bright weather had given place to freezing fog. But would he still feel like this when it was sunny here and spring again? Then the freezer and the carpet would seem the wiser option.

John Cooper was found guilty of breaking into and

entering Sterries and of stealing six silver spoons, and, since he had previous convictions, sent to prison for six months. Wexford was rather surprised to hear that one of these convictions, though long in the past, was for robbery with violence. Mrs Murray-Burgess was in court and she flushed brick-red with satisfaction when the sentence was pronounced. Throughout the proceedings she had been eyeing the dark, rather handsome, slouching Cooper in the awed and fascinated way one looks at a bull or a caged tiger.

It occurred to Wexford to call in at Sterries on his way back and impart the news to Natalie Arno. He had promised to let her know the outcome. She would very likely be as delighted as her neighbour, and she could have her spoons back now.

A man who tried to be honest with himself, he wondered if this could be his sole motive for a visit to Ploughman's Lane. After all, it was a task Sergeant Martin or even Constable Loring could more properly have done. Was he, in common with those encircling men, attracted by Natalie? Could she have said of him too, like Cleopatra with her fishing rod, 'Aha, you're caught'? Honestly he asked himself – and said an honest, almost unqualified no. She amused him, she intrigued him, he suspected she would be entertaining to watch at certain manipulating ploys, but he was not attracted. There remained with him a nagging little memory of how, in the music room at Sterries, before he had ever spoken to her, he had sensed her presence behind him as unpleasing. She was good to look at, she was undoubtedly clever, she was full of charm, yet wasn't there about her something snake-like? And although this image might dissolve when confronted by the real Natalie, out of her company he must think of her sinuous movements as reptilian and her marvellous eyes when cast down as hooded.

So in going to Sterries he knew he was in little danger. No one need tie him to the mast. He would simply be calling on Natalie Arno for an obligatory talk, perhaps a cup of tea, and the opportunity to watch a powerful personality at work with the weak. If the Zoffanys were still there, of course. He would soon know.

It was three o'clock on the afternoon of a dull day. Not a light showed in the Sterries windows. Still, many people preferred to sit in the dusk rather than anticipate the night too soon. He rang the bell. He rang and rang again, was pleased to find himself not particularly disappointed that there was no one at home.

After a moment's thought he walked down the path to Sterries Cottage. Ted Hicks answered his ring. Yes, Mrs Arno was out. In fact, she had returned to London. Her friends had gone and then she had gone, leaving him and his wife to look after the house.

'Does she mean to come back?'

'I'm afraid I've no idea about that, sir. Mrs Arno didn't say.' Hicks spoke respectfully. Indeed, he had far more the air of an old-fashioned servant than his wife. Yet again Wexford felt, as he had felt with Muriel Hicks, that at any moment the discreet speaker might break into abuse, either heaping insults on Natalie or dismissing her with contempt. But nothing like this happened. Hicks compressed his lips and stared blankly at Wexford, though without meeting his eyes. 'Would you care to come in? I can give you Mrs Arno's London address.'

Why bother with it? He refused, thanked the man, asked almost as an afterthought if the house was to be sold.

'Very probably, sir.' Hicks, stiff, soldierly almost, unbent a little. 'This house will be. The wife and me, we couldn't stick it here now Sir Manuel's gone.'

It seemed likely that Natalie had taken her leave of Kingsmarkham and the town would not see her again. Perhaps she meant to settle in London or even return to America. He said something on these lines to Sheila as he drove her up to London on the following morning. But she had lost interest in Sterries and its future and was preoccupied with the morning paper which was carrying a feature about her and the forthcoming wedding. On the whole she seemed pleased with it, a reaction that astonished Wexford and Dora. They had been appalled by the description of her as the 'beautiful daughter of a country policeman' and the full-length photograph which showed her neither as Stewardess Curtis nor in one of her Royal Shakespeare Company roles, but reclining on a heap of cushions in little more than a pair of spangled stockings and a smallish fur.

'Dorset Stores It' was the slogan on the side of the removal van that had arrived early in Hamilton Terrace. Two men sat in its cab, glumly awaiting the appearance of the owner of the flat. Recognition of who that owner was mollified them, and on the way up in the lift the younger man asked Sheila if she would give him her autograph for his wife who hadn't missed a single instalment of *Runway* since the serial began.

The other man looked very old. Wexford was thinking he was too old to be of much use until he saw him lift Sheila's big bow-fronted chest of drawers and set it like a light pack on his shoulders. The younger man smiled at Wexford's astonishment.

'Pity you haven't got a piano,' he said. 'He comes from the most famous piano-lifting family in the country.'

Wexford had never before supposed that talents of that kind ran in families or even that one might enjoy a reputation for such a skill. He looked at the old man, who seemed getting on for Camargue's age, with new respect.

'Where are you taking all this stuff?'

A list was consulted. 'This piece and them chairs and that chest up to Keats Grove and . . .'

'Yes, I mean what isn't going to Keats Grove.'

'Down the warehouse. That's our warehouse down Thornton Heath, Croydon way if you know it. The lady's not got so much she'll need more than one container.' He named the rental Sheila would have to pay per week for the storage of her tables and chairs.

'It's stacked up in this container, is it, and stored along with a hundred others? Suppose you said you wanted it stored for a year and then you changed your mind and wanted to get, say, one item out?'

'That'd be no problem, guv'nor. It's yours, isn't it? While you pay your rent you can do what you like about it, leave it alone if that's what you want like or inspect it once a week. Thanks very much, lady.' This last was addressed to Sheila who was dispensing cans of beer.

'Give us a hand, George,' said the old man.

He had picked up Sheila's four-poster on his own, held it several inches off the ground, then thought better of it. He and the man called George began dismantling it.

'You'd be amazed,' said George, 'the things that go on. We're like a very old-established firm and we've got stuff down the warehouse been stored since before the First War . . .'

'The Great War,' said the old man.

'OK, then, the *Great* War. We've got stuff been stored since before 1914. The party as stored it's dead and gone and the rent's like gone up ten, twenty times, but the family wants it kept and they go on paying. Furniture that's been stored twenty years, that's common, that's nothing out of the way. We got one lady, she put her grand piano in store 1936 and she's dead now, but her daughter, she keeps the rent up. She comes along every so often and we open up her container for her and let her have a look her piano's OK.'

'See if you can shift that nut, George,' said the old man.

By two they were finished. Wexford took Sheila out to lunch, to a little French restaurant in Blenheim

Terrace, a far cry from Mr Haq's. They shared a bottle of Domaine du Parc and as Wexford raised his glass and drank to her happiness he felt a rush of unaccustomed sentimentality. She was so very much his treasure. His heart swelled with pride when he saw people look at her, whisper together and then look again. For years now she had hardly been his, she had been something like public property, but after Saturday she would be Andrew's and lost to him for ever . . . Suddenly he let out a bark of laughter at these maudlin indulgences.

'What's funny, Pop darling?'

'I was thinking about those removal men,' he lied.

He drove her up to Hampstead where she was staying the night and began the long haul back to Kingsmarkham. Not very experienced in London traffic, he had left Keats Grove at four and by the time he came to Waterloo Bridge found himself in the thick of the rush. It was after seven when he walked, cross and tired, into his house.

Dora came out to meet him in the hall. She kept her voice low. 'Reg, that friend of Sheila's who was going to marry Manuel Camargue is here. Dinah Whatever-it-is.'

'Didn't you tell her Sheila wouldn't be back tonight?'

Dora, though aware that she must move with the times, though aware that Sheila and Andrew had been more or less living together for the past year, nevertheless still made attempts to present to the world a picture of her daughter as an old-fashioned maiden bride. Her husband's accusing look – he disapproved of this kind of Mrs Grundy-ish concealment – made her blush and say hastily:

'She doesn't want Sheila, she wants you. She's been here an hour, she insisted on waiting. She says . . .' Dora cast up her eyes. 'She says she didn't know till this morning that you were a policeman!'

Wedding presents were still arriving. The house wasn't big enough for this sort of influx, and now the larger items were beginning to take over the hall. He nearly tripped over an object which, since it was swathed in corrugated cardboard and brown paper, might have been a plant stand, a lectern or a standard lamp, and cursing under his breath made his way into the living room.

This time the Alsatian had been left behind. Dinah Sternhold had been sitting by the hearth, gazing into the heart of the fire perhaps while preoccupied with her own thoughts. She jumped up when he came in and her round pale face grew pink.

'Oh, I'm so sorry to bother you, Mr Wexford. Believe me, I wouldn't be here if I didn't think it was absolutely – well, absolutely vital. I've delayed so long and I've felt so bad and now I can't sleep with the worry . . . But it wasn't till this morning I found out you were a detective chief inspector.'

'You read it in the paper,' he said, smiling. '"Beautiful daughter of a country policeman."'

'Sheila never told me, you see. Why should she? I never told her my father's a bank manager.'

Wexford sat down. 'Then what you have to tell me is something serious, I suppose. Shall we have a drink? I'm a bit tired and you look as if you need Dutch courage.'

On doctor's orders, he could allow himself nothing stronger than vermouth but she, to his surprise, asked for whisky. That she wasn't used to it he could tell by the way she shuddered as she took her first sip. She lifted to him those greyish-brown eyes that seemed full of soft light. He had thought that face plain but it was not, and for a moment he could intuit what Camargue had seen in her. If his looks had been spiritual and sensitive so, superlatively, were hers. The old musician and this young creature had shared, he sensed, an approach to life that was gentle, impulsive and joyous.

There was no joy now in her wan features. They seemed convulsed with doubt and perhaps with fear.

'I know I ought to tell someone about this,' she began again. 'As soon as – as Manuel was dead I knew I ought to tell someone. I thought of his solicitors but I imagined them listening to me and knowing I wasn't to – well, inherit, and thinking it was all sour grapes . . . It seemed so – so *wild* to go to the police. But this morning when I read that in the paper – you see, I know you, you're Sheila's father, you won't . . . I'm afraid I'm not being very articulate. Perhaps you understand what I mean?'

'I understand you've been feeling diffident about giving some sort of information but I'm mystified as to what it is.'

'Oh, of course you are! The point is, I don't really believe it myself. I can't, it seems so – well, outlandish. But Manuel believed it, he was so sure, so I don't think I ought to keep it to myself and just let things go ahead, do you?'

'I think you'd better tell me straight away, Mrs Sternhold. Just tell me what it is and then we'll have the explanations afterwards.'

She set down her glass. She looked a little away from him, the firelight reddening the side of her face.

'Well, then. Manuel told me that Natalie Arno, or the woman who calls herself Natalie Arno, wasn't his daughter at all. He was absolutely convinced she was an impostor.'

6

He said nothing and his face showed nothing of what he felt. She was looking at him now, the doubt intensified, her hands lifted and clasped hard together under her chin. In the firelight the ruby on her finger burned and twinkled.

'There,' she said, 'that's it. It was something to – to hesitate about, wasn't it? But I don't really believe it. Oh, I don't mean he wasn't marvellous for his age and his mind absolutely sound. I don't mean that. But his sight was poor and he'd worked himself into such an emotional state over seeing her, it was nineteen years, and perhaps she wasn't very kind and – oh, I don't know! When he said she wasn't his daughter, she was an impostor, and he'd leave her nothing in his will, I . . .'

Wexford interrupted her. 'Why don't you tell me about it from the beginning?'

'Where is the beginning? From the time she, or whoever she is . . .'

'Tell me about it from the time of her return to this country in November.'

Dora put her head round the door. He knew she had come to ask him if he was ready for his dinner but she retreated without a word. Dinah Sternhold said:

'I think I'm keeping you from your meal.'

'It doesn't matter. Let's go back to November.'

'I only know that it was in November she came back. She didn't get in touch with Manuel until the middle of December – 12 December it was. She didn't say anything about our getting married, just could she come and see him and something about healing the breach. At first she wanted to come at Christmas but when Manuel wrote back that that would be fine and I should be there and my parents, she said no, the first time she wanted to see him alone. It sounds casual, putting it like that, Manuel writing back and inviting her, but in fact it wasn't a bit. Getting her first letter absolutely threw him. He was very – well, excited about seeing her and rather confused and it was almost as if he was afraid. I suggested he phone her – she gave a phone number – but he couldn't bring himself to that and it's true he was difficult on the phone if you didn't know him. His hearing was fine when he could *see* the speaker. Anyway, she suggested 10 January and we had the same excitement and nervousness all over again. I wasn't to be there or the Hickses, Muriel was to get the tea ready and leave him to make it and she was to get one of the spare rooms ready in case Natalie decided to stay.

'Well, two or three days before, it must have been about the 7th, a woman called Mrs Zoffany phoned. Muriel took the call. Manuel was asleep. This Mrs Zoffany said she was speaking on behalf of Natalie who couldn't come on the 10th because she had to go into hospital for a check-up and could she come on the 19th instead? Manuel got into a state when Muriel told him. I went over there in the evening and he was very depressed and nervous, saying Natalie didn't really want a reconciliation, whatever she may have intended at first, she was just trying to get out of seeing him. You can imagine. He went on about how he was going to die soon and at any rate that would be a blessing for me, not to be tied to an old man *et cetera*. All nonsense, of course, but natural, I think. he was *longing* to see her. It's a good thing I haven't got a jealous nature. Lots of women would have been jealous.'

Perhaps they would. Jealousy knows nothing of age discrepancies, suitability. Camargue, thought Wexford, had chosen for his second wife a surrogate daughter, assuming his true daughter would never reappear. No wonder, when she did, that emotions had run high. He said only:

'I take it that it was on the 19th she came?'

'Yes. In the afternoon, about three. She came by train from Victoria and then in a taxi from the station. Manuel asked the Hickses not to interrupt them and

Ted even took Nancy away for the afternoon. Muriel left tea prepared on the table in the drawing room and there was some cold duck and stuff for supper in the fridge.'

'So that when she came Sir Manuel was quite alone?'

'Quite alone. What I'm going to tell you is what he told me the next day, the Sunday, when Ted drove him over to my house in the morning.

'He told me he intended to be rather cool and distant with her at first.' Dinah Sternhold smiled a tender, reminiscent smile. 'I didn't have much faith in that,' she said. 'I knew him, you see. I knew it wasn't in him not to be warm and kind. And in fact, when he went down and opened the front door to her he said he forgot all about that resolve of his and just took her in his arms and held her. He was ashamed of that afterwards, poor Manuel, he was sick with himself for giving way.

'Well, they went upstairs and sat down and talked. That is, Manuel talked. He said he suddenly found he had so much to say to her. He talked on and on about his life since she went away, her mother's death, his retirement because of the arthritis in his hands, how he had built that house. She answered him, he said, but a lot of things she said he couldn't hear. Maybe she spoke low, but my voice is low and he could always hear me. However . . .'

'She has an American accent,' said Wexford.

'Perhaps that was it. The awful thing was, he said, that when he talked of the long time she'd been away he actually cried. I couldn't see it was important, but he was so ashamed of having cried. Still, he pulled himself together. He said they must have tea and he hoped she would stay the night and would she like to see over the house? He was always taking people over the house, I think it was something his generation did, and then . . .'

Wexford broke in, 'All this time he believed her to be his daughter?'

'Oh, yes! He was in no doubt. The way he said he found out – well, it's so crazy . . . Anyway, he actually told her he was going to make a new will after his marriage, and although he intended to leave me the house and its contents, everything else was to go to her, including what remained of her mother's fortune. It was a lot of money, something in the region of a million, I think.

'He showed her the bedroom that was to be hers, though she did say at this point that she couldn't stay, and then they went back and into the music room. Oh, I don't suppose you've ever been in the house, have you?'

'As a matter of fact, I have,' said Wexford.

She gave him a faintly puzzled glance. 'Yes. Well, you'll know then that there are alcoves all round the music room and in one of the alcoves is a flute made of gold. It was given to Manuel by a sort of patron and fan of his, an American of Italian origin called Aldo Cazzini, and it's a real instrument, it's perfectly *playable*, though in fact Manuel had never used it.

'He and Natalie went in there and Natalie took one look in the alcove and said, "You still have

Cazzini's golden flute," and it was at this point, he said, that he knew. He knew for certain she wasn't Natalie.'

Wexford said, 'I don't follow you. Surely recognizing the flute would be confirmation of her identity rather than proof she was an impostor?'

'It was the way she pronounced it. It ought to be pronounced Catzini and this woman pronounced it Cassini. Or so he said. Now the real Natalie grew up speaking English, French and Spanish with equal ease. She learnt German at school and when she was fifteen Manuel had her taught Italian because he intended her to be a musician and he thought some Italian essential for a musician. The real Natalie would never have mispronounced an Italian name. She would no more have done that, he said – these are his own words – than a Frenchman would pronounce Camargue to rhyme with Montague. So as soon as he heard her pronunciation of Cazzini he knew she couldn't be Natalie.'

Wexford could almost have laughed. He shook his head in dismissal. 'There must have been more to it.'

'There was. He said the shock was terrible. He didn't say anything for a moment. He looked hard at her, he studied her, and then he could *see* she wasn't his daughter. Nineteen years is a long time but she couldn't have changed that much and in that way. Her features were different, the colour of her eyes was different. He went back with her into the drawing room and then he said, "You are not my daughter, are you?"'

'He actually asked her, did he?'

'He asked her and – you understand, Mr Wexford, that I'm telling you what he said – I feel a traitor to him, doubting him, as if he were senile or mad – he wasn't, he was wonderful, but . . .'

'He was old,' said Wexford. A foolish, fond old man, fourscore years . . .' He was overwrought.'

'Oh, yes, exactly! But the point is he said he asked her and she admitted it.'

Wexford leaned forward, frowning a little, his eyes on Dinah Sternhold's intent face.

'Are you telling me this woman admitted to Sir Manuel that she wasn't Natalie Arno? Why didn't you say so before?'

'Because I don't believe it. I think that when he said she admitted she wasn't Natalie and seemed ashamed and embarrassed, I think he was – well, dreaming. You see, he told her to go. He was trembling, he was terribly distressed. It wasn't in him to shout at anyone or be violent, you understand, he just told her not to say any more but to go. He heard her close the front door and then he did something he absolutely never did. He had some brandy. He never touched spirits in the normal way, a glass of wine sometimes or a sherry, that was all. But he had some brandy to steady him, he said, and then he went to lie down because his heart was racing – and he fell asleep.'

'It was next day when you saw him?'

She nodded. 'Next day at about eleven. I think that while he was asleep he dreamt that bit about her admitting she wasn't Natalie. I told him so. I didn't humour him – ours wasn't that kind of relationship. I told him I thought he was mistaken. I told him all sorts of things that I believed and believe now – that eye colour fades and features change and one can forget a language as one can forget anything else. He wouldn't have any of it. He was so sweet and good and a genius – but he was terribly impulsive and stubborn as well.

'Anyway, he started saying he was going to cut her out of his will. She was a fraud and an impostor who was attempting to get hold of a considerable property by false pretences. She was to have nothing, therefore, and I was to have the lot. Perhaps you won't believe me if I say I did my best to dissuade him from that?'

Wexford slightly inclined his head. 'Why not?'

'It would have been in my own interest to agree with him. However, I did try to dissuade him and he was sweet to me as he always was but he wouldn't listen. He wrote to her, telling her what he intended to do, and then he wrote to his solicitors, asking one of the partners to come up to Sterries on February 4th – that would have been two days after our wedding.'

'Who are these solicitors?'

'Symonds, O'Brien and Ames,' she said, 'in the High Street here.'

Kingsmarkham's principal firm of solicitors. They had recently moved their premises into the new Kingsbrook Precinct. It was often Wexford's lot to have dealings with them.

'He invited Mr Ames to lunch with us,' Dinah Sternhold said, 'and afterwards he was to draw up a new will for Manuel. It must have been on the 22nd or the 23rd that he wrote to Natalie and on the 27th – he was drowned.' Her voice shook a little.

Wexford waited. He said gently, 'He had no intention of coming to us and he wasn't going to confide in his solicitor?'

She did not answer him directly. 'I think I did right,' she said. 'I prevented that. I couldn't dissuade him from the decision to disinherit her but I did manage to stop him going to the police. I told him he would make a – well, a scandal, and he would have hated that. What I meant to do was this. Let him make a new will if he liked. Wills can be unmade and remade. I knew Natalie probably disliked me and was jealous but I thought I'd try to approach her myself a month or so after we were married, say, and arrange another meeting. I thought that somehow we'd all meet and it would come right. It would turn out to have been some misunderstanding like in a play, like in one of those old comedies of mistaken identity.'

Wexford was silent. Then he said, 'Would you like to tell me about it all over again, Mrs Sternhold?'

'What I've just told?'

He nodded. 'Please.'

'But why?'

To test your veracity. He didn't say that aloud. If she were intelligent enough she would know without his saying, and her flush told him that she did.

Without digressions this time, she repeated her story. He listened concentratedly. When she had finished he said rather sharply:

'Did Sir Manuel tell anyone else about this?'

'Not so far as I know. Well, no, I'm sure he didn't.' Her face was pale again and composed. She asked him, 'What will you do?'

'I don't know.'

'But you'll do something to find out. You'll prove she *is* Natalie Arno?'

Or that she is not? He didn't say it, and before he had framed an alternative reply she had jumped up and was taking her leave of him in that polite yet child-like way she had.

'It was very good and patient of you to listen to me, Mr Wexford. I'm sure you understand why I had to come. Will you give my love to Sheila, please, and say I'll be thinking of her on Saturday? She did ask me to come but of course that wouldn't be possible. I'm afraid I've taken up a great deal of your time . . .'

He walked with her out to the Volkswagen which she had parked round the corner of the street on an ice-free patch. She looked back once as she drove away and raised her hand to him. How many times, in telling her story, had she said she didn't believe it? He had often observed how people will say they are sure of something when they truly mean they are unsure, how a man will hotly declare that he doesn't believe a word of it when he believes only too easily. If Dinah Sternhold had not believed, would she have come to him at all?

He asked himself if he believed and if so what was he going to do about it?

Nothing till after the wedding . . .

7

The success or failure of a wedding, as Wexford remarked, is no augury of the marriage itself. This wedding might be said to have failed. In the first place, the thaw set in the evening before and by Saturday morning it was raining hard. All day long it rained tempestuously. The expected crowd of well-wishers come to see their favourite married, a youthful joyous crowd of confetti-hurlers, became in fact a huddle of pensioners under umbrellas, indifferently lingering on after the Over-Sixties meeting in St Peter's Hall. But the press was there, made spiteful by rain and mud, awaiting opportunities. And these were many: a bridesmaid's diaphanous skirt blown almost over her head by a gust of wind, a small but dismaying accident when the bride's brother-in-law's car went into the back of a press photographer's car, and later the failure of the Olive and Dove management to provide luncheon places for some ten of the guests.

The Sunday papers made the most of it. Their pictures might have been left to speak for themselves, for the captions, snide or sneering, only added insult to injury. Dora wept.

'I suppose it's inevitable.' Wexford, as far as he could recall it and with a touch of paraphrase, quoted Shelley to her. 'They scatter their insults and their slanders without heed as to whether the poisoned shafts light on a heart made callous by many blows or one like yours composed of more penetrable stuff.'

'And is yours made callous by many blows?'

'No, but Sheila's is.'

He took the papers away from her and burnt them, hoping none would have found their way into the Burdens' bungalow where they were going to lunch. And when they arrived just after noon, escorted from their car by Burden with a large coloured golf umbrella, there was not a newspaper to be seen. Instead, on the coffee table, where the *Sunday Times* might have reposed, lay a book in a glossy jacket entitled *The Tichborne Swindle*.

In former days, during the lifetime of Burden's first wife and afterwards in his long widowerhood, no book apart from those strictly necessary for the children's school work was ever seen in that house. But when he re-married things changed. And it could not be altogether due to the fact that his wife's brother was a publisher, though this might have helped, that the inspector was becoming a reading man. It was even said, though Wexford refused to believe it, that Burden and Jenny read aloud to each other in the evenings, that they had got through Dickens and were currently embarking on the Waverley novels.

Wexford picked up the book. It had been, as he expected, published by Carlyon Brent, and was a reappraisal of the notorious nineteenth-century Tichborne case in which an Australian butcher attempted to gain possession of a great fortune by posing as heir to an English baronetcy. Shades of the tale he had been told by Dinah Sternhold . . . The coincidence of finding the book there decided him. For a little while before lunch he and Burden were alone together.

'Have you read this yet?'

'I'm about half-way through.'

'Listen.' He repeated the account he had been given baldly and without digressions. 'There aren't really very many points of similarity,' he said. 'From what I remember of the Tichborne case the claimant didn't even look like the Tichborne heir. He was much bigger and fatter for one thing and obviously not of the same social class. Lady Tichborne was a hysterical woman who would have accepted practically anyone who said he was her son. You've almost got the reverse here. Natalie Arno looks very much like the young Natalie Camargue and, far from accepting her, Camargue seems to have rumbled her within half an hour.'

'"Rumbled" sounds as if you think there might be something in this tale.'

'I'm not going to stomp up and down raving that I don't believe a word of it, if that's what you mean. I just don't know. But I'll tell you one thing. I expected you to have shouted you didn't believe it long before now.'

Burden gave one of his thin, rather complacent little smiles. In his domestic circle he behaved, much as he had during his first marriage, as if nobody but he had ever quite discovered the heights of marital felicity. Today he was wearing a new suit of smooth matt cloth the colour of a ginger nut. When happy he always seemed to grow thinner and he was very thin now. The smile was still on his mouth as he spoke. 'It's a funny old business altogether, isn't it? But I wouldn't say I don't believe it. It's fertile ground for that sort of con trick, after all. A nineteen-year absence, an old man on his own with poor sight, an old man who has a great deal of money . . . By the way, how do you know this woman looks like the young Natalie?'

'Dinah Sternhold sent me this.' Wexford handed him a snapshot. 'Camargue was showing her a family photograph album, apparently, and he left it behind in her house.'

The picture showed a dark, Spanish-looking girl, rather plump, full-faced and smiling. She was wearing a summer dress in the style known at the time when the photograph was taken as 'the sack' on account of its shapelessness and lack of a defined waist. Her black hair was short and she had a fringe.

'That could be her. Why not?'

'A whitely wanton with a velvet brow' said Wexford, 'and two pitchballs stuck in her face for eyes. Camargue said the eyes of the woman he saw were different from his daughter's and Dinah told him that eyes fade. I've never heard of eyes or anything else fading to black, have you?'

Burden refilled their glasses. 'If Camargue's sight was poor I think you can simply discount that sort of thing. I mean, you can't work on the premise that she's not Natalie Camargue because she looks different or he thought she did. The pronouncing of that name wrong, that's something else again, that's really weird.'

Wexford, hesitating for his figure's sake between potato crisps, peanuts or nothing at all, looked up in surprise. 'You think so?'

The thin smile came again. 'Oh, I know you reckon on me being a real philistine but I've got kids, remember. I've watched them getting an education if I've never had much myself. Now my Pat, she had a Frenchwoman teaching them French from when she was eleven, and when she speaks a French word she pronounces the R like the French, sort of rolls it in her throat. The point I'm making is, it happens naturally now, Pat couldn't pronounce a French word with an R in it any other way and *she never will.*'

'Mm hmm.' While pondering Wexford had absentmindedly sneaked two crisps. He held his hands firmly together in his lap. 'There's always the possibility Camargue *heard* the name incorrectly because of defective hearing while it was, in fact, pronounced in the proper way. What I'm sure of is that Dinah is telling the truth. I tested her and she told the same story almost word for word the second time as she had the first, dates, times, everything.'

'Pass over those crisp things, will you? I don't see what motive she'd have for inventing it, anyway. Even if Natalie were out of the way she wouldn't inherit.'

'No. Incidentally, we must find out who would. Dinah could have had spite for a motive, you know. If Natalie is the real Natalie no one of course could hope to prove she is not, and no doubt she could very quickly prove she *is*, but an inquiry would look bad for her, the mud would stick. If there were publicity about it and there very likely would be, there would be some people who would always believe her to be an impostor and many others who would feel a doubt.'

Burden nodded. 'And there must inevitably be an inquiry now, don't you think?'

'Tomorrow I shall have to pass on what I know to Symonds, O'Brien and Ames,' said Wexford, and he went on thoughtfully, 'It would be deception under the '68 Theft Act. Section Fifteen, I believe.' And he quoted with some small hesitations, 'A person who by any deception dishonestly obtains property belonging to another, with the intention of permanently depriving the other of it, shall on conviction on indictment be liable to imprisonment for a term not exceeding ten years.'

'No one's obtained anything yet. It'll take a bit

of time for the will to be proved.' Burden gave his friend and superior officer a dubious and somewhat wary look. 'I don't want to speak out of turn and no offence meant,' he said, 'but this could be the kind of thing you get – well, you get obsessional about.'

Wexford's indignant retort was cut off in mid-sentence by the entry of Jenny and Dora to announce lunch.

Kingsmarkham's principal firm of solicitors had moved their offices when the new Kingsbrook shopping precinct was built, deserting the medieval caverns they had occupied for fifty years for the top floor above the British Home Stores. Here all was light, space and purity of line. The offices had that rather disconcerting quality, to be constantly met with nowadays, of looking cold and feeling warm. It was much the same in the police station.

Wexford knew Kenneth Ames well by sight, though he couldn't recall ever having spoken to him before. He was a thin, spare man with a boyish face. That is, his face like his figure had kept its youthful contours, though it was by now seamed all over with fine lines as if a web had been laid upon the skin. He wore a pale grey suit that seemed too lightweight for the time of year. His manner was both chatty and distant which gave the impression, perhaps a false one, that his mind was not on what he was saying or listening to.

This made repeating Dinah Sternhold's account a rather uneasy task. Mr Ames sat with his elbows on the arms of an uncomfortable-looking metal chair and the tips of his fingers pressed together. He stared out of the window at St Peter's spire. As the story progressed he pushed his lips and gradually his whole jaw forward until the lower part of his face grew muzzle-like. This doggy expression he held for a moment or two after Wexford had finished. Then he said:

'I don't think I'd place too much credence on all that, Mr Wexford. I don't think I would. It sounds to me as if Sir Manuel rather got a bee in his belfry, you know, and this young lady, Mrs – er, Steinhalt, is it? – Mrs Steinhall maybe gilded the gingerbread.' Mr Ames paused and coughed slightly after delivering these confused metaphors. He studied his short clean fingernails with interest. 'Once Sir Manuel was married he'd have had to make a new will. There was nothing out of the way in that. We have no reason to believe he meant to disinherit Mrs Arno.' The muzzle face returned as Mr Ames glared at his fingernails and enclosed them suddenly in his fists as if they offended him. 'In point of fact,' he said briskly, 'Sir Manuel invited me to lunch to discuss a new will and to meet his bride, Mrs – er, Sternhill, but unfortunately his death intervened. You know, Mr Wexford, if Sir Manuel had really believed he'd been visited by an impostor, don't you think he'd have said something to us? There was over a week between the visit and his death and during that week he wrote to me and phoned me. No, if this extraordinary tale were true I fancy he'd have said something to his solicitors.'

'He seems to have said nothing to anyone except Mrs Sternhold.'

An elastic smile replaced the muzzle look. 'Ah, yes. People like to make trouble. I can't imagine why. You may have noticed?'

'Yes,' said Wexford. 'By the way, in the event of Mrs Arno not inheriting, who would?'

'Oh dear, oh dear, I don't think there's much risk of Mrs Arno not inheriting, do you, really?'

Wexford shrugged. 'Just the same, who would?'

'Sir Manuel had – has, I suppose I should say if one may use the present tense in connection with the dead – Sir Manuel has a niece in France, his dead sister's daughter. A Mademoiselle Thérèse Something. Latour? Lacroix? No doubt I can find the name for you if you really want it.'

'As you say, there may be no chance of her inheriting. Am I to take it then that Symonds, O'Brien and Ames intend to do nothing about this story of Mrs Sternhold's?'

'I don't follow you, Mr Wexford.' Mr Ames was once more contemplating the church spire which was now veiled in fine driving rain.

'You intend to accept Mrs Arno as Sir Manuel's heir without investigation?'

The solicitor turned round. 'Good heavens, no, Mr Wexford. What can have given you that idea?' He became almost animated, almost involved. 'Naturally, in view of what you've told us we shall make the most thorough and exhaustive inquiries. No doubt, you will too?'

'Oh, yes.'

'A certain pooling of our findings would be desirable, don't you agree? It's quite unthinkable that a considerable property such as Sir Manuel left could pass to an heir about whose provenance there might be the faintest doubt.' Mr Ames half closed his eyes. He seemed to gather himself together in order to drift once more into remoteness. 'It's only,' he said with an air of extreme preoccupation, 'that it doesn't really do, you know, to place too much credence on these things.'

As the receiver was lifted the deep baying of a dog was the first sound he heard. Then the soft gentle voice gave the Forby number.

'Mrs Sternhold, do you happen to know if Sir Manuel had kept any samples of Mrs Arno's handwriting from *before* she went away to America?'

'I don't know. I don't think so.' Her tone sounded dubious, cautious, as if she regretted having told him so much. Perhaps she did, but it was too late now. 'They'd be inside Sterries, anyway.' She didn't add what Wexford was thinking, that if Camargue had kept them and if Natalie was an impostor, they would by now have been destroyed.

'Then perhaps you can help me in another way. I gather Sir Manuel had no relatives in this country. Who is there I can call on who knew Mrs Arno when she was Natalie Camargue?'

Burden's Burberry was already hanging on the palm tree hatstand when Wexford walked into the Pearl of Africa. And Burden was already seated under the plastic fronds, about to start on his antipasto Ankole.

'I don't believe they have shrimps in Uganda,' said Wexford, sitting down opposite him.

'Mr Haq says they come out of Lake Victoria. What are you going to have?'

'Oh, God. Avocado with Victorian shrimps, I suppose, and maybe an omelette. Mike, I've been on to the California police through Interpol, asking them to give us whatever they can about the background of Natalie Arno, but if she's never been in trouble, and we've no reason to think she has, it won't be much. And I've had another talk with Dinah. The first – well, the only really – Mrs Camargue had a sister who's still alive and in London. Ever heard of a composer called Philip Cory? He was an old pal of Camargue's. Either or both of them ought to be able to tell us if this is the real Natalie.'

Burden said thoughtfully, 'All this raises something else, doesn't it? Or, rather, what we've been told about Camargue's will does. And in that area it makes no difference whether Natalie is Natalie or someone else.'

'What does it raise?'

'You know what I mean.'

Wexford did. That Burden too had seen it scarcely surprised him. A year or two before the inspector had often seemed obtuse. But happiness makes so much difference to a person, Wexford thought. It doesn't just make them happy, it makes them more intelligent, more aware, more alert, while unhappiness deadens, dulls and stupefies. Burden had seen what he had seen because he was happy, and happiness was making a better policeman of him.

'Oh, I know what you mean. Perhaps it was rather too readily assumed that Camargue died a natural death.'

'I wouldn't say that. It's just that then there was no reason to suspect foul play, nothing and no one suspicious seen in the neighbourhood, no known enemies, no unusual bruising on the body. A highly distinguished but rather frail old man happened to go too near a lake on a cold night in deep snow.'

'And if we had known what we know now? We can take it for granted that Natalie's aim – whether she is Camargue's daughter or an impostor – her aim in coming to her father was to secure his property or the major part of it for herself. She came to him and, whether he actually saw through her and denounced her or thought he saw through her and dreamed he denounced her, he at any rate apparently wrote to her and told her she was to be disinherited.'

'She could either attempt to dissuade him,' said Burden, 'or take steps of another sort.'

'Her loss wouldn't have been immediate. Camargue was getting married and had therefore to make a new will after his marriage. She might count on his not wishing to make a new will at once and then another after his marriage. She had two weeks in which to act.'

'There's a point too that, whereas she might have dissuaded him from cutting her out, she couldn't have dissuaded him from leaving Sterries to Dinah. But there don't seem to have been any efforts at dissuasion, do there? Dinah doesn't know of any or she'd have told you, nor did Natalie come to Sterries again.'

'Except perhaps,' said Wexford, 'on the night of Sunday, 27 January.'

Burden's answer was checked by the arrival of Mr Haq, bowing over the table.

'How are you doing, my dear?'

'Fine, thanks.' Any less hearty reply would have summoned forth a stream of abject apology and the cook from the kitchen as well as causing very real pain to Mr Haq.

'I can recommend the mousse Maherere.'

Mr Haq, if his advice was rejected, was capable of going off into an explanation of how this dish was composed of coffee beans freshly plucked in the plantations of Toro and of cream from the milk of the taper-horned Sanga cattle. To prevent this, and though knowing its actual provenance to be Sainsbury's instant dessert, Burden ordered it. Wexford always had the excuse of his shaky and occasional diet. A bowl of pale brown froth appeared, served by Mr Haq's own hands.

Quietly Wexford repeated his last remark.

'The night of 27 January?' echoed Burden. 'The night of Camargue's death? If he was murdered, and I reckon we both think he was, if he was pushed into that water and left to drown, Natalie didn't do it.'

'How d'you know that?'

'Well, in a funny sort of way,' Burden said almost apologetically, 'she told me so.'

'It was while we were up at Sterries about that burglary. I was in the dining room talking to Hicks when Natalie and the Zoffany couple came downstairs. She may have known I was within earshot but I don't think she did. She and Mrs Z. were talking and Natalie was saying she supposed she would have to get Sotheby's or someone to value Camargue's china for her. On the other hand, there had been that man she and Mrs Z. had met that someone had said was an expert on Chinese porcelain and she'd like to get hold of his name and phone number. Zoffany said what man did she mean and Natalie said he wouldn't know, he hadn't been there, it had been at so-and-so's party *last Sunday evening.*'

'A bit too glib, wasn't it?'

'Glib or not, if Natalie was at a party there'll be at least a dozen people to say she was, as well as Mrs Z. And if Camargue was murdered *we will never prove it.* If we'd guessed it at the time it would have been bad enough with snow lying everywhere, with snow falling to obliterate all possible evidence. No weapon but bare hands. Camargue cremated. We haven't a hope in hell of proving it.'

'You're over-pessimistic,' said Wexford, and he quoted softly, 'If a man will begin with certainties, he shall end in doubts, but if he will be content to begin with doubts he shall end in certainties.'

8

A shop that is not regularly open and manned seems to announce this fact to the world even when the 'open' sign hangs on its door and an assistant can be seen pottering inside. An indefinable air of neglect, of lack of interest, of precarious existence and threatened permanent closure hangs over it. So it was with the Zodiac, nestling in deep Victoriana, tucked behind a neo-Gothic square, on the borders of Islington and Hackney.

Its window was stacked full of paperback science fiction, but some of the books had tumbled down, and those which lay with their covers exposed had their gaudy and bizarre designs veiled in dust. Above the shop was a single storey – for this was a district of squat buildings and wide streets – and behind it a humping of rooms, shapelessly huddled and with odd little scraps of roof, gables protruding, seemingly superfluous doors and even a cowled chimney. Wexford pushed open the shop door and walked in. There was a sour, inky, musty smell, inseparable from secondhand books. These lined the shop like wallpaper, an asymmetrical pattern of red and green and yellow and black spines. They were all science fiction, *The Trillion Project, Nergal of Chaldea, Neuropodium, Course for Umbrial, The Triton Occultation.* He was replacing on the shelf a book whose cover bore a picture of what appeared to be a Boeing 747 coated in fish scales and with antennae, when Ivan Zoffany came in from a door at the back.

Recognition was not mutual. Zoffany showed intense surprise when Wexford said who he was, but it seemed like surprise alone and not fear.

'I'd like a few words with you.'

'Right. It's a mystery to me what about but I'm easy. I may as well close up for lunch anyway.'

It was ten past twelve. Could they hope to make any sort of living out of this place? Did they try? The 'open' sign was turned round and Zoffany led Wexford into the room from which he had come. By a window which gave on to a paved yard and scrap of garden and where the light was best, Jane Zoffany, in antique gown, shawl and beads, sat sewing. She appeared to be turning up or letting down the hem of a skirt and Wexford, whose memory was highly retentive about this sort of thing, recognized it as the skirt Natalie had been wearing on the day they were summoned after the burglary.

'What can we do for you?'

Zoffany had the bluff, insincere manner of the man who has a great deal to hide. Experience had taught Wexford that what such a nature is hiding is far more often some emotional disturbance or failure of nerve than guilty knowledge. He could hardly have indulged in greater self-deception than when he had said he was easy. There was something in Zoffany's eyes and the droop of his mouth when he was not forcing it into a grin that spoke of frightful inner suffering. And it was more apparent here, on his home ground, than it had been at Sterries.

'How long have you known Mrs Arno?'

Instinctively, Jane Zoffany glanced towards the ceiling. And at that moment a light footstep sounded overhead. Zoffany didn't look up.

'Oh, I'd say a couple of years, give or take a little.'

'You knew her before she came to this country then?'

'Met her when my poor sister died. Mrs Arno and my sister used to share a house in Los Angeles. Perhaps you didn't know that? Tina, my sister, she died the summer before last, and I had to go over and see to things. Grisly business but someone had to. There wasn't anyone else, barring my mother, and you can't expect an old lady of seventy – I say, what's all this in aid of?'

Wexford ignored the question as he usually ignored such questions until the time was ripe to answer them. 'Your sister and Mrs Arno shared a house?'

'Well, Tina had a flat in her house.'

'A room actually, Ivan,' said Jane Zoffany.

'A room in her house. Look, could you tell me why you want . . . ?'

'She must have been quite a young woman. What did she die of?'

'Cancer. She had cancer in her twenties while she was still married. Then she got divorced, but she didn't keep his name, she went back to her maiden name. She was thirty-nine if you want to know. The cancer came back suddenly, it was all over her, carcinomatosis, they called it. She was dead in three weeks from the onset.'

Wexford thought he spoke callously and with a curious kind of resentment. There was also an impression that he talked for the sake of talking, perhaps to avoid an embarrassing matter.

'I hadn't seen her for sixteen or seventeen years,' he said, 'but when she went like that someone had to go over. I can't think what you want with all this.'

It was on the tip of Wexford's tongue to retort that he had not asked for it. He said mildly, 'When you arrived you met Mrs Arno? Stayed in her house perhaps?'

Zoffany nodded, uneasy again.

'You got on well and became friends. After you came home you corresponded with her and when you heard she was coming back here and needed somewhere to live, you and your wife offered her the upstairs flat.'

'That's quite correct,' said Jane Zoffany. She gave a strange little skittish laugh. 'I'd always admired her from afar, you see. Just to think of my own sister-in-law living in Manuel Camargue's own daughter's house! I used to worship him when I was young. And Natalie and I are very close now. It was a really good idea. I'm sure Natalie has been a true friend to me.' She re-threaded her needle, holding the eye up against the yellowed and none-too-clean net curtain. 'Please, why are you asking all these questions?'

'A suggestion has been made that Mrs Arno is not in fact the late Sir Manuel Camargue's daughter but an impostor.'

He was interested by the effect of these words on his hearers. One of them expected this statement and was not surprised by it, the other was either flabbergasted or was a superb actor. Ivan Zoffany seemed stricken dumb with astonishment. Then he asked Wexford to repeat what he had said.

'That is the most incredible nonsense,' Zoffany said with a loaded pause between the words. 'Who has suggested it? Who would put about a story like that? Now just you listen to me . . .' Wagging a finger, he began lecturing Wexford on the subject of Natalie Arno's virtues and misfortunes. 'One of the most charming, delightful girls you could wish to meet, and as if she hasn't had enough to put up with . . .'

Wexford cut him short again. 'It's her identity, not her charm, that's in dispute.' He was intrigued by the behaviour of Jane Zoffany who was sitting hunched up, looking anywhere but at him, and who appeared to be very frightened indeed. She had stopped sewing because her hands would have shaken once she moved each out of the other's grasp.

He went back into the shop. Natalie Arno was standing by the counter on the top of which now lay an open magazine. She was looking at this and laughing with glee rather than amusement. When she saw Wexford she showed no surprise, but smiled, holding her head a little on one side.

'Good morning, Mr – er, Wexford, isn't it? And how are you today?' It was an Americanism delivered with an American lilt and one that seemed to require no reply. 'When you close the shop, Ivan,' she said, 'you should also remember to lock the door. All sorts of undesirables could come in.'

Zoffany said with gallantry, but stammering a little, 'That certainly doesn't include you, Natalie!'

'I'm not sure the chief inspector would agree with you.' She gave Wexford a sidelong smile. She knew. Symonds, O'Brien and Ames had lost no time in telling her. Jane Zoffany was afraid but she was not. Her black eyes sparkled. Rather ostentatiously, she closed the magazine she had been looking at, revealing the cover which showed it to belong to the medium hard genre of pornography. Plainly, this was Zoffany's under-the-counter solace that she had lighted on. He flushed, seized it rather too quickly from under her hands and thrust it between some catalogues in a pile. Natalie's face became pensive and innocent. She put up her hands to her hair and her full breasts in the sweater rose with the movement, which seemed to have been made quite artlessly, simply to tuck in a tortoiseshell pin.

'Did you want to interrogate me, Mr Wexford?'

'Not yet,' he said. 'At present I'll be content if you'll give me the name and address of the people whose party you and Mrs Zoffany went to on the evening of 27 January.'

She told him, without hesitation or surprise.

'Thank you, Mrs Arno.'

At the door of the room where Jane Zoffany was she paused, looked at him and giggled. 'You can call me Mrs X, if you like. Feel free.'

A housekeeper in a dark dress that was very nearly a uniform admitted him to the house in a cul-de-sac off Kensington Church Street. She was a pretty, dark-haired woman in her thirties who doubtless looked on her job as a career and played her part so well that he felt she *was* playing, was acting with some skill the role of a deferential servant. In a way she reminded him of Ted Hicks.

'Mrs Mountnessing hopes you won't mind going upstairs, Chief Inspector. Mrs Mountnessing is taking her coffee after luncheon in the little sitting room.'

It was a far cry from the house in De Beauvoir Square to which Natalie had sent him, a latter-day Bohemia where there had been Indian bedspreads draping the walls and a smell of marijuana for anyone who cared to sniff for it. Here the wall decorations were hunting prints, ascending parallel to the line of the staircase whose treads were carpeted in thick soft olive-green. The first-floor hall was wide, milk chocolate with white cornice and mouldings, the same green carpet, a *Hortus siccus* in a copper trough on a console table, a couple of fat-seated, round-backed chairs upholstered in golden-brown velvet, a twinkling chandelier and a brown table lamp with a cream satin shade. There are several thousand such interiors in the Royal Borough of Kensington and Chelsea. A panelled door was pushed open and Wexford found himself in the presence of Natalie Arno's Aunt Gladys, Mrs Rupert Mountnessing, the sister of Kathleen Camargue.

His first impression was of someone cruelly encaged and literally gasping for breath. It was a fleeting image. Mrs Mountnessing was just a fat woman in a too-tight corset which compressed her body from thighs to chest into the shape of a sausage and thrust a shelf of bosom up to buttress her double chin. This constrained flesh was sheathed in biscuit-coloured wool and upon the shelf rested three strands of pearls. Her face had become a cluster of pouches rather than a nest of wrinkles. It was thickly painted and surmounted by an intricate white-gold coiffure that was as smooth and stiff as a wig. The only area of Mrs Mountnessing which kept some hint of youth was her legs. And these were still excellent: slender, smooth, not varicosed, the ankles slim, the tapering feet shod in classic court shoes of beige glacé kid. They reminded him of Natalie's legs, they were exactly like. Did that mean anything? Very little. There are only a few types of leg, after all. One never said 'She has her aunt's legs' as one might say a woman had her father's nose or her grandmother's eyes.

The room was as beige and gold as its owner. On a low table was a coffee cup, coffee pot, sugar basin and cream jug in ivory china with a Greek key design on it in gold. Mrs Mountnessing rose when he came in and held out a hand much be-ringed, the old woman's claw-like nails filed to points and painted dark red.

'Bring another cup, will you, Miranda?'

It was the voice of an elderly child, petulant, permanently aggrieved. Wexford thought that the voice and the puckered face told of a lifetime of hurts, real or imagined. Rupert Mountnessing was presumably dead and gone long ago, and Dinah Sternhold had told him there had been no children. Would Natalie, real or false, hope for an inheritance here? Almost the first words uttered by Mrs Mountnessing told him that, if so, she hoped in vain.

'You said on the phone you wanted to talk to me about my niece. But I know nothing about my niece in recent years and I don't – I don't want to. I should have explained that to you, I realize that now. I shouldn't have let you come all this way when I've nothing at all to tell you.' Her eyes blinked more often or more obviously than most people's. The effect was to give the impression she fought off tears. 'Thank you, Miranda.' She took the coffee cup and listened, subsiding back into her chair as he told her the reason for his visit.

'Anastasia,' she said.

The Tichborne claimant had been recalled, now the Tsar's youngest daughter. Wexford did not relish the reminder, for wasn't it a fact that Anastasia's grandmother, the one person who could positively have identified her, had refused ever to see the claimant, and that as a result of that refusal no positive identification had ever been made?

'We hope it won't come to that,' he said. 'You seem to be her nearest relative, Mrs Mountnessing. Will you agree to see her in my presence and tell me if she is who she says she is?'

Her reaction, the look on her face, reminded him of certain people he had in the past asked to come and identify, not a living person, but a corpse in the mortuary. She put a hand up to each cheek. 'Oh no, I couldn't do that. I'm sorry, but it's impossible. I couldn't ever see Natalie again.'

He accepted it. She had forewarned him with her mention of Anastasia. If he insisted on her going with him the chances were she would make a positive identification simply to get the whole thing over as soon as possible. Briefly he wondered what it could have been that her niece, while still a young girl, had done to her, and then he joined her at the other end of the room where she stood contemplating a table that was used entirely as a stand for photographs in silver frames.

'That's my sister.'

A dark woman with dark eyes, but nevertheless intensely English. Perhaps there was something of the woman he knew as Natalie Arno in the broad brow and pointed chin.

'She had cancer. She was only forty-five when she

died. It was a terrible blow to my poor brother-in-law. He sold their house in Pomfret and built that one in Kingsmarkham and called it Sterries. Sterries is the name of the village in Derbyshire where my parents had their country place. Kathleen and Manuel first met there.'

Camargue and his wife were together among the photographs on the table. Arm-in-arm, walking along some Mediterranean sea front; seated side by side on a low wall in an English garden; in a group with a tall woman so like Camargue that she had to be his sister, and with two small dark-haired smiling girls. A ray of sunlight, obliquely slanted at three on a winter's afternoon, fell upon the handsome moustached face of a man in the uniform of a colonel of the Grenadier Guards. Rupert Mountnessing, no doubt. A little bemused by so many faces, Wexford turned away.

'Did Sir Manuel go to the United States after your niece went to live there?'

'Not to see *her*. I think he went there on a tour – yes, I'm sure he did, though it must be ten or twelve years since he gave up playing. His arthritis crippled him, poor Manuel. We saw very little of each other in recent years, but I was fond of him, he was a sweet man. I would have gone to the memorial service but Miranda wouldn't let me. She didn't want me to risk bronchitis in that terrible cold.'

Mrs Mountnessing, it seemed, was willing to talk about any aspect of family life except her niece. She sat down again, blinking back non-existent tears, held ramrod stiff by her corset. Wexford persisted.

'He went on a tour. Did he make any private visits?'

'He may have done.' She said it in the way people do when they dodge the direct affirmative but don't want to lie.

'But he didn't visit his daughter while he was there?'

'California's three thousand miles from the east coast,' she said, 'it's as far again as from here.'

Wexford shook his head dismissively. 'I don't understand that for nineteen years Sir Manuel never saw his daughter. It's not as if he was a poor man or a man who never travelled. If he had been a vindictive man, a man to bear a grudge – but everyone tells me how nice he was, how kind, how good. I might say I'd had golden opinions from all sorts of people. Yet for nineteen years he never made an effort to see his only child and allegedly all because she ran away from college and married someone he didn't know.'

She said so quietly that Wexford hardly heard her, 'It wasn't like that.' Her voice gained a little strength but it was full of distress. 'He wrote to her – oh, ever so many times. When my sister was very ill, was in fact dying, he wrote to her and asked her to come home. I don't know if she answered but she didn't come. My sister died and she didn't come. Manuel made a new will and wrote to her, telling her he was leaving her everything because it was right she should have his money and her mother's. She didn't answer and he gave up writing.'

I wonder how you come to know that? he asked

himself, looking at the crumpled profile, the chin that now trembled.

'I'm telling you all this,' said Mrs Mountnessing, 'to make you understand that my niece is cruel, cruel, a cruel unfeeling girl and violent too. She even struck her mother once. Did you know that?' The note in her voice grew hysterical and Wexford, watching the blinking eyes, the fingers clasping and unclasping in her lap, wished he had not mentioned the estrangement. 'She's a nymphomaniac too. Worse than that, it doesn't matter to her who the men are, her own relations, it's too horrible to talk about, it's too . . .'

He interrupted her gently. He got up to go. 'Thank you for your help, Mrs Mountnessing. I can't see a sign of any of these propensities in the woman I know.'

Miranda showed him out. As he crossed to the head of the stairs he heard a very soft whimpering sound from the room he had left, the sound of an elderly child beginning to cry.

9

A birth certificate, a marriage certificate, an American driving licence complete with immediately recognizable photograph taken three years before, a United States passport complete with immediately recognizable photograph taken the previous September, and perhaps most convincing of all, a letter to his daughter from Camargue, dated 1963, in which he informed her that he intended to make her his sole heir. All these documents had been readily submitted to Symonds, O'Brien and Ames, who invited Wexford along to their offices in the precinct over the British Home Stores to view them.

Kenneth Ames, distant and chatty as ever, said he had personally seen Mrs Arno, interviewed her exhaustively and elicited from her a number of facts about the Camargue family and her own childhood which were currently being verified. Mrs Arno had offered to take a blood test but since this could only prove that she was *not* Camargue's daughter, not that she was, and since no one seemed to know what Camargue's blood group had been, it was an impracticable idea. Mr Ames said she seemed heartily amused by the whole business, a point of course in her favour. She had even produced samples of her handwriting from when she was at the Royal Academy of Music to be compared with her writing of the present day.

'Do you know what she said to him?' Wexford said afterwards, meeting Burden for a drink in the Olive and Dove. 'She's got a nerve. "It's a pity I didn't do anything criminal when I was a teenager," she said. "They'd have my fingerprints on record and that would solve everything".'

Burden didn't smile. 'If she's not Natalie Camargue, when could the change-over have taken place?'

'Provided we accept what Zoffany says, not recently. Say more than two years ago but after the death of Vernon Arno. According to Ames, he would seem to have died in a San Francisco hospital in 1971.'

'He must have been young still.' Burden echoed Wexford's words to Ivan Zoffany. 'What did he die of?'

'Leukaemia. No one's suggesting there was anything odd about his death, though there's a chance we'll know more when we hear from the California police. But, Mike, if there was substitution, if this is an assumed identity, it was assumed for some other reason. That is, it wasn't put on for the sake of inheriting from Carmargue.'

Burden gave a dubious nod. 'It would mean the true Natalie was dead.'

'She may be but there are other possibilities. The true Natalie may be incurably ill in some institution or have become insane or gone to live in some inaccessible place. And the impostor could be someone who needed an identity because keeping her own was dangerous, because, for instance, she was some kind of fugitive from justice. That Camargue was rich, that Camargue was old, that Natalie was to be his sole heir, all these facts might be *incidental*, might be a piece of luck for the impostor which she only later decided to take advantage of. The identity would have been taken on originally as a safety measure, even perhaps as the only possible lifeline, and I think it was taken on at a point where the minimum of deception would have been needed. Maybe at the time the move was made from San Francisco to Los Angeles or much later, at the time when Tina Zoffany died.'

Burden, who seemed not to have been concentrating particularly on any of this, said suddenly, looking up from his drink and fixing Wexford with his steel-coloured eyes:

'Why did she come to this country at all?'

'To make sure of the dibs,' said Wexford.

'No.' Burden shook his head. 'No, that wasn't the reason. Impostor or real, she was in no doubt about what you call the dibs. She'd had that letter from Camargue, promising her her inheritance. She need do nothing but wait. There was no need to re-establish herself in his eyes, no need to placate him. If she'd felt there was she'd have tried it before. After all, he was getting on for eighty.

'And it's no good saying she came back because he was getting married again. No one knew he was getting married till 10 December when his engagement was in the *Telegraph*. She came back to this country in November but she made no attempt to see Camargue until after she read about his engagement. She was here for three or four weeks before that. Doing what? Planning what?'

Admiration was not something Wexford had often felt for the inspector in the past. Sympathy, yes, affection and a definite need, for Burden had most encouragingly fulfilled the function of an Achates or a Boswell, if not quite a Watson. But admiration? Burden was showing unexpected deductive powers that were highly gratifying to witness, and Wexford wondered if they were the fruit of happiness or of reading aloud from great literature in the evenings.

'Go on,' he said.

'So why did she come back? Because she was sentimental for her own home, her ain countree, as you might say?' As Scott might say, thought Wexford. Burden went on, 'She's a bit young for those feelings. She's an American citizen, she was settled in California. If she is Natalie Camargue she'd lived there longer than here, she'd no relatives here but a father and an aunt she didn't get on with, and no friends unless you count those Zoffanys.

'If she's an impostor, coming back was a mad thing to do. Stay in America and when Camargue dies his solicitors will notify her of the death, and though she'll no doubt then have to come here and swear affidavits and that sort of thing, *no one will question who she is.* No one would have questioned it if she hadn't shown herself to Camargue.'

'But she had to do that,' Wexford objected. 'Her whole purpose surely in going to see him was to persuade him not to re-marry.'

'She didn't know that purpose would even exist when she left the United States in November. And if she'd stayed where she was she might never have known of Camargue's re-marriage until he eventually died. What would that announcement have merited in a California newspaper? The *Los Angeles Times,* for instance? A paragraph tucked away somewhere. "Former world-famous British flautist . . ."'

'They say flutist over there.'

'Flautist, flutist, what does it matter? Until we know *why* she came here I've got a feeling we're not going to get at the truth about this.'

'The truth about who she is, d'you mean?'

'The truth about Camargue's death.' And Burden said with a certain crushing triumph, 'You're getting an obsession about who this woman is. I knew you would, I said so. What interests me far more is the murder of Camargue and who did it. Can't you see that in the context of the murder, who she is is an irrelevance?'

'No', said Wexford. 'Who she is is everything.'

*

The California police had nothing to tell Wexford about Natalie Arno. She was unknown to them, had never been in any trouble or associated with any trouble.

'The litigation in the Tichborne case,' said Burden gloomily, 'went on for three years and cost ninety thousand pounds. That was in 1874. Think what the equivalent of that would be today.'

'We haven't had any litigation yet,' said Wexford, 'or spent a single penny. Look on the bright side. Think of the claimant getting a fourteen-year sentence for perjury.'

In the meantime Kenneth Ames had interviewed two people who had known Camargue's daughter when she was an adolescent. Mavis Rolland had been at the Royal Academy of Music at the same time as Natalie Camargue and was now head of the music department at a girls' school on the South Coast. In her opinion there was no doubt that Natalie Arno was the former Natalie Camargue. She professed to find her not much changed except for her voice which she would not have recognized. On the other hand, Mary Woodhouse, a living-in maid who had worked for the Camargue family while they were in Pomfret, said she would have known the voice anywhere. In Ames's presence Mrs Woodhouse had talked to Natalie about Shaddough's Hall Farm where they had lived and Natalie had been able to recall events which Mrs Woodhouse said no impostor could have known.

Wexford wondered why Natalie had not proffered as witnesses for her support her aunt and that old family friend, Philip Cory. It was possible, of course, that in the case of her aunt (if she really was Natalie Arno) the dislike was mutual and that, just as he had feared Mrs Mountnessing would recognize her as her niece to avoid protracting an interview, so Natalie feared to meet her aunt lest animosity should make her refuse that recognition. But Cory she had certainly seen since she returned home, and Cory had so surely believed in her as to cling to her arm in the excess of emotion he had no doubt felt at his old friend's obsequies. Was there some reason she didn't want Cory brought into this?

In the early years of broadcasting Philip Cory had achieved some success by writing incidental music for radio. But this is not the kind of thing which makes a man's name. If Cory had done this at all it was on the strength of his light opera *Aimée*, based on the story of the Empress Josephine's cousin, the French Sultana. After its London season it had been enthusiastically taken up by amateur operatic societies, largely because it was comparatively easy to sing, had a huge cast, and the costumes required for it could double for *Entführung* or even *Aladdin*. This was particularly the case in Cory's own locality, where he was looked upon as something of a pet bard. Driving out to the environs of Myringham where the composer lived, Wexford noted in the villages at least three posters announcing that *Aimée* was to be performed yet again. It was likely then to be a disappointed man he was on his way to see. Local fame is gratifying only at the beginning of a career, and it could not have afforded much solace to Cory to see that his more frivolous work was to be staged by the Myfleet and District Operatic Society (tickets £1.20, licensed bar opens seven-thirty) while his tone poem *April Fire* and his ballet music for the *Flowers of Evil* were forgotten.

Parents can of course (as Wexford knew personally) enjoy success vicariously. Philip Cory might be scarcely remembered outside village-hall audiences, but his son Blaise Cory was a celebrity as only a television personality can be. His twice-weekly show of soul-searching interviews, drumming up support for charities, and professing aid for almost anyone out of a job, a home or a marriage, vied for pride of place with *Runway* in the popularity ratings. The name was as much a household word as Frost or Parkinson; the bland, handsome, rather larger-than-life face instantly familiar.

'But he doesn't live here, does he?' said Burden whose *bête noire* Blaise Cory was.

'Not as far as I know.' Wexford tapped the driver on the shoulder. 'Those are the gates up ahead, I think. On the left.'

It had been necessary to keep an eye out for Moidore Lodge which was in deep country, was three miles from the nearest village and, Cory had told Wexford on the phone, was invisible from the road. The pillars that supported the gates and on which sat a pair of stone wolves or possibly Alsatians – they very much resembled Nancy – were, however, unmistakable. The car turned in and, as the drive descended, entered an avenue of plane trees. And very strange and sinister they looked at this season, their trunks and limbs half covered in olive-green bark, half stripped to flesh colour, so that they appeared, or would have appeared to the fanciful, like shivering forms whose nakedness was revealed through rags. At the end of this double row of trees Moidore Lodge, three floors tall, narrow, and painted a curious shade of pale pea-green, glared formidably at visitors.

To ring the front-door bell it was necessary to climb half a dozen steps, though at the top of them there was no covered porch, nothing but a thin railing on each side. The wind blew sharply off the downs. Wexford, accustomed of late, as he remarked to Burden, to moving amongst those in the habit of being waited on, expected to be let in by a man or a maid or at least a cleaning woman, and was surprised when the door was opened by Cory himself.

He was no bigger than the impression of him Wexford had gained from that glimpse outside St Peter's, a little thin old man with copious white hair as silky as floss. Rather than appearing disappointed, he had a face that was both cheerful and peevish. He wore jeans and the kind of heavy navy-blue sweater that is called a guernsey, which gave him a look of youth, or the look perhaps of *a* youth who suffers from some terrible prematurely ageing disease. Before speaking, he looked them up and down closely. Indeed, they had passed through the over-heated, dusty, amazingly untidy and untended hall and were in the overheated, dusty rubbish heap of a living room before he spoke.

'Do you know,' he said, 'you are the first policemen I've ever actually had in my house. In any house I've ever lived in. Not the first I've ever *spoken* to, of course. I've *spoken* to them to ask the way and so forth. No doubt, I've lived a sheltered life.' Having done his best to make them feel like lepers or untouchables, Cory cracked his face into a nervous smile. 'The idea was distinctly strange to me. I've had to take two tranquillizers. As a matter of fact, my son is coming. I expect you've heard of my son.'

Burden's face was a mask of blankness. Wexford said, who hadn't? and proceeded to enlighten Cory as to the purpose of their visit. The result of this was that the old man had to take another Valium. It took a further full ten minutes to convince him there was a serious doubt about Natalie Arno's identity.

'Oh dear,' said Cory, 'oh dear, oh dear, how dreadful. Little Natalie. And she was so kind and considerate to me at poor Manuel's memorial service. Who could possibly have imagined she wasn't Natalie at all?'

'Well, she may be,' said Wexford. 'We're hoping you can establish that one way or the other.'

Looking at the distracted little man on whom tranquillizers seemed to have no effect, Wexford couldn't help doubting if the truth could be established through his agency. 'You want me to come with you and ask her a lot of questions? How horribly embarrassing that will be.' Cory actually ran his fingers through his fluffy hair. Then he froze, listening, and looking for all the world like an alerted rabbit. 'A car!' he cried. 'That will be Blaise. And none too soon. I must say, really, he knew what he was about when he insisted on being here to support me.'

If the father was no larger than Wexford had anticipated, the son was much smaller. The screen is a great deceiver when it comes to height. Blaise Cory was a small, wide man with a big face and eyes that twinkled as merrily as those of Santa Claus or a friendly elf. He came expansively into the room, holding out both hands to Wexford.

'And how is Sheila? Away on her honeymoon? Isn't that marvellous?' Forewarned, astute, one who had to make it his business to know who was who, he had done his homework. 'You know, she's awfully like you. I almost think I should have known if I hadn't known, if you see what I mean.'

'They want me to go and look at poor Manuel's girl and tell them if she's really her,' said Cory dolefully.

His son put up his eyebrows, made a soundless whistle. 'You don't mean it? Is *that* what it's about?'

He seemed less surprised than his father or Mrs Mountnessing had been. But perhaps that was only because he daily encountered more surprising things than they did.

'Do you also know her, Mr Cory?' Wexford asked.

'Know her? We took our first violin lessons together. Well, that's an exaggeration. Let me say we, as tots, went to the same master.'

'You didn't keep it up, Blaise,' said Cory senior.

'You were never a *concentrating* boy. Now little Natalie was very good. I remember little Natalie playing so beautifully to me when she was fifteen or sixteen, it was Bach's Chaconne from the D minor Partita and she . . .'

Blaise interrupted him. 'My dear father, it is twelve-thirty, and though I seem to remember promising to take you out to lunch, a drink wouldn't come amiss. With the possible exception of Macbeth, you must be the world's worst host.' He chuckled irrepressibly at his own joke. 'Now surely you have something tucked away in one of these glory holes?'

Once more Cory put his hands through his hair. He began to trot about the room, opening cupboard doors and peering along cluttered shelves as if he were as much a stranger to the house as they were. 'It's because I've no one to look after me,' he said distractedly. 'I asked Natalie – or whoever she is, you know – I asked her if she didn't want those Hickses and if she didn't, would they come and work for me? She was rather non-committal, said she'd ask them, but I haven't heard another word. How do *you* manage?'

Wexford was saved from replying by a triumphant shout from Blaise Cory who had found a bottle of whisky and one of dry sherry. It was now impossible to refuse a drink especially as Blaise Cory, with ferocious twinkles, declared that he knew for a fact policemen did drink on duty. The glasses were dusty and fingermarked, not to be too closely scrutinized. Nothing now remained but to fix a time with Philip Cory for visiting Natalie, and Wexford felt it would be wise, in spite of Burden's prejudice, to invite Blaise too.

'Ah, but I've already seen her. And frankly I wouldn't have the foggiest whether she was the late lamented Sir Manuel's daughter or not, I hadn't set eyes on her since we were teenagers. She said she was Natalie and that was good enough for me.'

'You were also at the memorial service?'

'Oh, no, no, no. Those morbid affairs give me the shivers. I'm a *life* person, Mr Wexford. No, I gave Natalie lunch. Oh, it must have been a good five or six weeks ago.'

'May I ask why you did that, Mr Cory?'

'Does one have to have a reason for taking attractive ladies out to lunch apart from the obvious one? No, I'm teasing you. It was actually Natalie who phoned me, recalled our former acquaintance and asked me if I could get a friend of hers a job, a man, she didn't say his name. I'm afraid it was all rather due to my programme. I don't know if a busy man like you ever has a moment to watch it? A poor thing, but mine own. I do make rather bold claims on it – not, however, without foundation *and* results – to aid people in finding – well, niches for themselves. This chap was apparently some sort of musician. Fancied himself on the box, I daresay. Anyway, I couldn't hold out much hope but I asked her to have lunch with me. Now I come to think of it, it was January 17th. I remember because that was the dear old dad's birthday.'

'I was seventy-four,' said Cory senior in the tone of

one intending to astonish nobody, as indeed he had.

'And when you met her that day you had no doubt she was the Natalie Camargue you had once known?'

'Now wait a minute. When it came to it, I didn't meet her that day. She cancelled on account of some medical thing she had to have, a biopsy, I think she said. We made a fresh date for the following Tuesday. She kept that and I must say we had a delightful time, she was absolutely charming, full of fun. I was only sorry to have to say I hadn't anything cooking for this bloke of hers. But, you know, I couldn't actually tell you if she was *our* Natalie. I mean, it obviously never occurred to me.' He let his eyes light on Burden as being closer to his own age than the others. 'Would you recognize a lady you hadn't seen since you were nineteen?'

Burden responded with a cold smile which had no disconcerting effect on Blaise Cory.

'It's all rather thrilling, isn't it? Quite a tonic it must be for the dear old dad.'

'No, it isn't,' said the composer. 'It's very upsetting indeed. I think I'll come back to London with you, Blaise, since I've got to be up there tomorrow. And I think I may stay awhile. I suppose you can put up with me for a couple of weeks?'

Blaise Cory put an arm round his father's shoulders and answered with merry affirmatives. Perhaps it was Wexford's imagination that the twinkle showed signs of strain.

The kind of coincidence that leads to one's coming

across a hitherto unknown word three times in the same day or receiving a letter from an acquaintance one has dreamed of the night before was no doubt responsible for the poster in the window of the Kingsbrook Precinct travel agents. *Come to sunny California, land of perpetual spring* . . . A picture of what might be Big Sur and next to it one of what might be Hearst Castle. Wexford paused and looked at it and wondered what the chief constable would say if he suggested being sent to the Golden West in quest of Natalie Arno's antecedents. He could just imagine Colonel Griswold's face.

Presently he turned away and went back to the police station. He had come from Symonds, O'Brien and Ames. Their handwriting expert had examined the writing of the eighteen-year-old Natalie Camargue and that of the thirty-seven-year-old Natalie Arno and expressed his opinion that, allowing for normal changes over a period of nearly two decades, the two samples had in all probability been made by the same person. Wexford had suggested the samples also be examined by an expert of police choosing. Without making any positive objection, Ames murmured that it would be unwise to spoil the ship with too many cooks.

Wexford thought he saw a better way.

'Mike,' he said, putting his head round the door of Burden's office, 'where can we get hold of a violin?'

10

Burden's wife was something of a paragon. She was a history teacher, she was well-read in English literature, she was an excellent cook and dressmaker and now it appeared she was musical too.

'You never told me Jenny played the violin,' said Wexford.

'As a matter of fact,' said Burden rather shyly, 'she used to be with the Pilgrim String Quartet.' This was a local ensemble that enjoyed a little more than local fame. 'I expect we could borrow her Hills if we were very careful with it.'

'Her *what*?'

'Her Hills. It's a well-known make of violin.'

'If you say so, Stradivarius.'

Burden brought the violin along in the morning.

They were going to call for Philip Cory at his son's home and drive him to De Beauvoir Place. It was a bright sunny day, the first since the snow had gone.

Blaise Cory lived on Campden Hill, not far from Mrs Mountnessing, and work seemed to have claimed him, for his father was alone in the big penthouse flat. Although he popped a Valium pill into his mouth as soon as he saw them, a night in London had evidently done him good. He was sprightly, his cheeks pink, and he had dressed himself in a dark suit with a thin red stripe, a pink shirt and a burgundy silk tie, more as if he were going to a smart luncheon party than taking part in a criminal investigation.

In the car he was inclined to be talkative.

'I think I shall write to those Hickses personally. I've no reason to believe they're not well-disposed towards me. I understand they like the country and the thing about Moidore Lodge is, it's in the real country. Charming as poor Manuel's place is, I always used to think there was something Metroland-ish about it. One might as well be living in Hampstead Garden Suburb. Do you know, I thought it would be quite an ordeal facing little Natalie today, but actually I feel rather excited at the prospect. London is such a stimulus, don't you find? It seems to tone up one's whole system. And if she isn't Natalie, there's nothing to be embarrassed about.'

Wexford had no intention of going into the bookshop. The door to the upstairs flat was at the side of the building, a panelled door with a pane of glass in it, set under a porch with a steep tiled roof. As they walked up the path, Wexford leading and Burden bringing up the rear with the violin, the door opened, a woman came out and it immediately closed again. The woman was elderly and so tiny as to be almost a midget. She wore a black coat and a brightly coloured knitted hat and gloves. Cory said:

'Good gracious me! It's Mrs Woodhouse, isn't it?'

'That's right, sir, and you're Mr Cory.' She spoke with a Sussex burr. 'How have you been keeping? Mustn't grumble, that's what I always say. I see Mr Blaise on the telly last night, he's a real scream, just the same as ever. You living in London now, are you?'

'Oh dear, no,' said Cory. 'Down in the same old place.' His eyes widened suddenly as if with inspiration. 'I haven't anyone to look after me. I don't suppose . . .'

'I'm retired, sir, and never had so much to do. I don't have a moment for myself let alone other folks, so I'll say bye-bye now and nice to see you after all this time.'

She scuttled off in the direction of De Beauvoir Square, looking at her watch like the White Rabbit as she went.

'Who was that?' said Burden.

'She used to work for poor Manuel and Kathleen when they lived at Shaddough's Hall Farm. I can't think what she's doing up here.'

The door, though closed, had been left on the latch. Wexford pushed it open and they went up the steep staircase. Natalie had come out on to the landing and was waiting for them at the top. Wexford had thought about her so much, had indeed become so obsessive about her, that since last seeing her he had created an image of her in his mind that was seductive, sinister, Mata Hari-like, corrupt, guileful and serpentine. Before the reality this chimera showed itself briefly for the absurd delusion it was and then dissolved. For here, standing before them, was a charming and pretty woman to whom none of these pejorative expressions could possibly apply. Her black hair hung loose to her shoulders, held back by a velvet Alice band. She wore the skirt Jane Zoffany had been altering and with it a simple white shirt and dark blue cardigan. It was very near a school uniform and there was something of the schoolgirl about her as she brought her face down to Cory's and kissed him, saying with the slightest edge of reproach:

'It's good to see you, Uncle Philip. I only wish the circumstances were different.'

Cory drew his face away. He said in a kind of sharp chirp, 'One must do one's duty as a citizen.'

She laughed at that and patted his shoulder. They all went into a small and unpretentious living room from which a kitchen opened. It was all a far cry from Sterries. The furnishings looked as if they had come down to the Zoffanys from defunct relatives who hadn't paid much for them when they were new. Nothing seemed to have been added by Natalie except a small shelf of paperbacks which could only be designated as non-Zoffany because none of them was science fiction.

There was an aroma of coffee and from the kitchen the sound, suggestive of some large hibernating creature snoring, that a percolator makes.

'Do sit down,' said Natalie, 'Make yourselves at home. Excuse me while I see to the coffee.' She seemed totally carefree and gave no sign of having noticed what Burden had brought into the flat. There's no art, thought Wexford, to find the mind's construction in the face.

The coffee, when it came, was good. 'The secret', said Natalie gaily, 'is to put enough in.' Uttering this cliché, she laughed. 'I'm afraid the British don't do that.'

She surely couldn't be enjoying herself like this if she was not Natalie, if there was any chance of her failing the test ahead of her. He glanced at Burden whose eyes were on her, who seemed to be studying her appearance and was recalling perhaps newspaper photographs or actual glimpses of Camargue. Having taken a sip of his coffee into which he ladled three spoonfuls of sugar, Cory started at once on his questioning. He would have made a good quizmaster. Perhaps it was from him that Blaise had inherited his talents.

'You and your parents went to live at Shaddough's Hall Farm when you were five. Can you remember what I gave you for your sixth birthday?'

She didn't hesitate. 'A kitten. It was a grey one, a British Blue.'

'Your cat had been run over and I gave you that one to replace it.'

'We called it Panther.'

Cory had forgotten that. But Wexford could see that now he remembered and was shaken. He asked less confidently: 'Where was the house?'

'On the Pomfret to Cheriton road. You'll have to do better than that, Uncle Philip. Anyone could have found out where Camargue lived.'

For answer he threw a question at her in French. Wexford wasn't up to understanding it but he gave Cory full marks for ingenuity. There was more to this old man than at first met the eye. She answered in fluent French and Cory addressed her in what Wexford took to be Spanish. This was something he was sure Symonds, O'Brien and Ames had not thought of. But what a sound test it was. Momentarily he held his breath, for she was not answering, her face had that puzzled foolish look people have when spoken to in a language they know less thoroughly than they have claimed.

Cory repeated what he had said. Burden cleared his throat and moved a little in his chair. Wexford held himself perfectly still, waiting, knowing that every second which passed made it more and more likely that she had been discovered and exposed. And then, as Cory was about to speak for the third time, she broke into a flood of fast Spanish so that Cory himself was taken aback, uncomprehending apparently, until she explained more slowly what it was that she had said.

Wexford drank his coffee and she, looking at

him mischievously, refilled his cup. On Burden she bestowed one of her sparkling smiles. Her long hair fell forward, Cleopatra-like, in two heavy tresses to frame her face. It was a young face, Wexford thought, even possibly too young for the age she professed to be. And wasn't it also *too Spanish*? Natalie Camargue's mother had been English, typically English, her father half-French. Would their daughter look quite so much like one of Goya's women? None of the evidence, convincing though it was, was as yet conclusive. Why shouldn't an imposter speak Spanish? If the substitution had taken place in Los Angeles she might even be Mexican. Why not know about the kitten and its name if she had been a friend of the true Natalie and had set out to absorb her childhood history?

'What was the first instrument you learned to play?' Cory was asking.

'The recorder.'

'How old were you when you began the violin?'

'Eight.'

'Who was your first master?'

'I can't remember,' she said.

'When you were fifteen you were living at Shaddough's Hall Farm and you were on holiday from school. It was August. Your father had just come back from a tour of – America, I think.'

'Canada.'

'I do believe you're right.' Cory, having been determined almost from Wexford's first words on the subject to consider her an impostor, grew more and more astonished as the interrogation went on. 'You're right, it was. God bless my soul. Do you remember my coming to dinner with your parents? I and my wife? Can you remember that evening?'

'I think so. I hadn't seen you for about a year.'

'Before dinner I asked you to play something for me and you did and . . .'

She didn't even allow him to finish.

'I played Bach's Chaconne from the D minor Partita.'

Cory was stunned into silence. He stared at her and then turned on Wexford an affronted look.

'It was too difficult for me,' she said lightly. 'You clapped but I felt I'd made a mess of it.' The expressions on the three men's faces afforded her an amused satisfaction. 'That's proof enough, isn't it? Shall we all have a drink to celebrate my reinstatement?' She jumped up, took the tray and went into the kitchen, leaving the door open.

It was perhaps this open door and the sound of their hostess humming lightheartedly that stopped Cory from rounding on Wexford. Instead he raised his whiskery white eyebrows almost into his fluffy white hair and shook his head vigorously, a gesture that plainly said he felt he had been brought here on a wild-goose chase. If she wasn't Natalie, Wexford thought, there was no way she could have known about that piece of music. It was impossible to imagine circumstances in which the true Natalie would have spoken of such a thing to the false. If she had done so it would presuppose her having recounted every occasion on which she had played to a friend, listing every friend and every piece of music, since it could never have been foreseen that this particular piece would be inquired about. That Cory would ask this question, a question that had no doubt come into his mind because of his reference to the Bach Chaconne on the previous day, could only have been guessed at by those who had been present at the time, himself, Burden and Blaise.

So one could almost agree with her and acclaim her reinstated as Camargue's heir. She had passed the test no impostor could have passed. He looked at her wonderingly as she returned to the room, the contents of the tray now exchanged for a couple of bottles and an ice bucket. If she was, as she now seemed undoubtedly to be, Natalie Arno, how had Camargue possibly been deceived in the matter? This woman would never have mispronounced a word or a name in a foreign language known to her. And if Camargue had indeed accused her of doing so, it had been in her power to correct that misapprehension at once and to furnish him with absolute proof of who she was. For now Wexford had no doubt that if Camargue had asked her she would have recalled for him the minutest details of her infancy, of the family, of esoteric domestic customs which no one living but he and she could have known. But Camargue had been an old man, wandering in his wits as well as short-sighted and growing deaf. That tiresome woman Dinah Sternhold had wasted their time, repeating to him what was probably only one amongst several of a dotard's paranoid delusions.

Burden looked as if he was ready to leave. He had reached down to grasp once more the handle of the violin case.

'Would you play that piece of music for us now, Mrs Arno?' Wexford said.

If she had noticed the violin, as she surely must have done, she had presumably supposed it the property of Cory and unconnected with herself, for with his question her manner changed. She had put the tray down and had been about to lift her hands from it, but her hands remained where they were and slightly stiffened. Her face was unaltered, but she was no longer quite in command of the situation and she was no longer amused.

'No, I don't think I would,' she said.

'You've given up the violin?'

'No, I still play in an amateurish sort of way, but I'm out of practice.'

'We'll make allowances, Mrs Arno,' said Wexford. 'The inspector and I aren't competent to judge, anyway.' Burden gave him a look implying that *he* might be. 'If you'll play the violin so as to satisfy Mr Cory I will myself be satisfied that Sir Manuel had – made a mistake.'

She was silent. She sat still, looking down, considering. Then she put out her hand for the violin case and drew it towards her. But she seemed not quite to know how to open it, for she fumbled with the catch.

'Here, let me,' said Burden.

She got up and looked at the tray she had brought

in. 'I forgot the glasses. Excuse me.'

Burden lifted out the violin carefully, then the bow. The sight of it restored Cory's temper and he touched one of the strings lightly with his finger. From the kitchen came a sudden tinkle of breaking glass, an exclamation, then a sound of water running.

'You may as well put that instrument away again,' said Wexford quietly.

She came and her face was white. 'I broke a glass.' Wrapped round her left hand was a bunch of wet tissues, rapidly reddening, and as she scooped the sodden mass away, Wexford saw a long thin cut, bright red across three fingertips.

11

It should have been the beginning, not the end. They should have been able to proceed with a prosecution for deception and an investigation of the murder of Sir Manuel Camargue. And Wexford, calling on Symonds, O'Brien and Ames with what he thought to be proof that Natalie Arno was not who she said she was, felt confident he had a case. She might speak French and Spanish, she might know the most abstruse details about the Camargues' family life, but she couldn't play the violin and that was the crux. She had not dared to refuse so she had deliberately cut her fingers on the tips where they must press the strings. Kenneth Ames listened to all this with a vagueness bordering on indifference which would have alarmed Wexford if he hadn't been used to the man's manner. He seemed reluctant to disclose the address of Mrs Mary Woodhouse but finally did so when pressed.

She lived with her son and daughter-in-law, both of whom were out at work, in a council flat on the Pomfret housing estate. While Wexford talked to her, explaining gently but at some length what he suspected, she at first sat still and attentive, but when the purpose of his visit became clear to her, she pushed her brows together and stuck out her underlip and picked up the work on which she had been engaged before he arrived. This was some sort of bed cover, vast in size, of dead-white cotton crochet work. Mrs Woodhouse's crochet hook flashed in and out as she expended her anger through her fingers.

'I don't know what you're talking about, I don't know what you mean.' She repeated these sentences over and over whenever he paused for a reply. She was a small, sharp-featured old woman whose dark hair had faded to charcoal colour. 'I went to see Mrs Arno because she asked me. Why shouldn't I? I've got a sister living in Hackney that's been a bit off-colour. I've been stopping with her and what with Mrs Arno living like only a stone's throw away, it's only natural I'd go and see her, isn't it? I've known her since she was a kiddy, it was me brought her up as much as her mother.'

'How many times have you seen her, Mrs Woodhouse?'

'I don't know what you mean. Hundreds of times, thousands of times. If you mean been to her place like this past week, just the twice. The time you saw me and two days previous. I'd like to know what you're getting at.'

'Were some of those "hundreds of times" last November and December, Mrs Woodhouse? Did Mrs Arno go and see you when she first arrived in this country?'

'I'll tell you when I first saw her. Two weeks back. When that solicitor, that Mr Ames, come here and asked me the same sort of nonsense you're asking me. Only he knew when he was beaten.' The crochet hook jerked faster and the ball of yarn bounced on Mary Woodhouse's lap. 'Had I any doubt Mrs Arno was Miss Natalie Camargue?' She put a wealth of scorn into her voice. 'Of course I hadn't, not a shadow of doubt.'

'I expect Mrs Arno asked you a great many questions, didn't she? I expect she asked you to remind her of things in her childhood which had slipped her mind. The name of a grey kitten, for instance?'

'Panther,' said Mrs Woodhouse. 'That was his name. Why shouldn't I tell her? She'd forgotten, she was only a kiddy. I don't know what you mean, asking me things like that. Of course I've got a good memory, I was famous in the family for my memory. Mr Camargue – he was Mr Camargue then – he used to say, Mary, you're just like an elephant, and people'd look at me, me being so little and thin, and he'd say, You never forget a thing.'

'I expect you understand what conspiracy is, don't you, Mrs Woodhouse? You understand what is meant by a conspiracy to defraud someone of what is theirs by right of law? I don't think you would want to be involved in something of that kind, would you? Something which could get you into very serious trouble?'

She repeated her formula fiercely, one hand clutching the crochet hook, the other the ball of yarn. 'I don't know what you mean. I don't know what you're talking about.'

Mavis Rolland, the music teacher, was next on his list to be seen. He had the phone in his hand, he was about to dial the school number and arrange an appointment with her when Kenneth Ames was announced.

It was as warm in Wexford's office as it was in the Kingsbrook Precinct, but Ames removed neither his black, waisted overcoat nor his black-and-grey check worsted scarf. He took the chair Wexford offered him and fixed his eyes on the northern aspect of St Peter's spire just as he was in the habit of contemplating its southern elevation from his own window.

The purpose of his call, he said, was to inform the police that Symonds, O'Brien and Ames had decided to recognize Mrs Natalie Kathleen Camargue Arno as Sir Manuel Camargue's rightful heir.

In fact, said Ames, it was only their regard for truth and their horror of the possibility of fraud that had led them to investigate in the first place what amounted to malicious slander.

'We were obliged to look into it, of course, though

it never does to place too much credence on that kind of mischief-making.'

'Camargue himself . . .' Wexford began.

'My dear chap, according to Mrs Steinbeck, according to *her*. I'm afraid you've been a bit led up the garden. Lost your sense of proportion too, if I may say so. Come now. You surely can't have expected my client to play you a pretty turn on that fiddle when she'd got a nasty cut on her hand.'

Wexford noted that Natalie Arno had become 'my client'. He was more surprised than he thought he could be by Ames's statement, he was shocked, and he sat in silence, digesting it, beginning to grasp its implications. Still staring skywards, Ames said chattily:

'There was never any real doubt, of course.' He delivered one of his strange confused metaphors. 'It was a case of making a mare's nest out of a molehill. But we do now have incontrovertible proof.'

'Oh yes?' Wexford's eyebrows went up.

'My client was able to produce her dentist, chappie who used to see to the Camargue family's teeth. Man called Williams from London, Wigmore Street, in point of fact. He'd still got his records and – well, my client's jaw and Miss Natalie Camargue's are indisputably one and the same. She hasn't even lost a tooth.'

Wexford made his appointment with Miss Rolland but was obliged to cancel it next day. For in the interim he had an unpleasant interview with the chief constable. Charles Griswold, with his uncanny resemblance to the late General de Gaulle, as heavily built, grave and intense a man as Ames was slight, shallow and *distrait*, stormed in upon him on the following morning.

'Leave it, Reg, forget it. Let it be as if you had never heard the name Camargue.'

'Because an impostor has seduced Ames into believing a pack of lies, sir?'

'*Seduced*?'

Wexford made an impatient gesture with his hand. 'I was speaking metaphorically, of course. *She is not Natalie Arno*. My firm belief is that ever since she came here she's been employing a former servant of the Camargue family to instruct her in matters of family history. As for the dentist, did Symonds, O'Brien and Ames check on him? Did they go to him or did he come to them? If this is a conspiracy in which a considerable number of people are involved . . .'

'You know I haven't the least idea what you're talking about, don't you? All I'm saying is, if a reputable firm of solicitors such as Symonds, O'Brien and Ames will accept this woman and permit her to inherit a very significant property, we will accept her too. And we'll forget way-out notions of pushing old men into frozen lakes when we have not a shred of evidence that Camargue died anything but a natural death. Is that understood?'

'If you say so, it must be, sir.'

'It must,' said the chief constable.

Not the beginning but the end. Wexford had become obsessional about cases before, and the path these obsessions took had been blocked by just such obstacles and opposition. The feeling of frustration was a familiar one to him but it was none the less bitter for that. He stood by the window, cursing under his breath, gazing at the opaque pale sky. The weather had become raw and icy again, a white mist lifting only at midday and then hanging threateningly at tree height. Sheila was coming back today. He couldn't remember whether she was due in at ten in the morning or ten at night and he didn't want to know. That way he couldn't worry too precisely about what was happening to her aircraft in the fog, unable to land maybe, sent off to try Luton or Manchester, running short of fuel . . . He told himself sternly, reminded himself, that air transport was the safest of all forms of travel, and let his thoughts turn back to Natalie Arno. Or whoever. Was he never to know now? Even if it were only for the satisfaction of his own curiosity, was he never to know who she was and how she had done it? The switch from one identity to another, the impersonation, the murder . . .

After what Griswold had said, he dare not, for his very job's sake, risk another interview with Mary Woodhouse, keep his appointment with Mavis Rolland, attempt to break down the obduracy of Mrs Mountnessing or set about exposing that fake dentist, Williams. What could he do?

The way home had necessarily to be via the Kingsbrook Precinct, for Dora had asked him to pick up a brace of pheasants ordered at the poulterers there. Proximity to the premises of Symonds, O'Brien and Ames angered him afresh, and he wished he might for a split moment become a delinquent teenager in order to daub appropriate graffiti on their brass plate. Turning from it, he found himself looking once more into the window of the travel agents.

A helpful young man spread a handful of brochures in front of him. What had been Dora's favourites? Bermuda, Mexico, anywhere warm in the United States. They had discussed it endlessly without coming to a decision, knowing this might be the only holiday of such magnitude they would ever have. The poster he had seen in the window had its twin and various highly coloured siblings inside. He glanced up and it was the skyscraper-scape of San Francisco that met his eyes.

The fog had thickened while he was in there. It seemed to lay a cold wet finger on the skin of his face. He drove home very slowly, thinking once more about Sheila, but as he put his key into the front door lock the door was pulled open and there she was before him, browner than he had ever seen her, her hair bleached pale as ivory.

She put out her arms and hugged him. Dora and Andrew were in the living room.

'Heathrow's closed and we had to land at Gatwick,' said Sheila, 'so we thought we'd come and see you on our way. We've had such a fabulous time, Pop, I've been telling Mother, you just have to go.'

Wexford laughed. 'We are going to California,' he said.

Part Two

12

The will, published in the *Kingsmarkham Courier*, as well as in the national press, showed Sir Manuel Camargue to have left the sum of £1,146,000 net. This modest fortune became Natalie Arno's a little more than two months after Camargue's death.

'I shouldn't call a million pounds modest,' said Burden.

'It is when you consider all the people who will want their pickings,' Wexford said. 'All the conspirators. No wonder she's put the house up for sale.'

She had moved into Sterries, but immediately put the house on the market, the asking price being £110,000. For some weeks Kingsmarkham's principal estate agents, Thacker, Prince and Co., displayed in their window coloured photographs of its exterior, the music room, the drawing room and the garden, while less distinguishable shots of it appeared in the local press. But whether the house itself was too stark and simplistic in design for most people's taste or whether the price was too high, the fact was that it remained on sale throughout that period of the year when house-buying is at its peak.

'Funny to think that we know for sure she's no business to be there and no right to sell it and no right to what she gets for it,' said Burden, 'and there's not a damn thing we can do about it.'

But Wexford merely remarked that summer had set in with its usual severity and that he was looking forward to going somewhere warm for his holiday.

The Wexfords were not seasoned travellers and this would be the farthest away from home either had ever been. Wexford felt this need not affect the preparations they must make, but Dora had reached a point just below the panic threshold. All day she had been packing and unpacking and re-packing, confessing shamefacedly that she was a fool and then beginning to worry about the possibility of the house being broken into while they were away. It was useless for Wexford to point out that whether they were known to be in San Francisco or Southend would make little difference to a prospective burglar. He could only assure her that the police would keep an eye on the house. If they couldn't do that for him, whom could they do it for? Sylvia had promised to go into the house every other day in their absence and he set off that evening to give her a spare key.

Wexford's elder daughter and her husband had in the past year moved to a newer house in north Kingsmarkham, and it was only a slightly longer way round to return from their home to his own by taking Ploughman's Lane. To go and look at the house Camargue had built, and on the night before he set out to prove Natalie Arno's claim to it fraudulent, seemed a fitting act. He drove into Ploughman's Lane by way of the side road which skirted the grounds of Kingsfield House. But if Sterries had been almost invisible from the roadway in January and February, it was now entirely hidden. The screen of hornbeams, limes and planes that had been skeletons when last he was there, were in full leaf and might have concealed an empty meadow rather than a house for all that could be seen of it.

It was still light at nearly nine. He was driving down the hill when he heard the sound of running feet behind him. In his rear mirror he saw a flying figure, a woman who was running down Ploughman's Lane as if pursued. It was Jane Zoffany.

There were no pursuers. Apart from her, the place was deserted, sylvan, silent, as such places mostly are even on summer nights. He pulled into the kerb and got out. She was enough in command of herself to swerve to avoid him but as she did so she saw who it was and immediately recognized him. She stopped and burst into tears, crying where she stood and pushing her knuckles into her eyes.

'Come and sit in the car,' said Wexford.

She sat in the passenger seat and cried into her hands, into the thin gauzy scarf which she wore swathed round her neck over a red and yellow printed dress of Indian make. Wexford gave her his handkerchief. She cried some more and laid her head back against the headrest, gulping, the tears running down her face. She had no handbag, no coat or jacket, though the dress was sleeveless, and on her stockingless feet were Indian sandals with only a thong to attach them. Suddenly she began to speak, pausing only when sobs choked her voice.

'I thought she was wonderful. I thought he was the most wonderful, charming, gifted, *kind* person I'd ever met. And I thought she liked me, I thought she actually wanted my company. I never thought she'd really noticed my husband much, I mean except as my husband, that's all I thought he was to her, I thought it was *me* . . . And now he says . . . oh God, what am I going to do? Where shall I go? What's going to become of me?'

Wexford was nonplussed. He could make little sense of what she said but guessed she was spilling all this misery out on to him only because he was there. Anyone willing to listen would have served her purpose. He thought too, and not for the first time, that there was something unhinged about her. You could see disturbance in her eyes as much when they were dry as when they were swollen and wet with tears. She put her hand on his arm.

'I did everything for her, I bent over backwards to make her feel at home, I ran errands for her, I even mended her clothes. She took all that from me and all the time she and Ivan had been – when he went out to California they had a relationship!'

He neither winced nor smiled at the incongruous word, relic of the already outdated jargon of her youth. 'Did she tell you that, Mrs Zoffany?' he asked gently.

'He told me. Ivan told me.' She wiped her face with the handkerchief. 'We came down here on Wednesday to stay, we meant to stay till – oh, Sunday or Monday. The shop's a dead loss anyway, no one ever comes in, it makes no difference whether we're there or not. She invited us and we came. I know why she did now. She doesn't want him but she wants him in love with her, she wants him on a string.' She shuddered and her voice broke again. 'He told me this evening, just now, half an hour ago. He said he'd been in love with her for two years, ever since he first saw her. He was longing for her to come and live here so that they could be together and then when she did come she kept fobbing him off and telling him to wait and now . . .'

'Why did he tell you all this?' Wexford interrupted.

She gulped, put out a helpless hand. 'He had to tell someone, he said, and there was no one but me. He overheard her talking to someone on the phone like he was her lover, telling him to come down once we'd gone but to be discreet. Ivan understood then. He's broken-hearted because she doesn't want him. He told his own wife that, that he doesn't know how he can go on living because another woman won't have him. I couldn't take it in at first, I couldn't believe it, than I started screaming. She came into our room and said what was the matter? I told her what he'd said and she said, "I'm sorry, darling, but I didn't know you then". She said that to *me*. "I didn't know you then," she said, "and it wasn't anything important anyway. It only happened three or four times, it was just that we were both lonely." As if that made it better!'

Wexford was silent. She was calmer now, though trembling. Soon she would begin regretting that she had poured out her heart to someone who was almost a stranger. She passed her hands over her face and dropped her shoulders with a long heavy sigh.

'Oh God. What am I going to do? Where shall I go? I can't stay with him, can I? When she said that to me I ran out of the house, I didn't even take my bag, I just ran and you were there and – oh God, I don't know what you must think of me talking to you like this. You must think I'm out of my head, crazy, mad. Ivan says I'm mad, "If you're going to carry on like that," he said, "a psychiatric ward's the best place for you."' She gave him a sideways look. 'I've been in those places, that's why he said that. If only I had a friend I could go to but I've lost all my friends, in and out of hospital the way I've been. People don't want to know you any more when they think you've got something wrong with your mind. In my case it's only depression, it's a disease like any other, but they don't realize.' She gave a little whimpering cry. 'Natalie wasn't like that, she knew about my depression, she was *kind*. I thought she was, but all the time . . . I've lost my only friend as well as my husband!'

Her mouth worked unsteadily from crying, her eyes were red. She looked like a hunted gypsy, the greying bushy hair hanging in shaggy bundles against her cheeks. And it was plain from her expression and her fixed imploring eyes that, because of his profession and his manner and his having caught her the way he had, she expected him to do something for her. Wreak vengeance on Natalie Arno, restore an errant husband or at least provide some dignified shelter for the night.

She began to speak rapidly, almost feverishly. 'I can't go back there, I can't face it. Ivan's going home, he said so, he said he'd go home tonight, but I can't be with him, I can't be alone with him, I couldn't bear it. I've got my sister in Wellridge but she won't want me, she's like the rest of them . . . There must be somewhere I could go, you must know somewhere, if you could only . . .'

There flashed into Wexford's mind the idea that he could take her home with him and get Dora to give her a bed for the night. The sheer nuisance this would be stopped him. They were going on holiday tomorrow, their flight went at one p.m, which meant leaving Kingsmarkham for Heathrow at ten. Suppose she refused to leave? Suppose Zoffany arrived? It just wasn't on.

She was still talking non-stop. 'So if I could possibly be with you there are lots of things I'd like to tell you. I feel if I could only get them off my chest I'd be that much better and they'd help you, they're things you'd want to know.'

'About Mrs Arno?' he said sharply.

'Well, not exactly about her, about *me*. I need someone to listen and be sympathetic, that does you more good than all the therapy and pills in the world, I can tell you. I can't be alone, don't you understand?'

Later he was to castigate himself for not giving in to that first generous impulse. If he had done he might have known the true facts that night and, more important, a life might have been saved. But as much as the unwillingness to be involved and to create trouble for himself, a feeling of caution prevented him. He was a policeman, the woman was a little mad . . .

'The best thing will be for me to drive you back up the hill to Sterries, Mrs Zoffany. Let me . . .'

'No!'

'You'll very probably find your husband is ready to leave and waiting for you. You and he would still be in time to catch the last train to Victoria. Mrs Zoffany, you have to realize he'll get over this, it's something that will very likely lose its force now he's brought it into the open. Why not try to . . .?'

'No!'

'Come, let me take you back.'

For answer, she gathered up her skirts and draperies and half jumped, half tumbled out of the car. In some consternation, Wexford too got out to help her, but she had got to her feet and as he put out his arm she threw something at him, a crumpled ball. It was his handkerchief.

She stood for a little while a few yards from him, leaning against the high jasmine-hung wall of one of these sprawling gardens. She hung her head, her hands up to her chin, like a child who has been scolded. It was deep dusk now and growing cool. Suddenly she began to walk back the way she had come. She walked quite briskly up the hill, up over the crown of the hill, to be lost amid the soft, hanging, darkening green branches.

He waited a while, he hardly knew what for. A car passed him just as he started his own, going rather fast down the hill. It was a mustard-coloured Opel, and although it was much too dark to see at all clearly, the woman at the wheel looked very much like Natalie Arno. It was a measure, of course, of how much she occupied his thoughts.

He drove home to Dora who had packed for the last time and was watching Blaise Cory's programme on the television.

13

Wexford was driving on the wrong side of the road. Or that was how he put it to himself. It wasn't as bad as he had expected, the San Diego Freeway had so many lanes and traffic moved at a slower pace than at home. What was alarming and didn't seem to get any better was that he couldn't judge the space he had on the right-hand side so that Dora exclaimed, 'Oh, Reg, you were only about an inch from that car. I was sure you were going to scrape!'

The sky was a smooth hazy blue and it was very hot. Nine hours' flying had taken its toll on both of them. Stopped at the lights – traffic lights hung somewhere up in the sky here – Wexford glanced at his wife. She looked tired, she was bound to, but excited as well. For him it wasn't going to be much of a holiday, unless you agreed with those who say that a change is as good as a rest, and he was beginning to feel guilty about the amount of time he would have to spend apart from her. He had tried to explain that if it wasn't for this quest of his they wouldn't be coming here at all, and she had taken it with cheerful resignation. But did she understand quite what he meant? It was all very well her saying she was going to look up those long-lost friends of hers, the Newtons. Wexford thought he knew just how much they would do for a visitor, an invitation to dinner was what that would amount to.

He had just got used to the road, was even beginning to enjoy driving the little red automatic Chevette he had rented at the airport, when the palms of Santa Monica were before them and they were on Ocean Drive. He had promised Dora two days here, staying in luxury at the Miramar, before they set off for wherever his investigations might lead them.

Where was he going to begin? He had one meagre piece of information to go on. Ames had given it to him back in February and it was Natalie Arno's address in Los Angeles. The magnitude of his task was suddenly apparent as, once they had checked in and Dora had lain down in their room to sleep, he stood under the eucalyptus trees, looking at the Pacific. Everything seemed so big, a bigger sea, a bigger beach, a vaster sky than he had ever seen before. And as their plane had come in to land he had looked down and been daunted by the size of the sprawling, glittering, metallic-looking city spread out there below them. The secret of Natalie Arno had appeared enormous in Kingsmarkham; here in Los Angeles it was surely capable of hiding itself and becoming for ever lost in one of a hundred million crannies.

But one of these crannies he would explore in the morning. Tuscarora Avenue, where Natalie had lived for eight years after coming south from San Francisco, Tuscarora Avenue in a suburb called Opuntia. The fancy names suggested to Wexford that he might expect a certain slumminess, for at home Vale Road would be the site of residential elegance and Valhalla Grove of squalor.

The shops were still open. He walked up Wilshire Boulevard and bought himself a larger and more detailed street plan of Los Angeles than the car hire company had provided.

The next morning when he went out Dora was preparing to phone Rex and Nonie Newton. A year or two before she met Wexford Dora had been engaged to Rex Newton; a boy-and-girl affair it had been, they were both in their teens, and Rex had been supplanted by the young policeman. Married for thirty years now, Rex had retired early and emigrated with his American wife to California. Wexford hoped wistfully that they would be welcoming to Dora, that Nonie Newton would live up to the promises she had made in her last letter. But he could only hope for the best. By ten he was on his way to Opuntia.

The names had misled him. Everything here had an exotic name, the grand and tawdry alike.

Opuntia wasn't shabby but paintbox bright with houses like Swiss chalets or miniature French chateaux set in garden plots as lush as jungles. He had previously only seen such flowers in florist's shops or the hothouses of public gardens, oleanders, bougainvilleas, the orange-and-blue bird-of-paradise flower, emblem of the City of the Angels. No wind stirred the fronds of the fan palms. The sky was blue, but white with smog at the horizon.

Tuscarora Avenue was packed so tightly with cars that two drivers could hardly pass each other. Wexford despaired of finding a niche for the Chevette up there, so he left it at the foot of the hill and walked. Though there were side streets called Mar Vista and Oceania Way, the sea wasn't visible, being blocked from view by huge apartment buildings which raised their penthouse tops out of a forest of palm and eucalyptus. 1121 Tuscarora, where Natalie Arno had lived, was a small squat house of pink stucco. It and its neighbours, a chocolate-coloured mini-castle and a baby hacienda painted lemon, reminded Wexford of the confections on the sweets trolley at the Miramar the previous night. He hesitated for a moment, imagining Natalie there, the light and the primary colours suiting her better than the pallor and chill of Kingsmarkham, and then he went up to the door of the nearest neighbour, the chocolate-fudge-iced 1123.

A man in shorts and a tee-shirt answered his ring. Wexford, who had no official standing in California, who had no right to be asking questions, had already decided to represent himself as on a quest for a lost relative. Though he had never before been to America, he knew enough of Americans to be pretty sure that this kind of thing, which might at home be received with suspicion, embarrassment and taciturnity, would here be greeted with warmth.

The householder, whose shirt campaigned in red printed letters for the Equal Rights Amendment, said he was called Leo Dobrowski and seemed to justify Wexford's belief. He asked him in, explained that his wife and children had gone to church, and within a few minutes Wexford found himself drinking coffee with Mr Dobrowski on a patio hung with the prussian-blue trumpets of morning glory.

But in pretending to a family connection with Tina Zoffany he had made a mistake. Leo Dobrowski knew all about Tina Zoffany and scarcely anything about Natalie Arno or any other occupants of 1121 Tuscarora. Hadn't Tina, in the two years she had lived next door, become Mrs Dobrowski's closest friend? It was a pleasure, though a melancholy one, for Mr Dobrowski at last to be able to talk about Tina to someone who *cared*. Her brother, he thought, had never cared, though he hoped he wasn't speaking out of turn in saying so. If Wexford was Tina's uncle, he would know what a sweet lovely person she had been and what a tragedy her early death was. Mrs Dobrowski herself had been made sick by the shock of it. If Wexford would care to wait until she came back from church he knew his wife had some lovely snapshots of Tina and could probably let him have some small keepsake of Tina's. Her brother had brought all her little odds and ends to them, wouldn't want the expense of sending them home, you could understand that.

'You sure picked the right place when you came to us,' said Mr Dobrowski. 'I guess there's not another family on Tuscarora knew Tina like we did. You have ESP or something?'

After that Wexford could scarcely refuse to meet the church-going wife. He promised to come back an hour later. Mr Dobrowski beamed his pleasure and the words on his tee-shirt – 'Equality of rights under the law shall not be denied or abridged by the United States or any state on account of sex' – expanded with his well-exercised muscles.

The occupants of 1125 – this time Wexford was a cousin of Natalie's and no nonsense about it – were new to the district and so were those who lived further down the hill in a redwood-and-stucco version of Anne Hathaway's cottage. He went to 1121 itself and picked up from the man he spoke to his first piece of real information, that the house had not been bought but was rented from Mrs Arno. Who was there in the neighbourhood, Wexford asked him, who might have known Mrs Arno when she lived here? Try 1122 on the opposite side, he was advised. In an ever-changing population, the people at 1122, the Romeros, had been in residence longest.

Natalie's cousin once more, he tried at 1122.

'You English?' said Mrs Donna Romero, a woman who looked even more Spanish than Natalie and whose jet-black hair was wound on to pink plastic rollers.

Wexford nodded.

'Natalie's English. She went home to her folks in London. That's all I know. Right now she's somewhere in London, England.'

'How long have you been living here?'

'I just love your accent,' said Mrs Romero. 'How long have we been here? I guess it'd be four years, right? We came the summer Natalie went on that long vacation up the coast. Must've been the summer of '76. I guess I just thought the house was empty, no one living there, you know, you get a lot of that round here, and then one day my husband says to me, there's folks moved into 1121, and that was Natalie.'

'But she'd lived there before?'

'Oh, sure she lived there before but we didn't, did we?' Donna Romero said this triumphantly as if she had somehow caught him out. 'She had these roomers, you know? There was this guy she had, he was living here illegally. Well, I guess everyone knew it, but my husband being in the Police Department – well, he had to do what he had to do, you know?'

'You mean he had him deported?'

'That's what I mean.'

Wexford decided he had better make himself scarce before an encounter threatened with the policeman husband. He contented himself with merely asking when this deportation had taken place. Not so long ago, said Mrs Romero, maybe only last fall, as far as she could remember.

It was now noon and growing fiercely hot. Wexford reflected that whoever it was who had first described the climate of California as perpetual spring hadn't had much experience of an English April. He went back across the road.

The presence on the drive of 1123 of a four-year-old manoeuvring a yellow and red truck and a six-year-old riding a blue bicycle told him Mrs Dobrowski was back. She greeted him so enthusiastically and with such glistening if not quite tearful eyes that he felt a thrust of guilt when he thought of her conferring later with the man at 1121 and with Patrolman (Lieutenant? Captain?) Romero. But it was too late now to abandon the role of Tina's uncle. He was obliged to listen to a catalogue of Tina's virtues while Mrs Dobrowski, small and earnest and wearing a tee-shirt campaigning for the conservation of the sea otter, pressed Tina souvenirs on him, a brooch, a pair of antique nail scissors, and a curious object she said was a purse ashtray.

At last he succeeded in leading the conversation to Natalie by saying with perfect truth that he had seen her in London before he left. It was immediately clear that Mrs Dobrowski hadn't approved of Natalie. Her way of life had not been what Mrs Dobrowski was used to or expected from people in a nice neighbourhood. Turning a little pink, she said she came from a family of Baptists, and when you had children you had standards to maintain. Clearly she felt that she had said enough on the subject and reverted to Tina, her prowess as what she called a stenographer, the sad fact of her childlessness, the swift onset of the disease which had killed her. Wexford made a second effort.

'I've often wondered how Tina came to live here.'

'I guess Natalie needed the money after Rolf Ilbert moved out. Johnny was the one who told Tina Natalie had a room for rent.'

Wexford made a guess. 'Johnny was Natalie's – er, friend?'

Mrs Dobrowski gave him a grim smile. 'I've heard it called that. Johnny Fassbender was her lover.'

The name sounded German but here might not be. When Wexford asked if he were a local man Mrs Dobrowski said no, he was Swiss. She had often told Tina that one of them should report him to the authorities for living here without a residence permit, and eventually someone must have done so, for he was discovered and deported.

'That would have been last autumn,' Wexford said.

'Oh, no. Whatever gave you that idea? It was all of three years ago. Tina was still alive.'

There was evidently a mystery here, but not perhaps one of pressing importance. It was Natalie's identity he was primarily concerned with, not her friendships. But Mrs Dobrowski seemed to feel that she had digressed too far for politeness and moved rapidly on to her visitor's precise relationship to Tina. Was he her true uncle or uncle only by marriage? Strangely, Tina had never mentioned him. But she had mentioned no one but the brother who came over when she died. She, Mrs Dobrowski, would have liked Ivan to have stayed at her house while he was in Los Angeles but hadn't known how to broach this as she had hardly exchanged a word with Natalie all the years they had lived there. Wexford pricked up his ears at that. No, it was true, she had never set foot inside 1121 or seen Natalie closer than across the yard.

Wexford noted that what she called the yard was, by Kingsmarkham standards, a large garden, dense with oleanders, peach trees and tall cacti. In order not to offend Mrs Dobrowski, he was obliged to carry off with him the brooch as a keepsake. Perhaps he could pass it on to the Zoffanys.

'It's been great meeting you,' said Mrs Dobrowski. 'I guess I can see a kind of look of Tina about you now. Around the eyes.' She gathered the four-year-old up in her arms and waved to Wexford from the porch. 'Say hello to Ivan for me.'

In the heat of the day he drove back to the Miramar and took Dora out to lunch in a seafood restaurant down by the boardwalk. He hardly knew how to tell her he was going to have to leave her alone for the afternoon as well. But he did tell her and she bore it well, only saying that she would make another attempt to phone the Newtons. In their room she dialled their number again while he consulted the directory, looking for Ilberts. There was no Rolf Ilbert in the Los Angeles phone book or in the slimmer Santa Monica directory, but in this latter he did find a Mrs Davina Lee Ilbert at a place called Paloma Canyon.

Dora had got through. He heard her say delightedly, 'Will you really come and pick me up? About four?' Considerably relieved, he touched her shoulder, got a wide smile from her, and then he ran out to the lift, free from guilt at least for the afternoon.

It was too far to walk, half-way to Malibu. He found Paloma Canyon without difficulty and encouraged the car up an impossibly steep slope. The road zig-zagged as on some alpine mountainside, opening up at each turn bigger and better views of the Pacific. But otherwise he might have been in Ploughman's Lane. All super residential areas the world over are the same, he thought, paraphrasing Tolstoy, it is only the slums that differ from each other. Paloma Canyon was Ploughman's Lane with palms. And with a bluer sky, daisy lawns and an architecture Spanish rather than Tudor.

She wasn't the wife but the ex-wife of the man called Rolf Ilbert. No, she didn't mind him asking, she would be only too glad if there was anything she could do to get back at Natalie Arno. Would he mind coming around to the pool? They always spent their Sunday afternoons by the pool.

Wexford followed her along a path through a shrubbery of red and purple fuchsias taller than himself. She was a tall thin woman, very tanned and with bleached blonde hair, and she wore a sky-blue terry-cloth robe and flat sandals. He wondered what it must be like to live in a climate where you took it for granted you spent every Sunday afternoon round the pool. It was extremely hot, too hot to be down there on the beach, he supposed.

The pool, turquoise blue and rectangular with a fountain playing at the far end, was in a patio formed by the balconied wings of the lemon-coloured stucco house. Davina Lee Ilbert had evidently been lying in a rattan lounging chair, for there was a glass of something with ice in it and a pair of sunglasses on the table beside it. A girl of about sixteen in a bikini was sitting on the rim of the fountain and a boy a bit younger was swimming lengths. They both had dark curly hair and Wexford supposed they must resemble their father. The girl said 'Hi' to him and slipped into the water.

'You care for iced tea?' Mrs Ilbert asked him.

He had never tasted it but he accepted. While she was fetching it he sat down in one of the cane peacock chairs, looking over the parapet to the highway and the beaches below.

'You want to know where Rolf met her?' Davina Ilbert took off her robe and stretched out on the lounger, a woman of forty with a good if stringy figure who had the discretion to wear a one-piece swimsuit. 'It was in San Francisco in '76. Her husband had died and she was staying with friends in San Rafael. The guy was a journalist or something and they all went into the city for this writers' conference that was going on, a cocktail party, I guess it was. Rolf was there.'

'Your former husband is a writer?'

'Movie and TV scripts,' she said. 'You wouldn't have heard of him. Whoever heard of script writers? You have a serial called *Runway* on your TV?'

Wexford said nothing, nodded.

'Rolf's done some of that. You know the episodes set at Kennedy? That's his stuff. And he's made a mint from it, thank God.' She made a little quick gesture at the balconies, the fountain, her own particular expanse of blue sky. 'It's Natalie you want to know about, right? Rolf brought her back to LA and bought that house on Tuscarora for her.'

The boy came out of the pool and shook himself like a dog. His sister said something to him and they both stared at Wexford, looking away when he met their eyes.

'He lived there with her?' he asked their mother.

'He kind of divided his time between me and her.' She drank from the tall glass. 'I was really dumb in those days, I trusted him. It took me five years to find out and when I did I flipped. I went over to Tuscarora and beat her up. No kidding.'

Wexford said impassively, 'That would have been in 1976?'

'Right. Spring of '76. Rolf came back and found her all bruised and with two black eyes and he got scared and took her on a trip up the coast to get away from me. It was summer, I don't suppose she minded. She was up there – two, three months? He'd go up and join her when he could but he never really lived with her again.' She gave a sort of tough chuckle. 'I'd thrown him out too. All he had was a hotel room in Marina del Rey.'

The sun was moving round. Wexford shifted into the shade and the boy and girl walked slowly away into the house. A humming bird, no larger than an insect, was hovering on the red velvet threshold of a trumpet flower. Wexford had never seen one before. He said:

'You said "up the coast". Do you know where?'

She shrugged. 'They didn't tell me their plans. But it'd be somewhere north of San Simeon and south of Monterey, maybe around Big Sur. It could have been a motel, but Rolf was generous, he'd have rented a house for her.' She changed her tone abruptly. 'Is she in trouble? I mean, real trouble?'

'Not at the moment,' said Wexford. 'She's just inherited a very nice house and a million from her father.'

'Dollars?'

'Pounds.'

'Jesus, and they say cheating never pays.'

'Mrs Ilbert, forgive me, but you said your former husband and Mrs Arno never lived together again after the summer of '76. Why was that? Did he simply get tired of her?'

She gave her dry bitter laugh. '*She* got tired of him. She met someone else. Rolf was still crazy about her. He told me so, he told me all about it.'

Wexford recalled Jane Zoffany. Husbands seemed to make a practice of confiding in their wives their passion for Natalie Arno. 'She met someone while she was away on this long holiday?'

'That's what Rolf told me. She met this guy and took him back to the house on Tuscarora – it was hers, you see, she could do what she wanted – and Rolf never saw her again.'

'*He never saw her again*?'

'That's what he said. She wouldn't see him or speak to him. I guess it was because he still hadn't divorced me and married her, but I don't know. Rolf went crazy. He found out this guy she was with was living here illegally and he got him deported.'

Wexford nodded. 'He was a Swiss called Fassbender.'

'Oh, no. Where d'you get that from? I don't recall his name but it wasn't what you said. He was English. Rolf had him deported to England.'

'Did *you* ever see her again?'

'Me? No, why would I?'

'Thank you, Mrs Ilbert. You've been very frank and I'm grateful.'

'You're welcome. I guess I still feel pretty hostile towards her for what she did to me and my kids. It wouldn't give me any grief to hear she'd lost that house and that million.'

Wexford drove down the steep hill, noticing attached to a house wall something he hadn't seen on the way up. A printed notice that said 'No Solicitors'. He chuckled. He knew very well that this was an American equivalent of the 'nice' suburb's injunction to hawkers or people delivering circulars, but it still made him laugh. He would have liked to prise it off the wall and take it home for Symonds, O'Brien and Ames.

Dora was out when he got back to the Miramar and there was a note for him telling him not to wait for dinner if she wasn't back by seven-thirty. Rex Newton, whom he had rather disliked in the days when they had been acquaintances, he now blessed. And tomorrow he would devote the whole day exclusively to Dora.

14

From the map it didn't look as if there was much in the way of habitation in the vicinity of Big Sur, and Wexford's idea that Natalie Arno's trail might therefore easily be followed was confirmed by an elderly lady in the hotel lobby. This was a Mrs Lewis from Denver, Colorado, who had spent, it appeared, at least twenty holidays in California. There was hardly a house, hotel or restaurant, according to Mrs Lewis, between San Simeon in the south and Carmel in the north. The coast was protected, Wexford concluded, it was conserved by whatever the American equivalent might be of the National Trust.

The Miramar's enormous lobby had carpet sculpture on the walls. Although it was probably the grandest hotel Wexford had ever stayed in, the bar was so dark as to imply raffishness or at least that it would be wiser not to see what one was drinking. In his case this was white wine, the pleasant, innocuous, rather weak Chablis which must be produced here by the millions of gallons considering the number of people he had seen swilling it down. What had become of the whisky sours and dry martinis of his reading? He sat alone – Dora and Mrs Lewis were swapping family snaps and anecdotes – reflecting that he should try to see Rolf Ilbert before he began the drive northwards. Ilbert was surely by now over Natalie and would have no objection to telling him the name of the place where she had stayed in the summer of 1976. Wexford finished his second glass of wine and walked down past the sculptured carpet palms to phone Davina Ilbert, but there was no reply.

In the morning, when he tried her number again, she told him her ex-husband was in London. He had been in London for two months, researching for a television series about American girls who had married into the English aristocracy. Wexford realized he would just have to trace Natalie on what he had. They drove off at lunchtime and stopped for the night at a motel in Santa Maria. It was on the tip of Wexford's tongue to grumble to Dora that there was nothing to do in Santa Maria, miles from the coast and with Route 101 passing through it. But then it occurred to him that a visitor might say exactly that about Kingsmarkham. Perhaps there was only ever something obvious to do in the centre of cities or by the sea. Elsewhere there was ample to do if you lived there and nothing if you didn't. He would have occupation soon enough and then his guilt about Dora would come back.

Over dinner he confided his theory to her.

'If you look at the facts you'll see that there was a distinct change of personality in 1976. The woman who went away with Ilbert had a different character from the woman who came back to Los Angeles. Think about it for a minute. Camargue's daughter had led a very sheltered, cared-for sort of life, she'd never been out in the world on her own. First there was a secure home with her parents, then elopement with and marriage to Arno, and when Arno died, Ilbert. She was always under the protection of some man. But what of the woman who appears *after* the summer of '76? She lets off rooms in her house to bring in an income. She doesn't form long steady relationships but has casual love affairs – with the Swiss Fassbender, with the Englishman who was deported, with Zoffany. She can't sell the house Ilbert bought for her so she lets it out and comes to England. Not to creep under her father's wing as Natalie Camargue might have done, but to shift for herself in a place of her own.'

'But surely it was a terrible risk to go to Natalie's own house and live there as Natalie? The neighbours would have known at once, and then there'd be her friends . . .'

'Good fences make good neighbours,' said Wexford. 'There's a lot of space between those houses, it's a shifting population, and if my idea is right Natalie Camargue was a shy, reserved sort of woman. Her neighbours never saw much of her. As to friends – if a friend of Natalie's phoned she had only to say Natalie was still away. If a friend comes to the house she has only to say that she herself is a friend who happens to be staying there for the time being. Mrs Ilbert says Ilbert never saw her after she came back. Now if the real Natalie came back it's almost impossible Ilbert never saw her. Never was alone with her maybe, never touched her, but never saw her? No, it was the impostor who fobbed him off every time he called with excuses, with apologies, and at last with direct refusals, allegedly on the part of the real Natalie, ever to see him again.'

'But, Reg, how could the impostor know so much about the real Natalie's past?'

He took her up quickly. 'You spent most of last evening talking to Mrs Lewis. How much do you know about her from, say, two hours' conversation?'

Dora giggled. 'Well, she lives in a flat, not a house. She's a widow. She's got two sons and a daughter. One of the sons is a realtor, I don't know what that is.'

'Estate agent.'

'Estate agent, and the other's a vet. Her daughter's called Janette and she's married to a doctor and they've got twin girls and they live in a place called Bismarck. Mrs Lewis has got a four-wheel drive Chevrolet for the mountain roads and a holiday house, a log cabin, in the Rockies and . . .'

'Enough! You found all that out in two hours and you're saying the new Natalie couldn't have formed a complete dossier of the old Natalie in – what? Five or six weeks? And when she came to England she had a second mentor in Mary Woodhouse.'

'All right, perhaps she could have.' Dora hesitated. He had had a feeling for some hours that she wanted to impart – or even break – something to him. 'Darling,' she said suddenly, 'You won't mind, will you? I told Rex and Nonie we'd be staying at the Redwood Hotel in Carmel and it so happens, I mean, it's a complete coincidence, that they'll be staying with Nonie's daughter in Monterey at the same time. If we had lunch with them once or twice – or I did – well, you won't mind, will you?'

'I think it's a wonderful idea.'

'Only you didn't used to like Rex, and I can't honestly say he's changed.'

'It's such a stupid name,' Wexford said unreasonably. 'Stupid for a man, I mean. It's all right for a dog.'

Dora couldn't help laughing. 'Oh, come. It only just misses being the same as yours.'

'A miss is as good as a mile. What d'you think of my theory then?'

'Well – what became of the old Natalie?'

'I think it's probable she murdered her.'

The road came back to the sea again after San Luis Obispo. It was like Cornwall, Wexford thought, the Cornish coast gigantically magnified both in size and in extent. Each time you came to a bend in the road another bay opened before you, vaster, grander, more majestically beautiful than the last. At San Simeon Dora wanted to see Hearst Castle, so Wexford drove her up there and left her to take the guided tour. He went down on the beach where shade was provided by eucalyptus trees. Low down over the water he saw a pelican in ponderous yet graceful flight. The sun shone with an arrogant, assured permanence, fitting for the finest climate on earth.

There wasn't much to San Simeon, a car park, a restaurant, a few houses. And if Mrs Lewis was to be believed, the population would be even sparser as he drove north. The Hearst Castle tour lasted a long time and they made no more progress that day, but as they set off next morning Wexford began to feel something like dismay. It was true that if you were used to living in densely peopled areas you might find the coast here sparsely populated, but it wasn't by any means *un*populated. Little clusters of houses – you could hardly call them villages – with a motel or two, a store, a petrol station, a restaurant, occurred more often than he had been led to believe. And when they came to Big Sur and the road wandered inland through the redwood forest, there were habitations and places to stay almost in plenty.

They reached the Redwood Hotel at about eight that night. Simply driving through Carmel had been enough to lower Wexford's spirits. It looked a lively place, a considerable seaside resort, and it was full of hotels. Another phone call to Davina Ilbert elicited only that she had no idea of Ilbert's London address. Wexford realized that there was nothing for it but to try all the hotels in Carmel, armed with his photograph of Natalie.

All he derived from that was the discovery that Americans are more inclined to be helpful than English people, and if this is because they are a nation of salesmen just as the English are a nation of small shopkeepers, it does little to detract from the overall pleasant impression. Hotel receptionists exhorted him on his departure to have a good day, and then when he was still at it after sundown, to have a nice evening. By that time he had been inside every hotel, motel and lobby of apartments-for-rent in Carmel, Carmel Highlands, Carmel Woods and Carmel Point, and he had been inside them in vain.

Rex Newton and his American wife were sitting in the hotel bar with Dora when he got back. Newton's skin had gone very brown and his hair very white, but otherwise he was much the same. His wife, in Wexford's opinion, looked twenty years older than Dora, though she was in fact younger. It appeared that the Newtons were to dine with them, and Newton walked into the dining room with one arm round his wife's waist and the other round Dora's. Dora had given them to understand he was there on official police business – what else could she have said? – and Newton spent most of his time at the table holding forth on the American legal system, American police, the geography and geology of California and the rival merits of various hotels. His wife was a meek quiet little woman. They were going to take Dora to Muir Woods, the redwood forest north of San Francisco, on the following day.

'If he knows so much,' Wexford grumbled later, 'he might have warned you there are more hotels up here than in the West End of London.'

'I'm sorry, darling. I didn't ask him. He does rather talk the hind leg off a donkey, doesn't he?'

Wexford didn't know why he suddenly liked Rex Newton very much and felt even happier that Dora was having such a good time with him.

For his own part, he spent the next day and the next making excursions down the coast the way they had come, visiting every possible place to stay. In each he got the same response – or worse, that the motel had changed hands or changed management and that there were no records for 1976 available. He was learning that in California change is a very important aspect of life and that Californians, like the Athenians of old, are attracted by any new thing.

Nonie Newton was confined to bed in her daughter's house with a migraine. Wexford cut short his inquiries in Monterey to get back to Dora, who would have been deserted by her friends. The least he could do for her was take her on the beach for the afternoon. He asked himself if he hadn't mismanaged everything. The trip wasn't succeeding either as an investigation or as a holiday. Dora was out when he got back, there was no note for him, and he spent the rest of the day missing his wife and reproaching himself. Rex Newton brought her back at ten and, in spite of Nonie's illness, sat in the bar for half an hour, holding forth on the climate of California, seismology and the San Andreas Fault. Wexford couldn't wait for him to be gone to unburden his soul to Dora.

'You could always phone Sheila,' she said when they were alone.

'Sure I could,' he said. 'I could phone Sylvia and talk to the kids. I could phone your sister and my nephew Howard and old Mike. It would cost a great deal of money and they'd all no doubt say hard cheese very kindly, but where would it get me?'

'To Ilbert,' she said simply.

He looked at her.

'Rolf Ilbert. You said he does part of the script for *Runway*. He's in London. Even if he's not working on *Runway* now, even if she's never met him, Sheila's in a position to find out where he is, she could easily do it.'

'So she could,' he said slowly. 'Why didn't I think of that?'

It was eleven o'clock on the Pacific coast but seven in London, and he was lucky to find her up. Her voice sounded as if she were in the next room. He knew exactly what her voice in the next room would sound like because his hotel neighbours had had *Runway* on for the past half-hour.

'I don't know him, Pop darling, but I'm sure I can find him. Nothing easier. I'll shop around some likely agents. Where shall I ring you back?'

'Don't call us,' said her father. 'We'll call you. God know where we'll be.'

'How's Mother?'

'Carrying on alarmingly with her old flame.'

He would have laughed as he said that if Dora had shown the least sign of laughing.

Because it wasn't his nature to wait about and do nothing he spent all the next day covering what remained of the Monterey Peninsula. Something in him wanted to say, forget it, make a holiday of the rest of it, but it was too late for that. Instead of relaxing, he would only have tormented himself with that constantly recurring question, where had she stayed? It was awkward phoning Sheila because of the time difference. All the lines were occupied when he tried at eight in the morning, tea time for her, and again at noon, her early evening. When at last he heard the ringing there was no answer. Next day, or the day after at the latest, they would have to start south and leave behind all the possible places where Natalie Arno might have changed her identity. They had only had a fortnight and eleven days of it were gone.

As he was making another attempt to phone Sheila from the hotel lobby, Rex Newton walked in with Dora. He sat down, drank a glass of Chablis, and held forth on Californian vineyards, migraine, the feverfew diet and the gluten-free diet. After half an hour he went, kissing Dora – on the cheek but very near the mouth – and reminding her of a promise to spend their last night in America staying at the Newtons' house. And also their last day.

'I suppose I'm included in that,' Wexford said in a rather nasty tone. Newton was still not quite out of earshot.

She was cool. 'Of course, darling.'

His investigation was over, failed, fruitless. He had rather hoped to have the last two days alone with his wife. But what a nerve he had and how he was punished for it!

'I'm hoist with my own petard, aren't I?' he said and went off to bed.

The Newtons were flying back that morning. It would be a long weary drive for Wexford. He and Dora set off at nine.

The first of the *Danaus* butterflies to float across the windscreen made them both gasp. Dora had seen one only once before, Wexford never. The Milkweed, the Great American Butterfly, the Monarch, is a rare visitor to the cold British Isles. They watched that one specimen drift out over the sea, seeming to lose itself in the blue meeting the blue, and then a cloud of its fellows were upon them, thick as autumnal leaves that strow the brooks in Vallombrosa. And like leaves too, scarlet leaves veined in black, they floated rather than flew across the span of California One, down from the cliffs of daisies, out to the ocean. The air was red with them. All the way down from Big Sur they came, wings of cinnabar velvet, butterflies in flocks like birds made of petals.

'The Spanish for butterfly is *mariposa,*' said Dora. 'Rex told me. Don't you think it's a beautiful name?'

Wexford said nothing. Even if he managed to get hold of Sheila now, even if she had an address or a phone number for him, would he have time to drive back perhaps a hundred miles along this route? Not when he had to be in Burbank or wherever those Newtons lived by nightfall. A red butterfly came to grief on his windscreen, smashed, fluttered, died.

They stopped for a late lunch not far north of San Luis Obispo. He tried in vain to get through to Sheila again and then Dora said she would try. She came back from the phone with a little smile on her lips. She looked young and tanned and happy, but she hadn't been able to reach Sheila. Wexford wondered why she should look like that if she hadn't been talking to anyone. The Newtons would have been back in their home for hours by now. He felt that worst kind of misery, that which afflicts us as the result entirely of our own folly.

The road that returned from inland to the coast wound down through yellow hills. Yuccas pushed their way up through the sun-bleached grass and the rounded mountains were crowned with olives. The hills folded and dipped and rose and parted to reveal more hills, all the same, all ochreish in colour, until through the last dip the blue ocean appeared again. Dora was occupied with her map and guide book.

There was a little seaside town ahead. A sign by the roadside said: Santa Xavierita, height above sea level 50.2 metres, population 482. Dora said:

'According to the book there's a motel here called the Mariposa. Shall we try it?'

'What for?' said Wexford crossly. 'Half an hour's kip? We have to be two hundred miles south of here by eight and it's five now.'

'We don't have to. Our plane doesn't go till tomorrow night. We could stay at the Mariposa, I think we're meant to, it was a sign.'

He nearly stopped the car. He chuckled. He had known her thirty-five years but he didn't know her yet. 'You phoned Newton back there?' he said but in a very different tone from the one he would have used if he had asked that question ten minutes before. 'You phoned Newton and said we couldn't make it?'

She said demurely, 'I think Nonie was quite relieved really.'

'I don't deserve it,' said Wexford.

Santa Xavierita had a wide straggly street with a dozen side turnings at right angles to it, as many petrol stations, a monster market, a clutch of restaurants and among a dozen motels, the Mariposa. Wexford found himself being shown, not to a room, but to a little house rather like a bungalow at home in Ramsgate or Worthing. It stood in a garden, one of a score of green oases in this corner of Santa Xavierita, and up against its front door was a pink and white geranium as big as a tree.

He walked back between sprinklers playing on the grass to the hotel reception desk and phoned Sheila on a collect call. In London it was two in the morning, but by now he was unscrupulous. Sheila had got Ilbert's address. She had had it for two days and couldn't understand why her father hadn't phoned. Ilbert was staying at Durrant's Hotel in George Street by Spanish Place. Wexford wrote down the number. He looked round for someone to inform that he intended to make a call to London.

There was no sign of the little spry man called Sessamy who had checked them in. No doubt he was somewhere about, watering the geraniums and fuchsias and the heliotrope that smelt of cherries. Wexford went back to find Dora and tell her the news, such as it was. She was in the kitchen of their bungalow, arranging in a glass bowl, piling like an Arcimboldo still life, the fruit they had bought.

'Reg,' she said, turning round, a nectarine in her hand, 'Reg, Mrs Sessamy who owns this place, she's English. And she says we're the first English people to stay here since – a Mrs Arno in 1976.'

15

'Tell me about it,' Wexford said.

'I don't know anything about it. I don't know any more than I've told you. Your Natalie Arno stayed here in 1976. After we've eaten we're to go and have coffee with Mrs Sessamy and she'll enlighten you.'

'Will she now? And how did you account for my curiosity? What did you tell her about me?'

'The truth. The idea of you being a real English policeman almost made her cry. She was a GI bride, I think, she's about the right age. I honestly think she expects you to turn up in a blue uniform and say 'ere, 'ere, what's all this about? and she'd love it!'

He laughed. It was rare for him to praise his

wife, almost unknown for him to call her by an endearment. That wasn't his way, she knew it and wouldn't have wanted it. It would have bracketed her with those he loved on the next level down. He put his hand on her arm.

'If something comes of all this,' he said, 'and one of us gets sent back here at the government's expense, can I come too?'

There was, of all things, a Lebanese restaurant in the main street of Santa Xavierita. They walked there and ate delicate scented versions of humous and kebab and honey cake. The sun had long gone, sunk almost with a fizzle into that blue sea, and now the moon was rising. The moonlight painted the little town white as with frost. It was no longer very warm. In the gardens, which showed as dark little havens of lushness in aridity, the sprinklers still rotated and sprayed.

Wexford marvelled at his wife and, with hindsight, at his own ignorant presumption. Instead of allowing herself to be a passive encumbrance, she had made him absurdly jealous and had hoodwinked him properly. By some sixth sense or some gift of serendipity, she had done in an instant what had eluded him for nearly a fortnight – found Natalie Arno's hideout. And like Trollope's Archdeacon of his wife, he wondered at and admired the greatness of that lady's mind.

The Sessamys lived in a white-painted frame building, half their home and half the offices of the motel. Their living room was old-fashioned in an unfamiliar way, furnished with pieces from a thirties culture more overblown and Hollywood-influenced than that which Wexford himself had known. On a settee, upholstered in snow-white grainy plastic, a settee that rather resembled some monstrous dessert, a cream-coated log perhaps, rolled in coconut, sat the fattest woman Wexford had ever seen. He and Dora had come in by way of the open French windows, as she had been instructed, and Mrs Sessamy struggled to get to her feet. Like a great fish floundering to raise itself over the rim of the keeper net, she went on struggling until her guests were seated. Only then did she allow herself to subside again. She gave a big noisy sigh.

'It's such a pleasure to see you! You don't know how I've been looking forward to it ever since Mrs Wexford here said who you was. A real bobby! I turned on the waterworks, didn't I, Tom?'

Nearly forty years' domicile in the United States had not robbed her of a particle of her old accent or given her a hint of new. She was a Londoner who still spoke the cockney of Bow or Limehouse.

'Bethnal Green,' she said as if Wexford had asked. 'I've never been back. My people all moved out to one of them new towns, Harlow. Been there, of course. Like every other year mostly we go, don't we, Tom?'

Her husband made no reply. He was a little brown monkey of a man with a face like a nut. He suggested they have a drink and displayed a selection of bottles ranged behind a small bar. There was no sign of the promised coffee. When Dora had apologetically refused bourbon, rye, Chablis, Hawaiian cocktail, Perrier, grape juice and gin, Mrs Sessamy announced that they would have tea. Tom would make it, the way she had taught him.

'It's such a pleasure to see you,' she said again, sinking comfortably back into white plastic. 'The English who come here, mostly they stop up at the Ramada or the Howard Johnson. But you picked the old Mariposa.'

'Because of the butterflies,' said Dora.

'Come again?'

'*Mariposa* – well, it means butterfly, doesn't it?'

'It does?' said Tom Sessamy, waiting for the kettle to boil. 'You hear that, Edie? How about that then?'

It seemed the policy of the Sessamys to question each other frequently but never to answer. Mrs Sessamy folded plump hands in her enormous lap. She was wearing green trousers and a tent-like green and pink flowered smock. In her broad moon face, in the greyish-fair hair, could still be seen traces of the pretty girl who had married an American soldier and left Bethnal Green for ever.

'Mrs Wexford said you wanted to know about that girl who lived here – well, stopped here. Though she must have been here three months. We thought she'd go on renting the chalet for ever, didn't we, Tom? We thought we'd got a real sinecure.'

'I'd heard it was up around Big Sur she stayed,' said Wexford.

'So it was at first. She couldn't stick it, not enough life for her, and it was too far to drive to Frisco. You can get up to San Luis in twenty minutes from here by car. She had her own car and he used to come up in a big Lincoln Continental.'

'Ilbert?'

'That's right, that was the name. I will say for her she never pretended, she never called herself Mrs Ilbert. Couldn't have cared less what people thought.'

Tom Sessamy came in with the tea. Wexford who, while in California, had drunk from a pot made with one teabag, had seen tea made by heating up liquid out of a bottle or by pouring warm water on to a powder, noted that Tom had been well taught by his wife.

'I never did fancy them bags,' said Edith Sessamy. 'You can get tea loose here if you try.'

'Hafta go to the specialty shop over to San Luis,' said Tom.

Mrs Sessamy put cream and sugar into her cup. 'What more d'you want to know about her?' she said to Wexford.

He showed her the photograph. 'Is that her?'

She put on glasses with pink frames and rhinestone decoration. Mrs Sessamy had become Californian in all ways but for her tea and her speech. 'Yes,' she said, 'yes, I reckon that's her.' Her voice was full of doubt.

'I guess that's her,' said Tom. 'It's kinda hard to say. She kinda wore her hair loose. She got this terrific tan and wore her hair loose. Right, Edie?'

Edith Sessamy didn't seem too pleased by her

husband's enthusiastic description of Natalie Arno. She said rather sharply, 'One man wasn't enough for her. She was two-timing that Ilbert the minute he was off to L.A. For instance, there used to be a young fella hung about here, kipped down on the beach, I reckon you'd have called him a beachcomber in olden times.'

'Kinda hippie,' said Tom.

'She carried on with him. I say he slept on the beach, that summer I reckoned he slept most nights in Natalie's chalet. Then there was an English chap, but it wasn't long before she left she met him, was it, Tom?'

'Played the guitar at the Maison Suisse over to San Luis.'

'Why did she leave?' Wexford asked.

'Now that I can't tell you. We weren't here when she left. We were at home, we were in England.'

'Visiting with her sister over to Harlow,' said Tom.

'She was living here like she'd stay for the rest of her life when we left. That'd have been the end of July, I reckon. Tom's cousin from Ventura, she come up to run the place like she always does when we're off on our holidays. She kept in touch, I reckon we got a letter once a week. I remember her writing us about that woman who got drowned here, don't you, Tom? But she never mentioned that girl leaving. Why should she? There was guests coming and going all the time.'

'You weren't curious yourselves?'

Edith Sessamy heaved up her huge shoulders and

dropped them again. 'So if we were? There wasn't much we could do about it, six thousand miles away. She wasn't going to tell Tom's cousin why she upped and went, was she? When we come back we heard that's what she'd done, a moonlight flit like. Ilbert come up the next day but the bird was flown. She went off in her car, Tom's cousin said, and she'd got a young chap with her, and she left that poor mug Ilbert to pay the bill.'

Wexford woke up very early the next morning. The sun was perhaps the brightest and the clearest he had ever seen and the little town looked as if it had been washed clean in the night. Yet Edith Sessamy had told him that apart from a few showers the previous December they had had no rain for a year. He bathed and dressed and went out. Dora was still fast asleep. He walked down the narrow straight road bordered with fan palms, feather dusters on long tapering handles, that led to Santa Xavierita state beach.

The sky was an inverted pan of speckless blue enamel, the sea rippling blue silk. Along the silver sand a young man in yellow tee-shirt and red shorts was jogging. Another, in swimming trunks, was doing gymnastic exercises, sit-ups, press-ups, toe-touching. There was no one in the water. In the middle of the beach was a chair raised up high on stilts for the use of the lifeguard who would sit on it and halloo through his trumpet at over-venturesome swimmers.

Wexford's thoughts reverted to the night before.

There was a question he ought to have asked, that he had simply overlooked at the time, because of the crushing disappointment he had felt at the paucity of Edith Sessamy's information. Disappointment had made him fail to select from that mass of useless matter the one significant sentence. He recalled it now, picking it out as the expert might pick out the uncut diamond from a handful of gravel.

Two hours later, as early as he decently could, he was waiting in the motel's reception area by the counter. Ringing the bell summoned Tom Sessamy in shortie dressing gown which left exposed hairless white legs and long white feet in sandals of plaited straw.

'Hi, Reg, you wanna check out?'

'I wanted to ask you and your wife a few more questions first if you'll bear with me.'

'Edie, are ya decent? Reg's here ta pick your brains.'

Mrs Sessamy was rather more decent than her husband in an all-enveloping pink kimono printed with birds of paradise. She sat on the white sofa drinking more strong black tea, and on her lap on a tray were fried eggs and fried bacon and hash browns and English muffins and grape jelly.

'It's been such a pleasure meeting you and Dora, I can't tell you.' She had told him at least six times already, but the repetition was somehow warming and pleasant to hear. Wexford returned the compliment with a few words about how much they had enjoyed themselves.

'You wanna cup of Edie's tea?' said Tom.

Wexford accepted. 'You said last night a woman was drowned here. While you were away. D'you know any more than that? Who she was? How it happened?'

'Not a thing. Only what I said, a woman was drowned. Well, it was a young woman, a girl really, I do know that, and I reckon I heard she was on holiday here from the East somewhere.'

'You hafta talk to the cops over to San Luis,' said Tom.

'Wait a minute, though – George Janveer was lifeguard here then, wasn't he, Tom? I reckon you could talk to George.'

'Why don't I call George right now?' said Tom.

He was dissuaded from this by his wife since it was only just after eight. They would phone George at nine. Wexford wasn't pressed for time, was he? No, he wasn't, not really, he had all day. He had a 200 mile drive ahead of him, of course, but that was nothing here. Edith Sessamy said she knew what he meant, it was nothing here.

He walked slowly back. At last a clear pattern was emerging from the confusion. The pieces fluttered and dropped into a design as the coloured fragments do when you shake a kaleidoscope. Camargue too had been drowned, he thought.

Just after nine he went back and paid his bill. Tom said apologetically that he had phoned George Janveer's home and talked to Mrs Janveer who said George had gone to Grover City but she expected him back by eleven.

'Oughta've called him at eight like I said,' said Tom.

Wexford and Dora put the cases in the car and went to explore what they hadn't yet seen of Santa Xavierita. Wouldn't it be best, Wexford asked himself, to head straight for San Luis Obispo and call on the police there and see what facts he could get out of them? But suppose he couldn't get any? Suppose, before they imparted anything to him, they required proof of who he was and what he was doing there? He could prove his identity, of course, and present them with bona fides but it would all take time and he hadn't much left. He had to be at Los Angeles international airport by six in time for their flight home at seven. Better wait for Janveer who would know as much as the police did and would almost certainly talk to him.

Mrs Janveer was as thin as Edith Sessamy was fat. She was in her kitchen baking something she called devil's food and her overweight black Labrador was sitting at her feet, hoping to lick out the bowl.

It was after eleven and her husband still hadn't come back from Grover City. Maybe he had met a friend and they had got drinking. Mrs Janveer did not say this in a shrewish or condemnatory way or even as if there were anything to be defensive about. She said it in exactly the same tone, casual, indifferent, even slightly complacent, she would have used to say he had met the mayor or gone to a meeting of the Lions.

Wexford was driven to ask her if she remembered anything about the drowned woman. Mrs Janveer put the tin of chocolate cake mixture into the oven.

The dog's tail began to thump the floor. No, she couldn't say she remembered much about it at all, except the woman's first name had been Theresa, she recalled that because it was hers too, and after the drowning some of her relations had come out to Santa Xavierita, from Boston, she thought it was, and stayed at the Ramada Inn. She put the mixing bowl under the tap and her hand to the tap. The dog let out a piteous squeal. Mrs Janveer shrugged, looking upset, and slapped the bowl down in front of the dog with a cross exclamation.

Wexford waited until half-past eleven. Janveer still hadn't come. 'Considering what I know now,' he said to Dora, 'they're bound to send me back here. It's only time I need.'

'It's a shame, darling, it's such bad luck.'

He drove quickly out of the town, heading for the Pacific Highway.

16

The difference between California and Kingsmarkham was a matter of colour as well as temperature. The one was blue and gold, the sun burning the grass to its own colour; the other was grey and green, the lush green of foliage watered daily by those massy clouds. Wexford went to work, not yet used to seeing grass verges instead of daisy lawns, shivering a little because the temperature was precisely what Tom Sessamy had told him it could fall to in Santa Xavierita in December.

Burden was waiting for him in his office. He had on a lightweight silky suit in a shade of taupe and a beige silk shirt. No one could possibly have taken him for a policeman or even a policeman in disguise. Wexford, who had been considering telling him at once what he had found out in California, now decided not to and instead asked him to close the window.

'I opened it because it's such a muggy stuffy sort of day,' said Burden. 'Not cold, are you?'

'Yes, I am. Very cold.'

'Jet lag. Did you have a good time?'

Wexford grunted. He wished he had the nerve to start the central heating. It probably wouldn't start, though, not in July. For all he knew, the chief constable had to come over himself on 1 November and personally press a button on the boiler. 'I don't suppose there've been any developments while I was away?' he said.

Burden sat down. 'Well, yes, there have. That's what I'm doing in here. I thought I ought to tell you first thing. Jane Zoffany has disappeared.'

Zoffany had not reported her missing until she had been gone a week. His story, said Burden, was that he and his wife had been staying at Sterries with their friend Natalie Arno, and on the evening of Friday, 27 June his wife had gone out alone for a walk and had never come back. Zoffany, when pressed, admitted that immediately prior to this he and his wife had quarrelled over an affair he had had with another woman. She had said she was going to leave him, she could never live with him again, and had left the house. Zoffany himself had left soon after, taking the 10.05 p.m. train to Victoria. He believed his wife would have gone home by an earlier train.

However, when he got to De Beauvoir Place she

wasn't there. Nor did she appear the next day. He concluded she had gone to her sister in Horsham. This had apparently happened once before after a quarrel. But Friday 4 July had been Jane Zoffany's birthday, her thirty-fifth, and a birthday card came for her from her sister. Zoffany then knew he had been wrong and he went to his local police station.

Where no one had shown much interest, Burden said. Why should they? That a young woman should temporarily leave her husband after a quarrel over his infidelity was hardly noteworthy. It happened all the time. And of course she wouldn't tell him where she had gone, that was the last thing she had wanted him to know. Burden only got to hear of it when Zoffany also reported his wife's disappearance to the Kingsmarkham police. He seemed genuinely worried. It would not be putting it too strongly to say he was distraught.

'Guilt,' said Wexford, and as he pronounced the word he felt it himself. It was even possible he was the last person – the last but one – to have seen Jane Zoffany alive. And he had let her go. Because he was off on holiday, because he didn't want to inconvenience Dora or upset arrangements. Of course she hadn't taken refuge with her sister or some friend. She had had no handbag, no money. He had let her go, overwrought as she was, to walk away into the dusk of Ploughman's Lane – to go back to Sterries and Natalie Arno.

'I had a feeling we ought to take it a bit more seriously,' Burden said. 'I mean, I wasn't really alarmed but I couldn't help thinking about poor old Camargue. We've got our own ideas about what kind of a death that was, haven't we? I talked to Zoffany myself, I got him to give me the names of people she could possibly have gone to. There weren't many and we checked on them all.'

'And what about Natalie? Have you talked to her?'

'I thought I'd leave that to you.'

'We'll have to drag the lake,' said Wexford, 'and dig up the garden if necessary. But I'll talk to her first.'

The effect of her inherited wealth was now displayed. A new hatchback Opel, mustard-coloured, automatic transmission, stood on the gravel circle outside the front door. Looking at her, staring almost, Wexford remembered the skirt Jane Zoffany had mended, the old blanket coat. Natalie wore a dress of some thin clinging jersey material in bright egg-yellow with a tight bodice and full skirt. Around her small neat waist was tied a belt of yellow with red, blue and purple stripes. It was startling and effective and very fashionable. Her hair hung loose in a glossy black bell. There was a white gold watch on one wrist and a bracelet of woven white gold threads on the other. The mysterious lady from Boston, he thought, and he wondered how you felt when you knew your relatives, parents maybe, and your friends thought you were dead and grieved for you while in fact you were alive and living in the lap of luxury.

'But Mr Wexford,' she said with her faint accent – a

New England accent? 'But, Mr Wexford, Jane never came back here that night.' She smiled in the way a model does when her mouth and not her eyes are to show in the toothpaste ad. 'Her things are still in the room she and Ivan used. Would you like to see?'

He nodded. He followed her down to the spare rooms. On the carved teak chest stood a Chinese bowl full of Peace roses. They went into the room where he had once before seen Jane Zoffany standing before the long mirror and fastening the collar of a Persian lamb coat. Her suitcase lay open on the top of a chest of drawers. There was a folded nightdress inside it, a pair of sandals placed heel to toe and a paperback edition of Daphne du Maurier's *Rebecca*. On the black-backed hairbrush on the dressing table and the box of talcum powder lay a fine scattering of dust.

'Has Mrs Hicks left you?'

'In the spirit if not the flesh yet, Mr Wexford. She and Ted are going to Uncle Philip.' She added, as if in explanation to someone who could not be expected to know intimate family usage, 'Philip Cory, that is. He was just crazy to have them and it's made him so happy. Meanwhile this place is rather neglected while they get ready to leave. They've sold their house and I think I've sold this one at last. Well, practically sold it. Contracts have been exchanged.' She chatted on, straightening the lemon floral duvet, opening a window, for all the world as if he too were a prospective purchaser rather than a policeman investigating an ominous disappearance. 'I'm having some of the furniture put in store and the rest will go to the flat I've bought in London. Then I'm thinking of going off on vacation somewhere.'

He glanced into the adjoining bathroom. It had evidently been cleaned before Muriel Hicks withdrew her services. The yellow bath and basin were immaculate and fresh honey-coloured towels hung on the rail. Without waiting for permission, he made his way into the next room, the one Natalie had rejected in favour of using Camargue's very private and personal territory.

There were no immediately obvious signs that this room had ever been occupied since Camargue's death. In fact, it seemed likely that the last people to have slept here were Dinah Sternhold's parents when they stayed with Camargue at Christmas. But Wexford, peering quickly, pinched from the frill that edged one of the green and blue flowered pillows, a hair. It was black but it was not from Natalie's head, being wavy and no more than three inches long.

This bathroom too lacked the pristine neatness and cleanliness of the other. A man no more than ordinarily observant might have noticed nothing, but Wexford was almost certain that one of the blue towels had been used. On the basin, under the cold tap, was a small patch of tide mark. He turned as Natalie came up softly behind him. She was not the kind of person one much fancied creeping up on one, and he thought, as he had done when he first met her, of a snake.

'That night,' he said, 'Mrs Zoffany ran out of the house and then afterwards her husband left. How long afterwards?'

'Twenty minutes, twenty-five. Shall we say twenty-two and a half minutes, Mr Wexford, to be on the safe side?'

He gave no sign that he had noticed the implicit mockery. 'He walked to the station, did he?'

'I gave him a lift in my car.'

Of course. Now he remembered that he had seen them. 'And after that you never saw Mrs Zoffany again?'

'Never.' She looked innocently at Wexford, her black eyes very large and clear, the lashes lifted and motionless. 'It's the most extraordinary thing I ever came across in my life.'

Considering what he knew of her life, Wexford doubted this statement. 'I should like your consent to our dragging the lake,' he said.

'That's just a polite way of saying you're going to drag it anyway, isn't it?'

'Pretty well,' he said. 'It'll save time if you give your permission.'

Out of the lake came a quantity of blanket weed, sour green and sour smelling; two car tyres, a bicycle lamp, half a dozen cans and a broken wrought-iron gate as well as a lot of miscellaneous rubbish of the nuts and bolts and nails variety. They also found Sir Manuel Camargue's missing glove, but there was no trace of Jane Zoffany. Wexford wondered if he had chosen the lake as the first possible place to search because of the other drownings associated with Natalie Arno.

It was, of course, stretching a point to touch the garden at all. But the temptation to tell the men to dig up the flowerbed between the lake and the circular forecourt was very great. It was, after all, no more than three or four yards from the edge of the lake and the soil in it looked suspiciously freshly turned and the bedding plants as if they had been there no more than a day or two. Who would put out bedding plants in July? They dug. They dug to about three feet down and then even Wexford had to admit no body was buried there. Ted Hicks, who had been watching them for hours, now said that he had dug the bed over a week ago and planted out a dozen biennials. Asked why he hadn't said so before, he said he hadn't thought it his place to interfere. By then it was too late to do any more, nine on a typical English July evening, twilight, greyish, damp and cool.

Wexford's phone was ringing when he got in. The chief constable. Mrs Arno had complained that he was digging up the grounds of her house without her permission and without a warrant.

'True,' said Wexford, because it was and it seemed easier to confess than to get involved in the ramifications of explaining. A scalding lecture exploded at him from the mouthpiece. Once again he was overstepping the bounds of his duty and his rights, once again he was allowing an obsession to warp his judgement. And this time the obsession looked as if it were taking the form of a vindictive campaign against Mrs Arno.

Had her voice on the phone achieved this? Or had she been to Griswold in person, in the yellow dress, holding him with her glowing black eyes, moving her long pretty hands in feigned distress? For the second time he promised to persecute Natalie Arno no more, in fact to act as if he had never heard her name.

What changed the chief constable's mind must have been the systematic searching of the Zodiac. Two neighbours of Ivan Zoffany went independently to the police, one to complain that Zoffany had been lighting bonfires in his garden by night, the other to state that she had actually seen Jane in the vicinity of De Beauvoir Place on the night of Sunday, 29 June.

The house and the shop were searched without result. Zoffany admitted to the bonfires, saying that he intended to move away and take up some other line of work, and it was his stock of science-fiction paperbacks he had been burning. Wexford applied for a warrant to search the inside of Sterries and secured one three days after the dragging of the lake.

17

The house was empty. Not only deserted by its owner but half-emptied of its furnishings. Wexford remembered that Natalie Arno had said she would be going away on holiday and also that she intended having some of the furniture put in store. Mrs Murray-Burgess, that inveterate observer of unusual vehicles, told Burden when he called at Kingsfield House that she had seen a removal van turn out of the Sterries drive into Ploughman's Lane at about three on Tuesday afternoon. It was now Thursday, 17 July.

With Wexford and Burden were a couple of men, detective constables, called Archbold and Bennett. They were prepared not only to search but to dismantle parts of the house if need be. They began in the double garage, examining the cupboards at the end of it and the outhouse tacked on to its rear. Since Sterries Cottage was also empty and had been since the previous day, Wexford intended it to be searched as well. Archbold, who had had considerable practice at this sort of thing, picked the locks on both front doors.

The cottage was bare of furniture and carpets. Like most English houses, old or new, it was provided with inadequate cupboard space. Its walls were of brick but were not cavity walls, and at some recent period, perhaps when Sir Manuel and the Hickses had first come, the floors at ground level had been relaid with tiles on a concrete base. No possibility of hiding a body there and nowhere upstairs either. They turned their attention to the bigger house.

Here, at first, there seemed even less likelihood of being able safely to conceal the body of a full-grown woman. It was for no more than form's sake that they cleared out the cloaks cupboard inside the front door, the kitchen broom cupboard and the small room off the kitchen which housed the central-heating boiler and a stock of soap powders and other cleansers. From the first floor a great many pieces had gone, including the pale green settee and armchairs, the piano and all the furniture from Camargue's bedroom and sitting room. Everywhere there seemed to be blank spaces or marks of discolouration on the walls where this or that piece had stood. The Chinese vase of Peace roses, wilted now, had been stuck on the floor up against a window.

Bennett, tapping walls, discovered a hollow space between the right-hand side of the hanging cupboard and the outside wall in Camargue's bedroom. And outside there were signs that it had been the intention on someone's part to use this space as a cupboard for garden tools or perhaps to contain a dustbin, for an arch had been built into which to fit a door and this arch subsequently filled in with bricks of a slightly lighter colour.

From the inside of the hanging cupboard Bennett set about unscrewing the panel at its right-hand end. Wexford wondered if he were getting squeamish in his old age. It was with something amounting to nausea that he stood there anticipating the body falling slowly forward as the panel came away, crumpling into Bennett's arms, the tall thin body of Jane Zoffany with a gauzy scarf and a red and yellow dress of Indian cotton for a winding sheet. Burden sat on the bed, rubbing away fastidiously at a small powder or plaster mark that had appeared on the hem of his light fawn trousers.

The last screw was out and the panel fell, Bennett catching it and resting it against the wall. There was nothing inside the cavity but a spider which swung across its webs. A little bright light and fresh air came in by way of a ventilator brick. Wexford let out his breath in a sigh. It was time to take a break for lunch.

Mr Haq, all smiles and gratified to see Wexford back, remarked that he was happy to be living in a country where they paid policemen salaries on which they could afford to have holidays in California.

With perfect sincerity, he said this made him feel more secure. Burden ordered for both of them, steak Soroti, an innocuous beef stew with carrots and onions. When Mr Haq and his son were out of earshot he said he often suspected that the Pearl of Africa's cook hailed from Bradford. Wexford said nothing.

'It's no good,' said Burden, 'we aren't going to find anything in that place. You may as well resign yourself. You're too much of an optimist sometimes for your own good.'

'D'you think I want the poor woman to be dead?' Wexford retorted. 'Optimist, indeed.' And he quoted rather crossly, 'The optimist proclaims that we live in the best of all possible worlds. The pessimist fears this is true.'

'You want Natalie Arno to be guilty of something and you don't much care what,' said Burden. 'Why should she murder her?'

'Because Jane Zoffany knew who she really is. Either that or she found out how the murder of Camargue was done and who did it. There's a conspiracy here, Mike, involving a number of conspirators and Jane Zoffany was one of them. But there's no more honour among conspirators than there is among thieves, and when she discovered how Natalie had betrayed her she saw no reason to be discreet any longer.' He told Burden what had happened when he encountered Jane Zoffany in Ploughman's Lane on 27 June. 'She had something to tell me, she would have told me then only I didn't realize, I didn't give her a word of encouragement. Instead she went back to Sterries and no doubt had the temerity to threaten Natalie. It was a silly thing to do. But she was a silly woman, hysterical and unstable.'

The steak Soroti came. Wexford ate in silence. It was true enough that he wanted Natalie Arno to have done something, or rather that he now saw that charging her with something was almost within his grasp. Who would know where she had gone on holiday? Zoffany? Philip Cory? Would anyone know? They had the ice cream eau-de-Nil to follow but Wexford left half of his.

'Let's get back there,' he said.

It had begun to rain. The white walls of Sterries were streaked with water. Under a lowering sky of grey and purple cloud the house had the shabby faded look which belongs particularly to English houses built to a design intended for the Mediterranean. There were lights on in the upper rooms.

Archbold and Bennett were working on the drawing room, Bennett having so thoroughly investigated the chimney as to clamber half-way up inside it. Should they take up the floor? Wexford said no, he didn't think so. No one could hope to conceal a body for long by burying it under the floor in a house which was about to change hands. Though, as Wexford now told himself, it wasn't necessarily or exclusively a body they were looking for. By six o'clock they were by no means finished but Wexford told them to leave the rest of the house till next day. It was still raining, though slightly now, little more than a drizzle. Wexford made his way down the path between the conifers to check that they had closed and locked the door of Sterries Cottage.

In the wet gloom the Alsatian's face looking out of a ground-floor window and almost on a level with his own made him jump. It evoked strange ideas, that there had been a time shift and it was six months ago and Camargue still lived. Then again, from the way some kind of white cloth seemed to surround the dog's head . . .

'Now I know how Red Riding Hood felt,' said Wexford to Dinah Sternhold.

She was wearing a white raincoat with its collar turned up and she had been standing behind the dog, surveying the empty room. A damp cotton scarf was tied under her chin. She smiled. The sadness that had seemed characteristic of her had left her face now. It seemed fuller, the cheeks pink with rain and perhaps with running.

'They've gone,' she said, 'and the door was open. It was a bit of a shock.'

'They're working for Philip Cory now.'

She shrugged. 'Oh well, I suppose there was no reason they should bother to tell me. I'd got into the habit of bringing Nancy over every few weeks just for them to see her. Ted loves Nancy.' She took her hand from the dog's collar and Nancy bounded up to Wexford as if they were old friends. 'Sheila said you'd been to California.'

'For our summer holiday.'

'Not entirely, Mr Wexford, was it? You went to find out if what Manuel thought was true. But you haven't found out, have you?'

He said nothing, and she went on quickly, perhaps thinking she had gone too far or been indiscreet. 'I often think how strange it is she could get the solicitors to believe in her and Manuel's old friends to believe in her and the police and people who'd known the Camargues for years, yet Manuel who wanted to believe, who was pretty well geared up to believe anything, saw her on that one occasion and didn't believe in her for more than half an hour.' She shrugged her shoulders again and gave a short little laugh. Then she said politely as was her way, 'I'm so sorry, I'm keeping you. Did you want to lock up?' She took hold of the dog again and walked her out into the rain. 'Has she sold the house?' Her voice suddenly sounded thin and strained.

Wexford nodded. 'So she says.'

'I shall never come here again.'

He watched her walk away down the narrow lane which led from the cottage to the road. Raindrops glistened on the Alsatian's fur. Water slid off the flat branches of the conifers and dripped on to the grass. Uncut for more than a week, it was already shaggy, giving the place an unkempt look. Wexford walked back to the car.

Burden was watching Dinah Sternhold shoving Nancy on to the rear seat of the Volkswagen. 'It's a funny thing,' he said. 'Jenny's got a friend, a Frenchwoman, comes from Alsace. But you can't call her an Alsatian, can you? That word always means a dog.'

'You couldn't call anyone a Dalmatian either,' said Wexford.

Burden laughed. 'Americans call Alsatians German Shepherds.'

'We ought to. That's their proper name and I believe the Kennel Club have brought it in again. When they were brought here from Germany after the First World War there was a lot of anti-German feeling – hence we used the euphemism "Alsatian". About as daft as refusing to play Beethoven and Bach at concerts because they were German.'

'Jenny and I are going to German classes,' said Burden rather awkwardly.

'What on earth for?'

'Jenny says education should go on all one's life.'

Next morning it was heavy and sultry, the sun covered by a thick yellow mist. Sterries awaited them, full of secrets. Before he left news had come in for Wexford through Interpol that the woman who drowned in Santa Xavierita in July1976 was Theresa or Tessa Lanchester, aged thirty, unmarried, a para-legal secretary from Boston, Massachusetts. The body had been recovered after having been in the sea some five days and identified a further four days later by Theresa Lanchester's aunt, her parents both being dead. Driving up to Sterries, Wexford thought about being sent back to California. He wouldn't mind a few days in Boston, come to that.

Archbold and Bennett got to work on the spare bedrooms but without positive result and after lunch they set about the study and the two bathrooms.

In the yellow bathroom they took up the honey-coloured carpet, leaving exposed the white vinyl tiles beneath. It was obvious that none of these tiles had been disturbed since they were first laid. The carpet was replaced and then the same procedure gone through in the blue bathroom. Here there was a shower cabinet as well as a bath. Archbold unhooked and spread out the blue and green striped shower curtain. This was made of semi-transparent nylon with a narrow machine-made hem at the bottom. Archbold, who was young and had excellent sight, noticed that the machine stitches for most of the seam's length were pale blue but in the extreme right-hand corner, for about an inch, they were not blue but brown. He told Wexford.

Wexford, who had been sitting on a window-sill in the study, thinking, watching the cloud shadows move across the meadows, went into the blue bathroom and looked at the curtain and knelt down. And about a quarter of an inch from the floor, on the panelled side of the bath, which had been covered for nearly half an inch by the carpet pile, were two minute reddish-brown spots.

'Take up the floor tiles,' said Wexford.

Would they find enough blood to make a test feasible? It appeared so after two of the tiles had been lifted and the edge of the one which had been alongside the bath panelling showed a thick dark encrustation.

18

'You might tell me where we're going.'

'Why? You're a real ignoramus when it comes to London.' Wexford spoke irritably. He was nervous because he might be wrong. The chief constable had said he was and had frowned and shaken his head and talked about infringements of rights and intrusions of privacy. If he was wrong he was going to look such a fool. He said to Burden, 'If I said we were going to Thornton Heath, would that mean anything to you?'

Burden said nothing. He looked huffily out of the window. The car was passing through Croydon, through industrial complexes, estates of small red terraced houses, shopping centres, big spreadeagled roundabouts with many exits. Soon after Thornton

Heath station Wexford's driver turned down a long bleak road that was bounded by a tall wire fence on one side and a row of sad thin poplars on the other. Thank God there were such neighbours about as Mrs Murray-Burgess, thought Wexford. A woman endowed with a memory and a gimlet eye as well as a social conscience.

'An enormous removal van,' she had said, 'a real pantechnicon, and polluting what's left of our country air with clouds of the filthiest black diesel fumes. Of course I can tell you the name of the firm. I sat down and wrote to their managing director at once to complain. William Dorset and Company. I expect you've seen that slogan of theirs, "Dorset Stores It", it's on all their vans.'

The company had branches in north and south London, in Brighton, Guildford, and in Kingsmarkham, which was no doubt why both Sheila and Natalie Arno had employed them. Kingsmarkham people moving house or storing furniture mostly did use Dorset's.

Here and there along the road was the occasional factory as well as the kind of long, low, virtually windowless building whose possible nature or use it is hard for the passerby to guess at. Perhaps all such buildings, Wexford thought as they turned into the entrance drive to one of them, served the same purpose as this one.

It was built of grey brick and roofed with red sheet iron. What windows it had were high up under the roof. In the concrete bays in front of the iron double doors stood two monster vans, dark red and lettered 'Dorset Stores It' in yellow.

'They're expecting us,' Wexford said. 'I reckon that's the office over there, don't you?'

It was an annexe built out on the far side. Someone came out before they reached the door. Wexford recognized him as the younger of the two men who had moved Sheila's furniture, the one whose wife had not missed a single episode of *Runway*. He looked at Wexford as if he thought he had seen him somewhere before but knew just the same that he was mistaken.

'Come in, will you, please? Mr Rochford's here, our deputy managing director. He reckoned he ought to be here himself.'

Wexford's heart did not exactly sink but it floundered a little. He would so much rather have been alone, without even Burden. Of course he could have stopped all these people coming with him, he had the power to do that, but he wouldn't. Besides, two witnesses would be better than one and four better than two. He followed the man who said his name was George Prince into the office. Rochford, a man of Prince's age and in the kind of suit which, while perfectly clean and respectable, looks as if it has been worn in the past for emergency manual labour and could be put to such use again if the need arose, sat in a small armchair with an unopened folder on his knees. He jumped up and the folder fell on the floor. Wexford shook hands with him and showed him the warrant.

Although he already knew the purpose of the visit, he turned white and looked nauseous.

'This is a serious matter,' he said miserably, 'a very serious matter.'

'It is.'

'I find it hard to believe. I imagine there's a chance you're wrong.'

'A very good chance, sir.'

'Because,' said Rochford hopefully and extremely elliptically, 'in summertime and after – well, I mean, there's been nothing of that sort, has there, George?'

Not yet, thought Wexford. 'Perhaps we might terminate this suspense,' he said, attempting a smile, 'by going and having a look?'

'Oh yes, yes, by all means. This way, through here. Perhaps you'll lead the way, George. I hope you're wrong, Mr Wexford, I only hope you're wrong.'

The interior of the warehouse was cavernous and dim. The roof, supported by girders of red iron, was some thirty feet high. Up there sparrows flitted about and perched on these man-made branches. The sunlight was greenish, filtering through the tinted panes of high, metal-framed windows. George Prince pressed a switch and strip lighting came on, setting the sparrows in flight again. It was chilly inside the warehouse, though the outdoor temperature had that morning edged just into the seventies.

The place had the air of a soulless and shabby township erected on a grid plan. A town of caravans, placed symmetrically a yard or two apart and with streets crossing each other at right angles to give access to them. It might have been a camp for refugees or the rejected spill-over of some newly constituted state, or the idea of such a place in grim fiction or cinema, a settlement in a northern desert without a tree or a blade of grass. Wexford felt the fantasy and shook it off, for there were no people, no inhabitants of this container camp but himself and Burden and George Prince and Rochford padding softly up the broadest aisle.

Of these rectangular houses, these metal cuboids ranked in rows, iron red, factory green, camouflage khaki, the one they were making for stood at the end of the topmost lane to debouch from the main aisle. It stood up against the cream-washed wall under a window. Prince produced a key and was about to insert it into the lock on the container door when Rochford put out a hand to restrain him and asked to see the warrant again. Patiently, Wexford handed it to him. They stood there, waiting while he read it once more. Wexford had fancied for minutes now that he could smell something sweetish and foetid but this became marked the nearer he got to Rochford and it was only the stuff the man put on his hair or his underarms. Rochford said:

'Mrs N. Arno, 27a De Beauvoir Place, London, N1. We didn't move it from there, did we, George? Somewhere in Sussex, didn't you say?'

'Kingsmarkham, sir. It was our Kingsmarkham branch done it.'

'Ah, yes. And it was put into store indefinitely at the rate of £5.50 per week starting from 15 July?'

Wexford said gently, 'Can we open up now, sir, please?'

'Oh, certainly, certainly. Get it over, eh?'

Get it over . . . George Prince unlocked the door and Wexford braced himself for the shock of the foul air that must escape. But there was nothing, only a curious staleness. The door swung silently open on oiled hinges. The place might be sinister and evocative of all manner of disagreeable things, but it was well-kept and well-run for all that.

The inside of the container presented a microcosm of Sterries, a drop of the essence of Sir Manuel Camargue. His desk was there and the austere furnishings from the bedroom and sitting room in his private wing, the record player too and the lyre-backed chairs from the music room and the piano. If you closed your eyes you could fancy hearing the first movement from the Flute and Harp Concerto. You could smell and hear Camargue and nothing else. Wexford turned away to face the furniture from the spare bedrooms, a green velvet ottoman in a holland cover, two embroidered footstools, sheathed in plastic, a pair of golden Afghan rugs rolled up in hessian, and under a bag full of quilts and cushions, the carved teak chest, banded now with two stout leather straps.

The four men looked at it. Burden humped the quilt bag off on to the ottoman and knelt down to undo the buckles on the straps. There was a rattly intake of breath from Rochford. The straps fell away and Burden tried the iron clasps. They were locked. He looked inquiringly at Prince who hesitated and then muttered something about having to go back to the office to check in his book where the keys were.

Wexford lost his temper. 'You knew what we'd come for. Couldn't you have checked where the keys were before we came all the way down here? If they can't be found I'll have to have it broken open.'

'Look here . . .' Rochford was almost choking. 'Your warrant doesn't say anything about breaking. What's Mrs Arno going to say when she finds her property's been damaged? I can't take the responsibility for that sort of . . .'

'Then you'd better find the keys.'

Prince scratched his head. 'I reckon she said they were in that desk. In one of the pigeonholes in that desk.'

They opened the desk. It was entirely empty. Burden unrolled both rugs, emptied the quilt bag, pulled out the drawers of the bedside cabinet from Camargue's bedroom.

'You say you've got a note of where they are in some book of yours?' said Wexford.

'The note says there in the desk,' said Prince.

'Right. We break the chest open.'

'They're down here,' said Burden. He pulled out his hand from the cleft between the ottoman's arm and seat cushion and waved at them a pair of identical keys on a ring.

Wexford fitted one key into the lock on the right-hand side, turned it, and then unlocked the left-hand side. The clasps opened and he raised the lid. The chest seemed to be full of black heavy-duty polythene sheeting. He grasped a fold of it and pulled.

The heavy thing that was contained in this cold

glossy slippery shroud lurched against the wooden wall and seemed to roll over. Wexford began to unwrap the black stuff and then a horrible thing happened. Slowly, languidly, as if it still retained life, a yellowish-white waxen arm and thin hand rose from the chest and loomed trembling over it. It hung in the air for a moment before it subsided. Wexford stepped back with a grunt. The icy thing had brushed his cheek with fingers of marble.

Rochford let out a cry and stumbled out of the container. There was a sound of retching. But George Prince was made of tougher stuff and he came nearer to the chest with awe. With Burden's help, Wexford lifted the body on to the floor and stripped away its covering. Its throat had been cut and the wound wadded with a bloody towel, but this had not kept blood off the yellow dress, which was splashed and stained with red all over like some bizarre map of islands.

Wexford looked into the face, knowing he had been wrong, feeling as much surprise as the others, and then he looked at Burden.

Burden shook his head, appalled and mystified, and together they turned slowly back to gaze into the black dead eyes of Natalie Arno.

19

'*Cui bono*?' said Kenneth Ames. 'Who benefits?' He made a church steeple of his fingers and looked out at St Peter's spire. 'Well, my dear chap, the same lady who would have benefited had you been right in your preposterous assumption that poor Mrs Arno was not Mrs Arno. Or to cut a tall story short, Sir Manuel's niece in France.'

'You never did tell me her name,' said Wexford.

He did not then. 'It's an extraordinary thing. Poor Mrs Arno simply followed in her father's footmarks. It's no more than a week ago she asked me if she should make a will and I naturally advised her to do so. But, as was true in the case of Sir Manuel, she died before a will was drawn up. She too had been going to get married, you know, but she changed her mind.'

'No, I didn't know.'

Ames made his doggy face. 'So, as I say, the beneficiary will be this French lady, there being no other living relatives whatsoever. I've got her name somewhere.' He hunted in a drawer full of folders. 'Ah, yes. A Mademoiselle Thérèse Lerèmy. Do you want her precise address?'

The transformation of Moidore Lodge was apparent long before the house was reached. The drive was swept, the signboard bearing the name of the house had been re-painted black and white, and Wexford could have sworn the bronze wolves (or Alsatians) had received a polish.

Blaise Cory's Porsche was parked up in front of the house and it was he, not Muriel Hicks, who opened the door. They send for him like other people might send for their solicitor, thought Wexford. He stepped into a hall from which all dust and clutter had been removed, which even seemed lighter and airier. Blaise confided, looking once or twice over his shoulder:

'Having these good people has made all the difference to the dear old dad. I do hope you're not here to do anything which might – well, in short, which might put a spanner in the works.'

'I hardly think so, Mr Cory. I have a question or two to ask Mrs Hicks, that's all.'

'Ah, that's what you people always say.' He gave the short, breathy, fruity laugh with which, on his show, he was in the habit of receiving the more outrageous of the statements made by his interviewees. 'I believe she's about the house, plying her highly useful equipment.'

The sound of a vacuum cleaner immediately began overhead as if on cue, and Wexford would have chosen to go straight upstairs but he found himself instead ushered into Philip Cory's living room.

Ted Hicks was cleaning the huge Victorian French windows, the old man, once more attired in his boy's jeans and guernsey, watching him with fascinated approval. Hicks stopped work the moment Wexford came in and took up his semi-attention stance.

'Good morning, sir!'

'Welcome, Chief Inspector, welcome.' Cory spread out his meagre hands expansively. 'A pleasure to see you, I'm sure. It's so delightful for me to have visitors and not be ashamed of the old place, not to mention being able to find things. Now, for instance, if you or Blaise were to require a drink I shouldn't have to poke about looking for bottles. Hicks here would bring them in a jiffy, wouldn't you, Hicks?'

'I certainly would, sir.'

'So you have only to say the word.'

It being not yet ten in the morning, Wexford was not inclined to utter any drink-summoning word but asked if he might have a talk in private with Mrs Hicks.

'I saw in the newspaper about poor little Natalie,' said Cory. 'Blaise thought it would upset me. Blaise was always a very *sensitive* boy. But I said to him, how can I be upset when I don't know if she was Natalie or not?'

Wexford went upstairs, Hicks leading the way. Moidore Lodge was a very large house. Several rooms had been set aside to make a dwelling for the Hickses without noticeably depleting the Cory living space. Muriel Hicks, who had been cleaning Cory's own bedroom with its vast four-poster, came into her own rooms, drying her newly washed hands on a towel. She had put on weight since last he saw her and her pale red hair had grown longer and bushier. But her brusque and taciturn manner was unchanged.

'Mrs Arno was going away on her holidays. She says to me to see to the moving when the men came next day. It wasn't convenient, we were leaving ourselves and I'd got things to do, but that was all the same to her, I daresay.' Her husband flashed her an admonitory look, implying that respect should be accorded to *all* employers, or else perhaps that she must in no way hint at ill of the dead. Her pink face flushed rosily. 'Well, she said that was the only day Dorset's could do it, so it was no use arguing. She'd had a chap there staying the weekend . . .'

'A *gentleman*,' said Hicks.

'All right, Ted, a gentleman. I thought he'd gone by the Sunday, and maybe he had, but he was back the Monday afternoon.'

'You saw him?'

'I *heard* him. I went in about six to check up with her what was going and what was staying, and I heard them talking upstairs. They heard me come in and they started talking French so I wouldn't understand, and she laughed and said in English,

"Oh, your funny Swiss accent!" By the time I got upstairs he'd hid himself.'

'Did you hear his name, Mrs Hicks?'

She shook her head. 'Never heard his name and never saw him. She was a funny one, she didn't mind me knowing he was there and what he was to her like, but she never wanted me nor anyone to actually see him. I took it for granted they both went off on their holidays that same evening. She said she was going, she told me, and the car was gone.'

'What happened next day?'

'The men came from Dorset's nine in the morning. I let them in and told them what to take and what not to. She'd left everything labelled. When they'd gone I had a good clear-up. There was a lot of blood about in the blue bathroom, but I never gave it a thought, reckoned one of them had cut theirselves.' Wexford remembered the deliberate cutting of Natalie's fingertips in the bathroom in De Beauvoir Place and he almost shuddered. Muriel Hicks was more stolid about it than he. 'I had a bit of a job getting it off the carpet,' she said. 'I saw in the paper they found her at Dorset's warehouse. Was she . . . ? I mean, was *it* in that chest?'

He nodded.

She said indifferently, 'The men did say it was a dead weight.'

Blaise Cory walked out to the car with him. It was warm today, the sky a serene blue, the leaves of the plane trees fluttering in a light frisky breeze. Blaise said suddenly and without his usual affected geniality:

'Do you know Mrs Mountnessing, Camargue's sister-in-law?'

'I've seen her once.'

'There was a bit of a scandal in the family. I was only seventeen or eighteen at the time and Natalie and I – well, it wasn't an affair or anything, we were like brother and sister. We were close, she used to tell me things. The general made a pass at her and the old girl caught them kissing.'

'The general?' said Wexford.

Blaise made one of his terrible jokes. 'Must have been caviare to him.' He gave a yelp of laughter. 'Sorry. I mean old Roo Mountnessing, General Mountnessing. Mrs M told her sister and made a great fuss, put all the blame on poor little Nat, called her incestuous and a lot of crap like that. As if everyone didn't know the old boy was a satyr. Camargue was away on a tour of Australia at the time or he'd have intervened. Mrs Camargue and her sister tried to lock Nat up, keep her a sort of prisoner. She got out and hit her mother. She hit her in the chest, quite hard, I think. I suppose they had a sort of brawl over Natalie trying to get out of the house.'

'And?'

'Well, when Mrs Camargue got cancer Mrs Mountnessing said it had been brought on by the blow. I've heard it said that can happen. The doctors said no but Mrs M. wouldn't listen to that and she more or less got Camargue to believe it too. I've always thought that's why Natalie went off with Vernon Arno, she couldn't stand things at home.'

'So that was the cause of the breach,' said Wexford. 'Camargue blamed her for her mother's death.'

Blaise shook his head. 'I don't think he did. He was just confused by Mrs M. and crazy with grief over his wife dying. The dear old dad says Camargue tried over and over again to make things right between himself and Nat, wrote again and again, offered to go out there or pay her fare home. I suppose it wasn't so much him blaming her for her mother's death as her blaming herself. It was guilt kept her away.'

Wexford looked down at the little stocky man.

'Did she tell you all this when you had lunch with her, Mr Cory?'

'Good heavens, no. We didn't talk about that. I'm a *present* person, Chief Inspector, I live in the moment. And so did she. Curious,' he said reflectively, 'that rumour which went around back in the winter that she was some sort of impostor.'

'Yes,' said Wexford.

It was not a long drive from Moidore Lodge to the village on the borders of St Leonard's Forest. It was called Bayeux Green, between Horsham and Wellridge, and the house Wexford was looking for bore the name Bayeux Villa. Well, it was not all that far from Hastings, there was another village nearby called Doomsday Green, and very likely the name had something to do with the tapestry.

He found the house without having to ask. It was in the centre of the village, a narrow, detached, late nineteenth-century house, built of small pale grey bricks and with only a small railed-in area separating it from the pavement. The front door was newer and inserted in it was a picture in stained glass of a Norman soldier in chain mail. Wexford rang the bell and got no answer. He stepped to one side and looked in at the window. There was no sign of recent habitation. The occupants, at this time of the year, were very likely away on holiday. It seemed strange that they had made no arrangements for the care of their houseplants. Tradescantias, peperomias, a cissus that climbed to the ceiling on carefully spaced strings, a Joseph's coat, a variegated ivy, all hung down leaves that were limp and parched.

He walked around the house, looking in more windows, and he had a sensation of being watched, though he could see no one. The two little lawns looked as if they had not been cut for a month and there were weeds coming up in the rosebed. After he had rung the bell again he went to the nearest neighbour, a cottage separated from Bayeux Villa by a greengrocer's and a pair of garages.

It was a comfort to be himself once more, to have resumed his old standing. The woman looked at his warrant card.

'They went off on holiday – oh, it'd be three weeks ago. When I come to think of it, they must be due back today or tomorrow. They've got a caravan down in Devon, they always take three weeks.'

'Don't they have friends to come in and keep an eye on the place?'

She said quickly, 'Don't tell me it's been broken into.'

He reassured her. 'Nobody's watered the plants.'

'But the sister's there. She said to me on the Saturday, my sister'll be staying while we're away.'

This time he caught her off guard. He came up to the kitchen window and their eyes met. She had been on the watch for him too, creeping about the house, looking out for him. She was still wearing the red and yellow dress of Indian cotton, she had been shut up in there for three weeks, and it hung on her. Her face looked sullen, though not frightened. She opened the back door and let him in.

'Good morning, Mrs Zoffany,' he said. 'It's a relief to find you well and unharmed.'

'Who would harm me?'

'Suppose you tell me that. Suppose you tell me all about it.'

She said nothing. He wondered what she had done all by herself in this house since 27 July. Not eaten much, that was obvious. Presumably, she had not been out. Nor even opened a window. It was insufferably hot and stuffy and a strong smell of sweat and general unwashedness emanated from Jane Zoffany as he followed her into the room full of dying plants. She sat down and looked at him in wary silence.

'If you won't tell me,' he said, 'shall I tell you? After you left me on that Friday evening you went back to Sterries and found the house empty. Mrs Arno had driven your husband to the station. As a matter of fact, her car passed me as I was driving down the hill.' She continued to eye him uneasily. Her eyes had more madness in them than when he had last seen her. 'You took your handbag but you left your suitcase; didn't want to be lumbered with it, I daresay. There's a bus goes to Horsham from outside St Peter's. You'd have had time to catch the last one, or else maybe you had a hire car.'

She said stonily, 'I haven't money for hire cars. I didn't know about the bus, but it came and I got on.'

'When you got here you found your sister and her husband were leaving for their summer holiday the next day. No doubt they were glad to have someone here to keep an eye on the place while they were gone. Then a week later you got yourself a birthday card . . .'

'No.' She shook her head vehemently. 'I only posted it. My sister had bought a card for me and written in it and done the envelope and everything. She said, here, you'd better have this now, save the postage. I went out at night and posted it.' She gave a watery vague smile. 'I liked hiding, I enjoyed it.'

He could understand that. The virtue for her would be twofold. To some extent she would lose her identity, that troubling self, she would have hidden here from herself as successfully as she had hidden from others. And there would be the satisfaction of becoming for a brief while important, of causing anxiety, for once of stimulating emotions.

'What I don't see,' he said, 'is how you managed when the police came here making inquiries.'

She giggled. 'That was funny. They took me for my sister.'

'I see.'

'They just took it for granted I was my sister and they kept on talking about Mrs Zoffany. Did I have any idea where Mrs Zoffany might be? When had I last seen her? I said no and I didn't know and they had to believe me. It was funny, it was a bit like . . .' She put her fingers over her mouth and looked at him over the top of them.

'I shall have to tell your husband where you are. He's been very worried about you.'

'Has he? Has he *really*?'

Had she, during her semi-incarceration, watched television, heard a radio, seen a newspaper? Presumably not, since she had not mentioned Natalie's death. He wouldn't either. She was safe enough here, he thought, with the sister coming back. Zoffany himself would no doubt come down before that. Would they perhaps get her back into a mental hospital between them? He had no faith that the kind of treatment she might get would do her good. He wanted to tell her to have a bath, eat a meal, open the windows, but he knew she would take no advice, would hardly hear it.

'I thought you'd be very angry with me.'

He treated that no more seriously than if the younger of his grandsons had said it to him. 'You and I are going to have to have a talk, Mrs Zoffany. When you've settled down at home again and I've got more time. Just at present I'm very busy and I have to go abroad again.'

She nodded. She no longer looked sullen. He let himself out into Bayeux Green's little high street, and when he glanced back he saw her gaunt face at the window, the eyes following him. In spite of what he had said, he might never see her again, he might never need to, for in one of those flashes of illumination that he had despaired of ever coming in this case, he saw the truth. She had told him. In a little giggly confidence she had told him everything there still remained for him to know.

In the late afternoon he drove out to the home of the chief constable, Hightrees Farm, Millerton. Mrs Griswold exemplified the reverse of the Victorian ideal for children; she was heard but not seen. Some said she had been bludgeoned into passivity by forty years with the colonel. Her footsteps could sometimes be heard overhead, her voice whispering into the telephone. Colonel Griswold himself opened the front door, something which Wexford always found disconcerting. It was plunging in at the deep end.

'I want to go to the South of France, sir.'

'I daresay,' said Griswold. 'I shall have to settle for a cottage in north Wales myself.'

In a neutral voice Wexford reminded him that he had already had his holiday. The chief constable said yes, he remembered, and Wexford had been somewhere very exotic, hadn't he? He had wondered once or twice how that sort of thing would go down with the public when the police started screaming for wage increases.

'I want to go to the South of France,' Wexford said more firmly, 'and I know it's irregular but I would like to take Mike Burden with me. It's a little place *inland* – ' Griswold's lips seemed silently to be forming the syllables St Tropez, ' – and there's a woman there who will inherit Camargue's money and property. She's Camargue's niece and her name is Thérèse Lerèmy.'

'A French citizen?'

'Yes, sir, but . . .'

'I don't want you going about putting people's backs up, Reg. Particularly foreign backs. I mean, don't think you can go over there and arrest this woman on some of your thin suspicions and . . .'

But before Wexford had even begun to deny that this was his intention he knew from the moody truculent look which had replaced obduracy in Griswold's face that he was going to relent.

20

From the city of the angels to the bay of the angels. As soon as they got there the taxi driver took them along the Promenade des Anglais, though it was out of their way, but he said they had to see it, they couldn't come to Nice and just see the airport. While Wexford gazed out over the Baie des Anges, Burden spoke from his newly acquired store of culture. Jenny had a reproduction of a picture of this by a painter called Dufy, but it all looked a bit different now.

It was still only late morning. They had come on the early London to Paris flight and changed planes at Roissy-Charles de Gaulle. Now their drive took them through hills crowned with orange and olive trees. Saint-Jean-de-l'Éclaircie lay a few miles to the north of Grasse, near the river Loup. A bell began to chime noon as they passed through an ivy-hung archway in the walls into the ancient town. They drove past the ochre-stone cathedral into the Place aux Eaux Vives where a fountain was playing and where stood Picasso's statue 'Woman with a Lamb', presented to the town by the artist (according to Wexford's guide book) when he lived and worked there for some months after the war. The guide book also said that there was a Fragonard in the cathedral, some incomparable Sevres porcelain in the museum, the Fondation Yeuse, and a mile outside the town the well-preserved remains of a Roman amphitheatre. The taxi driver said that if you went up into the cathedral belfry you could see Corsica on the horizon.

Wexford had engaged rooms for one night – on the advice of his travel agent in the Kingsbrook Precinct – at the Hotel de la Rose Blanche in the *place*. Its vestibule was cool and dim, stone-walled, stone-flagged, and with that indefinable atmosphere that is a combination of complacency and gleeful anticipation and which signifies that the food is going to be good. The chef's in his kitchen, all's right with the world.

Kenneth Ames had known nothing more about Mademoiselle Lerèmy than her name, her address and her relationship to Camargue. It was also known that her parents were dead and she herself unmarried. Recalling the photograph of the two little girls shown him by Mrs Mountnessing, Wexford concluded she must be near the age of Camargue's daughter. He looked her up in the phone book, dialled the number apprehensively because of his scanty French, but got no reply.

They lunched off seafood, bread that was nearly all crisp crust, and a bottle of Monbazillac. Wexford said in an abstracted sort of voice that he felt homesick already, the hors d'oeuvres reminded him of Mr Haq and antipasto Ankole. He got no reply when he attempted once more to phone Thérèse Lerèmy, so there seemed nothing for it but to explore the town.

It was too hot to climb the belfry. On 24 July Saint-Jean-de-l'Éclaircie was probably at its hottest. The square was deserted, the narrow steep alleys that threaded the perimeter just inside the walls held only the stray tourist, and the morning market which had filled the Place de la Croix had packed up and gone. They went into the cathedral of St Jean Baptiste, dark, cool, baroque. A nun was walking in the aisle, eyes cast down, and an old man knelt at prayer. They looked with proper awe at Fragonard's 'Les Pains et Les Poissons', a large hazy canvas of an elegant Christ and an adoring multitude, and then they returned to the bright white sunshine and hard black shadows of the *place*.

'I suppose she's out at work,' said Wexford. 'A single woman would be bound to work. It looks as if we'll have to hang things out a few hours.'

'It's no hardship,' said Burden. 'I promised Jenny I wouldn't miss the museum.'

Wexford shrugged. 'O.K.'

The collection was housed in a sienna-red stucco

building with Fondation Yeuse lettered on a black marble plaque. Wexford had expected it to be deserted inside but in fact they met other tourists in the rooms and on the winding marble staircase. As well as the Sevres, Burden had been instructed to look at some ancient jewellery discovered in the Condamine, and Wexford, hearing English spoken, asked for directions from the woman who had been speaking correctly but haltingly to an American visitor. She seemed to be a curator, for she wore on one of the lapels of her dark red, near-uniform dress an oval badge inscribed Fondation Yeuse. He forced himself not to stare – and then wondered how many thousands before him had forced themselves not to stare. The lower part of her face was pitted densely and deeply with the scars of what looked like smallpox but was almost certainly acne. In her careful stumbling English she instructed him where to find the jewellery. He and Burden went upstairs again where the American woman had arrived before them. The sun penetrating drawn Venetian blinds shone on her flawless ivory skin. She had hands like Natalie Arno's, long and slender, display stands for rings as heavy and roughly made as those on the linen under the glass.

'We may as well get on up there,' said Wexford after they had bought a *flacon* of Grasse perfume for Dora and a glazed stoneware jar in a Picasso design for Jenny. 'Get on up there and have a look at the place.'

The two local taxis, which were to be found between the fountain and the Hotel de la Rose Blanche, were not much in demand at this hour.

Their driver spoke no English but as soon as Wexford mentioned the Maison du Cirque he understood and nodded assent.

On the north-eastern side of the town, outside the walls, was an estate of depressing pale grey flats and brown wooden houses with scarlet switchback roofs. It was as bad as home. Worse? ventured Burden. But the estate was soon left behind and the road ran through lemon groves. The driver persisted in talking to them in fast, fluent, incomprehensible French. Wexford managed to pick out two facts from all this, one that Saint-Jean-de-l'Éclaircie held a lemon festival each February, and the other that on the far side of the hill was the amphitheatre.

They came upon the house standing alone at a bend in the road. It was flat-fronted, unprepossessing but undoubtedly large. At every window were wooden shutters from which most of the paint had flaked away. Big gardens, neglected now, stretched distantly towards olive and citrus groves, separated from them by crumbling stone walls.

'Mariana in the moated grange,' said Wexford. 'We may as well go to the circus while we're waiting for her.'

The driver took them back. The great circular plain which was the base of the amphitheatre was strangely green as if watered by a hidden spring. The tiers of seating, still defined, still unmistakable, rose in their parallel arcs to the hillside, the pines, the crystalline blue of the sky. Wexford sat down where some prefect or consul might once have sat.

'I hope we're in time,' he said. 'I hope we can

get to her before any real harm has been done. The woman has been dead nine days. He's been here, say, eight . . .'

'If he's here. The idea of him being here is all based on your ESP. We don't know if he's here and, come to that, we don't know who he is or what he looks like or what name he'll be using.'

'It's not as bad as that,' said Wexford. 'He would naturally come here. This place, that girl, would draw him like magnets. He won't want to lose the money now, Mike.'

'No, not after plotting for years to get it. How long d'you reckon we're going to be here?'

Wexford shrugged. The air was scented with the herbs that grew on the hillsides, sage and thyme and rosemary and bay, and the sun was still very warm. 'However long it may be,' he said enigmatically, 'to me it would be too short.' He looked at his watch. 'Martin should have seen Williams by now and done a spot of checking up for me at Guy's Hospital.'

'Guy's Hospital?'

'In the course of this case we haven't remembered as often as we should that Natalie Arno went into hospital a little while before Camargue died. She had a biopsy.'

'Yes, what *is* that?'

'It means to look at living tissue. It usually describes the kind of examination that is done to determine whether certain cells are cancerous or not.'

Once this subject would have been a highly emotive one for Burden, an area to be avoided by all his sensitive acquaintances. His first wife had died of cancer. But time and his second marriage had changed things. He responded not with pain but only with an edge of embarrassment to his voice.

'But she didn't have cancer.'

'Oh, no.'

He sat down in the tier below Wexford. 'I'd like to tell you what I think happened, see if we agree.' On the grass beside him the shadow of Wexford's head nodded. 'Well, then. Tessa Lanchester went on holiday to that place in California, Santa – what was it?'

'Santa Xavierita.'

'And while she was there she met a man who played the guitar or whatever in a restaurant in the local town. He was living in America illegally and was very likely up to a good many other illegal activities as well. He was a con man. He had already met Natalie Arno and found out from her who her father was and what her expectations were. He introduced Tessa to Natalie and the two women became friends.

'He persuaded Tessa not to go back home to Boston but to remain longer in Santa Xavierita learning all she could about Natalie's life and past. Then he took Natalie out swimming by night and drowned her and that same night left with Tessa for Los Angeles in Natalie's car with Natalie's luggage and the key to Natalie's house. From then on Tessa became Natalie. The changes Natalie's body had undergone after five days in the sea made a true identification impossible and, since Tessa was missing, the corpse was identified as that of Tessa.

'Tessa and her accomplice then set about their plan to inherit Camargue's property, though this was somewhat frustrated by Ilbert's intervening and the subsequent deportation. Tessa tried in vain to sell Natalie's house. I think at this time she rather cooled off the plan. Otherwise I don't know how to account for a delay of more than three years between making the plan and putting it into practice. I think she cooled off. She settled into her new identity, made new friends and, as we know, had two further love affairs. Then one of these lovers, Ivan Zoffany, wrote from London in the autumn of 1979 to say he had heard from his sister-in-law who lived near Wellridge that Camargue was about to re-marry. That alerted her and fetched her to England. There she was once more able to join forces with the man who had first put her up to the idea. They had the support and help of Zoffany and his wife. How am I doing so far?'

Wexford raised his eyebrows. 'How did they get Williams and Mavis Rolland into this? Bribery?'

'Of course. It would have to be a heavy bribe. Williams's professional integrity presumably has a high price. I daresay Mrs Woodhouse could be bought cheaply enough.'

'I never took you for a snob before, Mike.'

'It's not snobbery,' said Burden hotly. 'It's simply that the poorer you are the more easily you're tempted. Shall I go on?'

The shadow nodded.

'They hesitated a while before the confrontation. Tessa was naturally nervous about this very important encounter. Also she'd been ill and had to have hospital treatment. When she finally went down to Sterries she blundered, not in having failed to do her homework – she knew every fact about the Camargue household she could be expected to, she knew them like she knew her own family in Boston – but over the pronunciation of an Italian name. Spanish she knew – many Americans do – French she knew, but it never occurred to her she would have to pronounce Italian.

'The rest we know. Camargue told her she would be cut out of his will, so on the following Sunday she made a sound alibi for herself by going to a party with Jane Zoffany. *He* went down to Sterries, waited for Camargue in the garden and drowned him in the lake.'

Wexford said nothing.

'Well?'

As befitted a person of authority sitting in the gallery of an amphitheatre, Wexford turned down his thumbs. 'The last bit's more or less right, the drowning bit.' He got up. 'Shall we go?'

Burden was still muttering that it had to be that way, that all else was impossible, when they arrived back at the Maison du Cirque. Ahead of them a bright green Citroen 2 CV had just turned into the drive.

The woman who got out of it, who came inquiringly towards them, was the curator of the Fondation Yeuse.

21

The sun shone cruelly on that pitted skin. She had done her best to hide it with heavy make-up, but there would never be any hiding it. And now as she approached these two strangers she put one hand up, half covering a cheek. Close to, she had a look of Camargue, all the less attractive traits of the Camargue physiognomy were in her face, too-high forehead, too-long nose, too-fleshy mouth, and added to them that acne-scarred skin. She was sallow and her hair was very dark. But she was one of those plain people whose smiles transform them. She smiled uncertainly at them, and the change of expression made her look kind and sweet-tempered.

Wexford introduced them. He explained that he had seen her earlier that day. Her surprise at being called upon by two English policemen seemed unfeigned. She was astonished but not apparently nervous.

'This is some matter concerning the *musée* – the museum?' she asked in her heavily accented English.

'No, mademoiselle,' said Wexford, 'I must confess I'd never heard of the Fondation Yeuse till this morning. You've worked there long?'

'Since I leave the university – that is, eighteen years. M. Raoul Yeuse, the Paris art dealer, he is, was, the brother of my father's sister. He has founded the museum, you understand? Excuse me, monsieur, I fear my English is very bad.'

'It is we who should apologize for having no French. May we go into the house, Mademoiselle Lerèmy? I have something to tell you.'

Did she know already? The announcement of the discovery of the body at Dorset's would have scarcely appeared in the French newspapers until three days ago. And when it appeared would it have merited more than a paragraph on an inside page? A murder, in England, of an obscure woman? The dark eyes of Camargue's niece looked merely innocent and inquiring. She led them into a large high-ceilinged room and opened latticed glass doors on to a terrace. From the back of the Maison du Cirque you could see the green rim of the amphitheatre and smell the scented hillsides. But the house itself was shabby and neglected and far too big. It had been built for a family and that family's servants in days when perhaps money came easily and went a long way.

Now that they were indoors and seated she had become rather pale. 'This is not bad news, I hope, monsieur?' She looked from one to the other of them with a rising anxiety that Wexford thought he understood. He let Burden answer her.

'Serious news,' said Burden. 'But not personally distressing to you, Miss Lerèmy. You hardly knew your cousin Natalie Camargue, did you?'

She shook her head. 'She was married. I have not heard her husband's name. When last I am seeing her she is sixteen, I seventeen. It is many years . . .'

'I'm afraid she's dead. To put it bluntly, she was murdered and so was your uncle. We're here to investigate these crimes. It seems the same person killed them both. For gain. For money.'

Both hands went up to her cheeks. She recoiled a little.

'But this is terrible!'

Wexford had decided not to tell her of the good fortune this terrible news would bring her. Kenneth Ames could do that. If what he thought was true she would be in need of consolation. He must now broach the subject of this belief of his. Strange that this time he could be so near hoping he was wrong . . .

Her distress seemed real. Her features were contorted into a frown of dismay, her tall curved forehead all wrinkles. 'I am so sorry, this is so very bad.'

'Mademoiselle Lerèmy . . .'

'When I am a little girl I see him many many times, monsieur. I stay with them in Sussex. Natalie is, was, nice, I think, always laughing, always very gay, have much sense of *humeur*. The world has become a very bad place, monsieur, when such things as this happen.' She paused, bit her lip. 'Excuse me, I must not say "sir" so much, is it not so? This I am learning to understand . . .' She hesitated and hazarded, 'Lately? Recently?'

Her words brought him the thrill of knowing he was right – and sickened him too. Must he ask her? Burden was looking at him.

The telephone rang.

'Please excuse me,' she said.

The phone was in the room where they were, up beside the windows. She picked up the receiver rather too fast and the effect on her of the voice of her caller was pitiful to see. She flushed deeply and it was somehow apparent that this was a flush of intense fearful pleasure as well as embarrassment.

She said softly, 'Ah, Jean . . . We see each other again tonight? Of course it is all right, it is fine, very good.' She made an effort, for their benefit or her caller's, to establish formality. 'It will be a great pleasure to see you again.'

He was here all right then, he was talking to her. But where was he? She had her back to them now. 'When you have finished your work, yes. *Entends*, Jean, I will fetch – pick up – pick you up. Ten o'clock?' Suddenly she changed into rapid French. Wexford could not understand a word but he understood *her*. She had been speaking English to a French speaker so that her English hearers would know she had a boy friend, a lover. For all her scarred face, her plainness, her age, her obscure job in this backwater, she had a lover to tell the world about.

She put the phone down after a murmured word or two, a ripple of excited laughter. Wexford was on his feet, signalling with a nod to Burden.

'You do not wish to ask me questions concerning my uncle and my *cousine* Natalie, monsieur?'

'It is no longer necessary, mademoiselle.'

The taxi driver had gone to sleep. Wexford woke him with a prod in his chest.

'La Rose Blanche, *s'il vous plaît.*'

The sun was going down. There were long violet shadows and the air was sweet and soft.

'He's a fast worker if ever there was one,' said Burden.

'The material he is working on could hardly be more receptive and malleable.'

'Pardon? Oh, yes, I see what you mean. Poor girl. It's a terrible handicap having all that pitting on her face, did you notice? D'you think he knew about that? Before he came here, I mean? The real Natalie might have known – you usually get that sort of acne in your teens – but Tessa Lanchester wouldn't have. Unless she picked it up when she was gathering all the rest of her info in Santa Xavierita.'

'Mrs Woodhouse might have known,' said Wexford. 'At any rate, he knew she was unmarried and an heiress and no doubt that she worked in the museum here. It was easy enough for him to scrape up an acquaintance.'

'Bit more than an acquaintance,' said Burden grimly.

'Let's hope it hasn't progressed far yet. Certainly his intention is to marry her.'

'Presumably his intention was to marry that other woman, but at the last she wouldn't have him and for that he killed her.' Burden seemed gratified to get from Wexford a nod of approval. 'Once he'd done that he'd realize who the next heir was and come here as fast as he could. But there's something here doesn't make sense. In putting her body in that chest he seems to have meant to keep it concealed for months, possibly even years, but the paradox there is that until the body was found death wouldn't be presumed and Thérèse Lerèmy wouldn't get anything.'

Wexford looked slyly at him. 'Suppose he intended by some means or other to prove, as only he could, that it was Natalie Arno and not Tessa Lanchester who drowned at Santa Xavierita in 1976? If that were proved Thérèse would become the heir at once and in fact *would have been* the rightful possessor of Sterries and Camargue's money for the past six months.'

'You really think that was it?'

'No, I don't. It would have been too bold and too risky and fraught with problems. I think this was what was in his mind. He didn't want the body found at once because if he then started courting Thérèse even someone as desperate as she might suspect he was after her money. But he wanted it found at some time in the not too distant future or his conquest of Thérèse would bring him no profit at all. What better than that the presence of a corpse in that warehouse should make itself apparent after, say, six months? And if it didn't he could always send the police an anonymous letter.'

'That's true,' said Burden. 'And there was very little to connect him with it, after all. If you hadn't been to California we shouldn't have known of his existence.'

Wexford laughed shortly. 'Yes, there was some profit in it.' They walked into the hotel. Outside Burden's room where they would have separated prior to dressing, or at least sprucing up, for dinner, Burden said, 'Come in here a minute. I want to ask you something.' Wexford sat on the bed. From the window you could see, not the square and the fountain but a mazy mosaic of little roofs against the backdrop of the city walls. 'I'd like to know what we're going to charge those others with. I mean, Williams and Zoffany and Mary Woodhouse. Conspiracy, I suppose – but not conspiracy to murder?'

Wexford pondered. He smiled a little ruefully. 'We're not going to charge them with anything.'

'You mean their evidence will be more valuable as prosecution witnesses?'

'Not really. I shouldn't think any of them would be a scrap of use as witnesses of any kind. They didn't witness anything and they haven't done anything. They all seem to me to be perfectly blameless, apart from a spot – and I'd guess a very small spot – of adultery on the part of Zoffany.' Wexford paused.

'That reconstruction of the case you gave me while we were at the amphitheatre, didn't it strike you there was something unreal about it?'

'Sort of illogical, d'you mean? Maybe, bits of it. Surely that's because they were so devious that there are aspects which aren't clear and never will be?'

Wexford shook his head. 'Unreal. One can't equate it with what one knows of human nature. Take, for instance, their foresight and their patience. They kill Natalie in the summer of 1976 and Tessa impersonates her. Fair enough. Why not go straight to England, make sure Natalie is the beneficiary under Camargue's will and then kill Camargue?'

'I know there's a stumbling block. I said so.'

'It's more than a stumbling block, Mike, it's a bloody great barrier across the path. Think what you – and I – believed they did. Went back to Los Angeles, ran the risk of being suspected by the neighbours, exposed by Ilbert – returned to and settled in what of all cities in the world was the most dangerous to them. And for what?'

'Surely she stayed there to sell the house?'

'Yet she never succeeded in selling it, did she? No, a delay of three-and-a-half years between the killing of Natalie and the killing of Camargue was too much for me to swallow. I can come up with just one feeble reason for it – that they were waiting for Camargue to die a natural death. But, as I say, that's a feeble reason. He might easily have lived another ten years.' Wexford looked at his watch. 'I'll leave you to your shaving and showering or whatever.

A wash and brush-up will do me. Laquin won't be here before seven.'

They met again in the bar where they each had a Stella Artois. Wexford said:

'Your suggestion is that Tessa came to England finally because, through Zoffany's sister-in-law, she heard that Camargue intended to marry again. Doesn't it seem a bit thin that Jane Zoffany's sister should come to know this merely because she lives in a village near the Kathleen Camargue School?'

'Not if she was set by the others to watch Camargue.'

Wexford shrugged. 'The others, yes. There would be five of them, our protagonist and her boy friend, the Zoffanys and Jane Zoffany's sister. Five conspirators working for the acquisition of Camargue's money. Right?'

'Yes, for a start,' said Burden. 'There were finally more like eight or nine.'

'Mary Woodhouse to give Tessa some advanced coaching, Mavis Rolland to identify her as an old school chum, and Williams the dentist.' Wexford gave a little shake of the head. 'I've said I was amazed at their foresight and their patience, Mike, but that was nothing to the trouble they took. That staggered me. All these subsidiary conspirators were persuaded to lie, to cheat or to sell their professional integrity. Tessa studied old samples of Natalie's handwriting, had casts made of her jaw, took lessons to perfect her college French and Spanish – though she neglected to polish up her Italian – while one of the others made a survey of the lie of the land round Sterries and of Camargue's habits. Prior to this Zoffany's sister-in-law was sending a secret agent's regular dispatches out to Los Angeles. Oh, and let's not forget – Jane Zoffany was suborning her neighbours into providing a fake alibi. And all this machinery was set in motion and relentlessly kept in motion for the sake of acquiring a not very large house in an acre of ground and an *unknown sum of money* that, when the time came, would have to be split between eight people.

'I've kept thinking of that and I couldn't believe in it. I couldn't understand why those two had chosen Camargue as their prey. Why not pick on some tycoon? Why not some American oil millionaire? Why an old musician who wasn't and never had been in the tycoon class?'

Burden supplied a hesitant answer. 'Because his daughter fell into their hands, one supposes. Anyway, there's no alternative. We know there was a conspiracy, we know there was an elaborate plan, and one surely simply comments that it's impossible fully to understand people's motivations.'

'But isn't there an alternative? You said I was obsessed, Mike. I think more than anything I became obsessed by the complexity of this case, by the deviousness of the protagonist, by the subtlety of the web she had woven. It was only when I saw how wrong I'd been in these respects that things began to clear for me.'

'I don't follow you.'

Wexford drank his beer. He said rather slowly, 'It was only then that I began to see that this case wasn't complicated, there was no deviousness, there was no plotting, no planning ahead, no conspiracy whatsoever, and that even the two murders happened so spontaneously as really to be unpremeditated.' He rose suddenly, pushing back his chair. Commissaire Mario Laquin of the Compagnies Republicaines de Securité of Grasse had come in and was scanning the room. Wexford raised a hand. He said absently to Burden as the commissaire came towards their table, 'The complexity was in our own minds, Mike. The case itself was simple and straightforward, and almost everything that took place was the result of accident or of chance.'

It was a piece of luck for Wexford that Laquin had been transferred to Grasse from Marseilles some six months before, for they had once or twice worked on cases together and since then the two policemen and their wives had met when M. and Mme Laquin were in London on holiday. It nevertheless came as something of a shock to be clasped in the commissaire's arms and kissed on both cheeks. Burden stood by, trying to give his dry smile but succeeding only in looking astonished.

Laquin spoke English that was almost flawless. 'You pick some charming places to come for your investigations, my dear Reg. A little bird tells me you have already had two weeks in California. I should be so lucky. Last year when I was in pursuit of Honorat L'Eponge, where does he lead me to but Dusseldorf, I ask you!'

'Have a drink,' said Wexford. 'It's good to see

you. I haven't a clue where this chap of ours is. Nor do I know what name he's going under while here.'

'Or even what he looks like,' said Burden for good measure. He seemed cheered by the presence of Laquin whom he had perhaps expected to speak with a Peter Sellers accent.

'I know what he looks like,' said Wexford. 'I've seen him.'

Burden glanced at him in surprise. Wexford took no notice of him and ordered their drinks.

'You'll dine with us, of course?' he said to Laquin.

'It will be a pleasure. The food here is excellent.'

Wexford grinned wryly. 'Yes, it doesn't look as though we'll be here to enjoy it tomorrow. I reckon we're going to have to take him at the Maison du Cirque, in that wretched girl's house.'

'Reg, she has known him no time at all, a mere week at most.'

'Even so quickly can one catch the plague . . . You're right, of course.'

'A blessing for her we're going to rid her of him, if you ask me,' said Burden. 'A couple of years and he'd have put her out of the way as well.'

'She implied he was working here . . .'

'Since Britain came in the European Economic Community, Reg, there is no longer need for your countrymen to have work permits or to register. Therefore to trace his whereabouts would be a long and laborious business. And since we know that later on tonight he will be at the Maison du Cirque . . .'

'Sure, yes, I know. I'm being sentimental, Mario, I'm a fool.' Wexford gave a grim little laugh. 'But not such a fool as to warn her and have him hop off on the next plane into Switzerland.'

After *bouillabaisse* and a fine *cassoulet* with brie to follow and a small armagnac each, it was still only nine. Ten-thirty was the time fixed on by Wexford and Laquin for their visit to the house by the amphitheatre. Laquin suggested they go to a place he knew on the other side of the Place aux Eaux Vives where there was sometimes flamenco dancing.

In the evening there was some modest floodlighting in the square. Apparently these were truly living waters and the fountain was fed by a natural spring. While they dined tiers of seating had been put up for the music festival of Saint Jean-de-l'Éclaircie, due to begin on the following day. A little warm breeze rustled through the plane and chestnut leaves above their heads.

The flamenco place was called La Mancha. As they passed down the stairs and into a kind of open, deeply sunken courtyard or cistern, a waiter told Laquin there would be no dancing tonight. The walls were made of yellow stone over which hung a deep purple bougainvillea. Instead of the dancers a thin girl in black came out and sang in the manner of Piaf. Laquin and Burden were drinking wine but Wexford took nothing. He felt bored and restless. Nine-thirty. They went up the stairs again and down an alley into the cobbled open space in front of the cathedral.

The moon had come up, a big golden moon flattened like a tangerine. Laquin had sat down at a table in a pavement café and was ordering coffee for all three men. From here you could see the city walls, part Roman, part medieval, their rough stones silvered by the light from that yellow moon.

Some teenagers went by. They were on their way, Laquin said, to the discotheque in the Place de la Croix. Wexford wondered if Camargue had ever, years ago, sat on this spot where they were. And that dead woman, when she was a child . . . ? It was getting on for ten. Somewhere in St Jean she would be meeting him now in the little green Citroen. The yellow hatchback Opel was presumably left in the long-term car park at Heathrow. He felt a tautening of tension and at the same time relief when Laquin got to his feet and said in his colloquial way that they should be making tracks.

Up through the narrow winding defile once more, flattening themselves tolerantly against stone walls to let more boys and girls pass them. Wexford heard the music long before they emerged into the Place aux Eaux Vives. A Mozart serenade. The serenade from *Don Giovanni,* he thought it was, that should properly be played on a mandolin.

Round the last turn in the alley and out into the wide open square. A group of young girls, also no doubt on their way to the discotheque, were clustered around the highest tier of the festival seating. They clustered around a man who sat on the top, playing a guitar, and they did so in the yearning, worshipping fashion of muses or nymphs on the plinth of some statue of a celebrated musician. The man sat aloft, his tune changed now to a Latin American rhythm, not looking at the girls, looking across the square, his gaze roving as if he expected at any moment the person he waited for to come.

'That's him,' said Wexford.

Laquin said, 'Are you sure?'

'Absolutely. I've only seen him once before but I'd know him anywhere.'

'I know him too,' said Burden incredulously. 'I've seen him before. I can't for the life of me think where, but I've seen him.'

'Let's get it over.'

The little green 2CV was turning into the *place* and the guitarist had seen it. He drew his hand across the strings with a flourish and jumped down from his perch, nearly knocking one of the girls over. He didn't look back at her, he made no apology, he was waving to the car.

And then he saw the three policemen, recognizing them immediately for what they were. His arm fell to his side. He was a tall thin man in his late thirties, very dark with black curly hair. Wexford steadfastly refused to look over his shoulder to see her running from the car. He said:

'John Fassbender, it is my duty to warn you that anything you say will be taken down and may be used in evidence . . . '

22

They were in the Pearl of Africa, having what Wexford called a celebration lunch. No one could possibly feel much in the way of pity for Fassbender, so why not celebrate his arrest? Burden said it ought to be called an elucidation lunch because there were still a lot of things he didn't understand and wanted explained. Outside it was pouring with rain again. Wexford asked Mr Haq for a bottle of wine, *good* Moselle or a Riesling, none of your living waters from Lake Victoria. They had got into sybaritic habits during their day in France. Mr Haq bustled off to what he called his cellar through the fronds of polyethylene Spanish moss.

'Did you mean what you said about there having been no conspiracy?'

'Of course I did,' Wexford said, 'and if we'd had a moment after that I'd have told you something else, something I realized before we ever went to France. The woman we knew as Natalie Arno, the woman Fassbender murdered, was never Tessa Lanchester. Tessa Lanchester was drowned in Santa Xavierita in 1976 and we've no reason to believe either Natalie or Fassbender even met her. The woman who came to London in November of last year came solely because Fassbender was in London. She was in love with Fassbender and since he had twice been deported from the United States he could hardly return there.'

'How could he have been deported twice?' asked Burden.

'I wondered that until the possibility of dual nationality occurred to me and then everything about Fassbender became simple. I'd been asking myself if she had two boyfriends, an Englishman and a Swiss. There was a good deal of confusion in people's minds over him. He was Swiss. He was English. He spoke French. He spoke French with a Swiss accent. He was deported to London. He was deported to Geneva. Well, I'll come back to him in a minute. Suffice it to say that it was after he had been deported a second time that she followed him to London.'

He stopped. Mr Haq, beaming, teeth flashing, was bringing the wine, a quite respectable-looking white Médoc. He poured Wexford a trial half-glassful. Wexford sipped it, looking serious. He had sometimes said, though, that he would rather damage his liver than upset Mr Haq by sending back a bottle. Anyway, the only fault with this wine was that it was at a temperature of around twenty-five degrees Celsius.

'Excellent,' he said to Mr Haq's gratification, and just stopped himself from adding, 'Nice and warm.' He continued to Burden as Mr Haq trotted off, 'She had a brief affair with Zoffany during Fassbender's first absence. I imagine this was due to nothing more than loneliness and that she put it out of her head once Zoffany had departed. But he kept up a correspondence with her and when she needed a home in London he offered her a flat. Didn't I tell you it was simple and straightforward?

'Once there, she saw that Zoffany was in love with her and hoped to take up their relationship (to use Jane Zoffany's word) where it had ended a year and a half before. She wasn't having that, she didn't care for Zoffany at all in that way. But it made things awkward. If she had Fassbender to live with her there, would Zoffany be made so jealous and angry as to throw her out? She couldn't live with Fassbender, he was living in one room. The wisest thing obviously was to keep Fassbender discreetly in the background until such time as he got a job and made some money and they could afford to snap their fingers at Zoffany and live together. We know that Fassbender was in need of work and that she tried to get him a job through Blaise Cory. The point I'm making is that Zoffany never knew of Fassbender's existence until he overheard Natalie talking on the phone to him *last month.*

'I suspect, though I don't know for certain, that there was no urgency on her part to approach Camargue. Probably she gave very little thought to Camargue. It was the announcement of his engagement that brought her to get in touch with him – perhaps reminded her of his existence. But there was no complex planning about that approach, no care taken with the handwriting or the style of the letter, no vetting of it by, say, Mrs Woodhouse . . .'

Young Haq came with their starter of prawns Pakwach. This was a shocking pink confection into which Burden manfully plunged his spoon before saying, 'There must have been. It may be that the identity of the woman we found in that chest will never be known, but we know very well she was an impostor and a fraudulent claimant.'

'Her identity is known,' said Wexford. 'She was Natalie Arno, Natalie Camargue, Camargue's only child.'

Pouring more wine for them, Mr Haq burst into a flowery laudation of various offerings among the entrées. There was caneton Kioga, wild duck breasts marinated in a succulent sauce of wine, cream and basil, or T-bone Toro, tender steaks *flambés*. Burden's expression was incredulous, faintly dismayed. Fortunately, his snapped 'Bring us some of that damned duck,' was lost on Mr Haq who responded only to Wexford's gentler request for two portions of caneton.

'I don't understand you,' Burden said coldly when Mr Haq had gone. 'Are you saying that the woman Camargue refused to recognize, the woman who deliberately cut her hand to avoid having to play the violin, whose antecedents you went rooting out all over America – that woman was Camargue's daughter all the time? We were wrong. Ames was right, Williams and Mavis Rolland and Mary Woodhouse and Philip Cory were right, but we were wrong. Camargue was wrong. Camargue was a senile half-blind old man who happened to make a mistake. Is that it?'

'I didn't say that,' said Wexford. 'I only said that Natalie Arno was Natalie Arno. Camargue made no mistake, though it would be true to say he misunderstood.' He sighed. 'We were such fools, Mike – you, me, Ames, Dinah Sternhold. Not one of us saw the simple truth, that though the woman who visited Camargue was not his daughter, she was not his daughter, if I may so put it, for just one day.'

'You see,' he went on, 'an illusion was created, as if by a clever trick. Only it was a trick we played upon ourselves. We were the conjurers and we held the mirrors. Dinah Sternhold told me Camargue said the woman who went to see him wasn't his daughter. I jumped to the conclusion – you did, Dinah did, we all did – that therefore the woman *we* knew as Natalie Arno wasn't his daughter. It never occurred to us he could be right and yet she might still be his daughter. It never occurred to us that the woman he saw might not be the woman who claimed to be his heir and lived in his house and inherited his money.'

'It wasn't Natalie who went there that day but it was Natalie before and always Natalie after that?' Burden made the face people do when they realize they have been conned by a stratagem unworthy of their calibre. 'Is that what you're saying?'

'Of course it is.' Wexford grinned and gave a rueful shake of the head. 'I may as well say here and now that Natalie wasn't the arch-villainess I took her for. She was cruel and devious and spiteful only in my imagination. Mind you, I'm not saying she was an angel of light. She may not have killed her father or plotted his death, but she connived at it afterwards and she had no scruples about taking an inheritance thus gained. Nor did she have any scruples about appropriating other women's husbands either on a temporary or a permanent basis. She was no paragon of virtue but she was no Messalina either. Why did I ever think she was? Largely, I'm ashamed to say, because Dinah Sternhold told me so.

'Now Dinah Sternhold is a very nice girl. If she blackened Natalie's character to me before I'd even met her, I'm sure it was unconscious. The thing with Dinah, you see, is that odd though it undoubtedly seems, she was genuinely in love with that old man. He was old enough to be her grandfather but she was as much in love with him as if he'd been fifty years younger. Have you ever noticed that it's only those who suffer most painfully from jealousy that say, "I haven't a jealous nature"? Dinah said that to me. She was deeply jealous of Natalie and perhaps with justification. For in marrying her, wasn't Camargue looking to replace his lost daughter? How then must she have felt when that lost daughter turned up? Dinah was jealous and in her jealousy, all unconsciously, without malice, she painted Natalie as a scheming adventuress and so angled the tale of the visit to Camargue to make her appear at once as a fraudulent claimant.'

'I'd like to hear your version of that visit.'

Wexford nodded. The duck had arrived, modestly veiled in a thick brown sauce. Wexford took a sip of his wine instead of a long draught, having decided with some soul-searching that it would hardly do to send for a second bottle. He sampled the duck, which wasn't too bad, and said after a few moments:

'The first appointment Natalie made with her father she couldn't keep. In the meantime something very disquieting had happened to her. She discovered a growth in one of her breasts.'

'How d'you know that?'

'A minute scar where the biopsy was done showed at the post-mortem,' said Wexford. 'Natalie went to her doctor and was sent to Guy's Hospital, the appointment being on the day she had arranged to go down to Sterries. She didn't want to talk to her father on the phone – I think we can call that a perfectly natural shrinking in the circumstances – so she got Jane Zoffany to do it. Shall I say here that Natalie was a congenital slave-owner and Jane Zoffany a born slave?

'Well, Jane made the call and a new date for the 19th. Natalie went to the hospital where they were unable to tell her whether the growth was malignant or not. She must come into their Hedley Atkins Unit in New Cross for a biopsy under anaesthetic.

'Now we're all of us afraid of cancer but Natalie maybe had more reason than most of us. She had seen her young husband die of leukaemia, a form of cancer, her friend Tina too, but most traumatic for her, her mother had died of it and died, it had been implied, through her daughter's actions. Moreover, at the time she had only been a few years older than Natalie then was. Small wonder if she was terrified.

'Then – due no doubt to some aberration on the part of the Post Office – the letter telling her she was to go into the Hedley Atkins Unit on 17 January didn't arrive till the morning before. This meant she couldn't go to Kingsmarkham on the 19th. I imagine she was past caring. All that mattered to her now was that she shouldn't have cancer, shouldn't have her beautiful figure spoilt, shouldn't live in dread of a recurrence or an early death. Jane Zoffany could deal with her father for her, phone or write or send a telegram.'

From staring down at his empty plate, Burden now lifted his eyes and sat bolt upright. 'It was Jane Zoffany who came down here that day?'

Wexford nodded. 'Who else?'

'She too is thin and dark and about the right age . . . But why? Why pose as Natalie? For whatever possible purpose?'

'It wasn't deliberate,' Wexford said a shade testily. 'Haven't I said scarcely anything in this case was deliberate, planned or premeditated? It was just typical silly muddled Jane Zoffany behaviour. And what months it took me to guess it! I suppose I had an inkling of the truth, that wet day in the garden at Sterries, when Dinah said how strange it was Natalie could get the solicitors and Camargue's old friends to believe in her, yet Camargue who wanted to believe, who was longing to believe, saw her *on that one occasion* and didn't believe in her for more than half an hour. And when Jane Zoffany said how the police had taken her for her own sister and then stuck her hand up over her mouth – I knew then, I didn't need to be told any more.'

'But she did tell you more?'

'Sure. When I talked to her last night. She filled in the gaps.'

'Why did she go down to Sterries at all?' asked Burden.

'Two reasons. She wanted to see the old man for herself – she'd been an admirer of his – and she didn't want his feelings hurt. She knew that if she phoned and told him Natalie had yet again to keep a hospital appointment he'd think she was making excuses not to see him and he'd be bitterly hurt. For nineteen years his daughter had stayed away from him and now that she had come back and they were on the brink of a reunion, he was to be fobbed off with a phone call – and a second phone call at that. So she decided to go down and see him herself. But not, of course, with any idea of posing as Natalie, nothing of that sort entered her head. It's just that she's a rather silly muddled creature who isn't always quite mentally stable.'

'You mean,' said Burden, 'that she came down here simply because it seemed kinder and more polite to call in person? She came to explain why Natalie couldn't come and – well, sort of assure him of Natalie's affection for him? Something like that?'

'Something very much like that. And also to get a look at the man who had been acclaimed the world's greatest flautist.' Wexford caught Mr Haq's eye for their coffee. 'Now Camargue,' he said, 'was the first person to cast a doubt on Natalie's identity, it was Camargue who started all this, yet it was Camargue himself who took Jane Zoffany for his daughter because it was *his daughter that he expected to see.*

'He had waited for nineteen years – eventually without much hope. Hope had reawakened in the past five weeks and he was keyed up to a pitch of very high tension. He opened the door to her and put his arms round her and kissed her before she could speak. Did she try to tell him then that he had made a mistake? He was deaf. He was carried away with emotion. She has told me she was so confused and aghast that she played along with him while trying to decide what to do. She says she was embarrassed, she was afraid to disillusion him.

'She humoured him by speaking of the Cazzini gold flute – which Natalie had possibly mentioned to her but which was in any case clearly labelled – and having no knowledge of Italian, she mispronounced the name. We know what happened then. Camargue accused her of imposture. But it was no dream of Camargue's, no senile fantasy, that his visitor confessed. Jane Zoffany freely admitted what she had been longing to admit for the past half-hour – but it did her no good. Camargue was convinced by then this was a deception plotted to secure Natalie's inheritance and he turned her out of the house.

'And that, Mike, was all this so-called imposture ever amounted to, half an hour's misunderstanding between a well-meaning neurotic and a "foolish, fond old man."'

While Burden experimented yet again with ice cream eau-de-Nil, Wexford contented himself with coffee.

'Natalie,' he said, 'came out of hospital on January 20th and she was so elated that the biopsy had shown the growth to be benign that instead of being angry she was simply amused by Jane's activities. As I've said, she had a very lively sense of fun. I think it must have tickled her to imagine the pair of them at cross-purposes, the wretched Jane Zoffany confessing and the irate Camargue throwing her out. What did it matter, anyway? She hadn't got cancer, she was fit and well and on top of the world and she could easily put that nonsense with her father right again. Let her only see if she could get a job out of Blaise Cory for her Johnny and then she'd see her father and patch things up.

'Before she could get around to that Camargue had written to her, informing her she should inherit nothing under the new will he intended to make.'

'Which led her,' said Burden, 'to plan on killing him first.'

'No, no, I've told you. There was no planning. Even after that letter I'm sure Natalie was confident she could make things smooth with her father. Perhaps she even thought, as Dinah says *she* did, that this could best be effected after the marriage. Natalie was not too concerned. She was amused. The mistake she made was in telling Fassbender. Probably for the first time Fassbender realized just how potentially wealthy a woman his girl friend actually was.'

'Why do you say for the first time?'

'If he'd known it before,' Wexford retorted, 'why hadn't he married her while they were both in California? That would have been a way of ensuring he didn't get deported. She was an American citizen. In those days, no doubt, she would have been willing enough to marry him, so if they didn't it must have been because he couldn't see there was anything in it for him. But now he did. Now he could see there was a very pleasant little sinecure here for the rest of their lives if only she wasn't so carefree and idle as to cast it all away.

'That Sunday Natalie went to a party with Jane Zoffany. She went because she liked parties, she liked enjoying herself, her whole life had been blithely dedicated to enjoying herself. There was no question of establishing an alibi. Nor, I'm sure, did she know Fassbender had taken himself off down to Kingsmarkham to spy out the land and have a look at the house and the affluence Natalie was apparently so indifferent to. It was on the impulse of the moment, in a sudden frenzy of – literally –

taking things at the flood, that he seized Camargue and forced him into the water under the ice.'

For a moment they were both silent. Then Burden said:

'He told her what he'd done?'

A curious look came into Wexford's face. 'I suppose so. At any rate, she knew. By the time of the inquest she knew. How much she cared I don't know. She hadn't seen her father for nineteen years, but still he was her father. She didn't care enough to shop Fassbender, that's for sure. Indeed, you might say she cared so little that she was prepared to take considerable risks to *defend* Fassbender. No doubt, she liked what she got out of it. Life had been a bit precarious in the past four years, hadn't it? Once rid of Ilbert, it was a hand-to-mouth affair, and one imagines that while she was in De Beauvoir Place she was living solely on the rent from her house in Los Angeles. But now she had Sterries and the money and everything was fine. I'd like to think it was his murdering her father that began the process of going off Fassbender for Natalie, but we've no evidence of that.'

'What I don't understand is, since she *was* Natalie Arno, why did she play around half pretending she wasn't? It was a hell of a risk she was taking. She might have lost everything.'

'There wasn't any risk,' said Wexford. 'There wasn't the slightest risk. If she wasn't Natalie there might be many ways of apparently proving she was. But since she was Natalie it could never possibly be proved that she was not.'

'But why? Why do it?'

Burden had never had much sense of humour. And lately, perhaps since his marriage, Wexford thought, this limited faculty had become quiescent. 'For fun, Mike,' he said, 'for fun. Don't you think she got enormous fun out of it? After all, by that time she believed there was no question of our associating Camargue's death with foul play. What harm could she do herself or Fassbender by just ever so slightly hinting she might be the impostor Dinah Sternhold said she was? And it must have been fun, I can see that. It must have been hilarious dumbfounding us by answering Cory's questions and then really giving me hope by nicking her fingers with a bit of glass.

'I said we were fools. I reckon I was an arch fool. Did I really believe an impostor would have had her instructor with her on the very morning she knew we were coming? Did I really believe in such an enormous coincidence as Mary Woodhouse leaving that flat by chance the moment we entered it? What fun Natalie must have got out of asking her old nanny or whatever she was to come round for a cup of coffee and then shooing her out when our car stopped outside. Oh, yes, it was all great fun, and as soon as it had gone far enough she had only to call in her dentist and prove beyond the shadow of a doubt who she was. For Williams is genuinely her dentist, a blameless person of integrity who happens to keep all his records and happens to have been in practice a long time.' Wexford caught Mr Haq's eye. 'D'you want any more coffee?'

'Don't think so,' said Burden.

'I may as well get the bill then.' Mr Haq glided over through the jungle. 'Once,' Wexford said, 'she had proved herself Natalie Arno to the satisfaction of Symonds, O'Brien and Ames, everything was plain sailing. The first thing to do was sell Sterries because it wouldn't do to have Fassbender show his face much around Kingsmarkham. But I think she was already beginning to go off Fassbender. Perhaps she saw that though he hadn't been prepared to marry her in America, even for the reward of legal residence there, he was anxious to do so now she was rich. Perhaps, after all, she simply decided there was no point in marrying. She hadn't done much of it, had she? Once only and she'd been a widow for nine years. And what would be the point of marrying when she now had plenty of money of her own and was happily independent? Still, this sort of speculation is useless. Suffice it to say that she had intended to marry Fassbender but she changed her mind. They quarrelled about it on the very eve of their going away on holiday together, and in his rage at being baulked of possession of the money he had killed for, had been to prison for, he attacked her and cut her throat.

'The body he put into that chest, which he locked, knowing it would be removed by Dorset's on the following day. Then off he went in the yellow Opel to Heathrow to use one of the two air tickets they had bought for their holiday in the South of France.'

Wexford paid the bill. It was modest, as always. By rights he ought, months ago, to have run Mr Haq in for offences under the Trade Descriptions Act.

He would never do that now. They walked out into the High Street where the sun had unaccountably begun to shine. The pavements were drying up, the heavy grey clouds rushing at a great rate away to the horizon. At too great a rate, though, for more than temporary disappearance.

The Kingsbrook tumbled under the old stone bridge like a river in winter spate. Burden leaned over the parapet. 'You knew Fassbender when we came upon him in that place in France,' he said. 'I've been meaning to ask you how you did. You hadn't seen him in America, had you?'

'Of course I hadn't. He wasn't in America while I was. He'd been back here for over a year by then.'

'Then where had you seen him?'

'Here. Back at the very start of this case. Back in January just after Camargue died. He was at Sterries too, Mike. Can't you remember?'

'You saw him too,' Wexford went on. 'You said when we spotted him, "I've seen him somewhere before."'

Burden made a gesture of dismissal. 'Yes, I know I did. But I was mistaken. I couldn't have seen him, I was mixing him up with someone else. One wouldn't forget that name.'

Instead of replying, Wexford said, 'Fassbender's father was a Swiss who lived here without ever becoming naturalized. I don't know what his mother was or is, it hardly matters. John Fassbender was born here and has dual nationality, Swiss and British, not at all an uncommon thing. Ilbert had him deported to this country in 1976 but of course there was nothing to stop him going back into America again on his Swiss passport. When Romero shopped him three years later he was sent back to Switzerland but he soon returned here. Presumably, he liked it better here. Maybe he just preferred the inside of our prisons – he'd seen enough of them.'

'He's got a record, has he?'

Wexford laughed. 'Don't happen to have your German dictionary on you, do you?'

'Of course I don't carry dictionaries about with me.'

'Pity. I don't know why we've walked all the way up here. We'd better take shelter, it's going to rain again heavens hard.'

He hustled Burden down the steps into the Kingsbrook Precinct. A large drop of rain splashed against the brass plate of Symonds, O'Brien and Ames, a score more against the travel agency's window, blurring the poster that still invited customers to sunny California.

'In here,' said Wexford and pushed open the door of the bookshop. The dictionaries section was down at the back on the left-hand side. Wexford took down a tome in a green-and-yellow jacket. 'I want you to look up a word. It won't be much use to you in your studies, I'm afraid, but if you want to know where you saw Fassbender before you'll have to find out what his name means.'

Burden put the book down on the counter and started on the Fs. He looked up. 'Spelt Fassbinder, a barrel maker, a maker of casks . . .'

'Well?'

'A cooper . . .' He hesitated, then said slowly, 'John Cooper, thirty-six, Selden Road, Finsbury Park. He broke into Sterries the night after the inquest on Camargue.'

Wexford took the dictionary away from him and replaced it on the shelf. 'His father called himself Cooper during the war – Fassbender wasn't generally acceptable then, on the lines of Beethoven and German Shepherds, one supposes. Fassbender held his British passport in the name of Cooper and his Swiss as Fassbender.

'That burglary was the only bit of planning he and Natalie did and that was done on the spur of the moment. It was a desperate measure taken in what they saw as a desperate situation. What alerted Natalie, of course, was Mrs Murray-Burgess telling Muriel Hicks she'd seen a suspicious-looking character in the Sterries grounds and that without a doubt she'd know him again. The only thing was, she couldn't quite remember which night. Natalie and Fassbender knew which night, of course. They knew it was the night Camargue drowned. So they faked up a burglary. Natalie slept in her late father's room, not to keep away from the amorous marauding Zoffany, still less to wound the feelings of Muriel Hicks, but to be in a room where she could credibly have heard breaking glass and seen the van's number.

'She had to have seen that to facilitate our rapidly getting our hands on Fassbender. Then Mrs Murray-Burgess could do her worst – it was a burglar she had seen and not a killer. In the event, he served four months. He came out in June, with two months' remission for good conduct.'

'I only saw him once,' said Burden. 'I saw him down the station here when we charged him.'

'With nicking six silver spoons,' said Wexford. 'Come on, the rain's stopped.'

They went outside. Once more a bright sun had appeared, turning the puddles into blinding mirrors.

Burden said doubtfully, 'It was a bit of a long shot, wasn't it? I mean, weren't they – well, over-reacting? They were supposing in the first place that Mrs Murray-Burgess would come to us and secondly that if she did we'd connect the presence of a man in the Sterries garden on an unspecified night with an old man's accidental death.'

'There was more to it than that,' said Wexford with a grin. 'She'd seen me, you see.'

'Seen you? What d'you mean?'

'At the inquest. You said at the time people would think things and you were right. Someone must have told Natalie who I was, and that was enough. I only went there because our heating had broken down, I was looking for somewhere to get warm, but she didn't know that. She thought I was there because at that early stage we suspected foul play.'

Burden started to laugh.

'Come,' said Wexford, 'let us shut up the box and the puppets, for our play is played out.'

And in the uncertain sunshine they walked up the street to the police station.

THE NEW WEXFORD CASE

The Monster in the Box

Ruth Rendell

Wexford had almost made up his mind that he would never again set eyes on Eric Targo's short, muscular figure. And yet there he was, back in Kingsmarkham, still with that cocky, strutting walk. Years earlier, when Wexford was a young police officer, a woman called Elsie Carroll had been found strangled in her bedroom. Although many still had their suspicions that her husband was guilty, no one was convicted.

Another woman was strangled shortly afterwards, and every personal and professional instinct told Wexford that the killer was still at large. And it was Eric Targo, A psychopath who would kill again . . .

As the Chief Inspector investigates a new case, Ruth Rendell looks back to the beginning of Wexford's career, even to his courtship of the woman who would later become his wife. The past is a haunted place, with clues and passions that leave an indelible imprint on the here and now.

arrow books

A WEXFORD CASE NOVEL

No More Dying Then

Ruth Rendell

The truth is never far from home

On a stormy February afternoon, little Stella Rivers disappeared – and was never seen again. There were no clues, no demands and no traces. And there was nowhere else for Wexford and his team to look. All that remained was the cold fear and awful dread that touched everyone in Kingsmarkham.

Just months later, another child vanishes – five-year-old John Lawrence. Wexford and Inspector Burden are launched into another investigation and, all too quickly, chilling similarities to the Stella Rivers case emerge.

Then the letters begin. Horrifying, evil, threatening letters of a madman. And suddenly Wexford is fighting against time to find the missing boy, before he meets the same fate as poor Stella . . .

'One of the best novelists writing today' P. D. James

arrow books

A WEXFORD CASE NOVEL

Murder Being Once Done

Ruth Rendell

She feared losing everything. And it left her with nothing . . .

It seems fitting that the final resting place of a girl's body should be in a graveyard. But this is no peaceful burial. This is a brutal murder scene.

On strict orders from his doctor, Wexford is sent to London for a break away from the pressures of the Kingsmarkham constabulary. But then he discovers his nephew Howard is heading the investigation into the macabre murder of Loveday Morgan, whose body was found abandoned in Kenbourne Cemetery.

Despite opposition from Howard and his team Wexford is drawn to the case. And when he unearths Loveday's connection to a religious cult whose leader was imprisoned for sexual abuse, he relentlessly pursues this sinister new lead . . .

'She can make a scene between two women sitting in a café as violent as anything you've seen between a couple of guys with baseball bats'
Mark Billingham

arrow books

A WEXFORD CASE NOVEL

Some Lie and Some Die

Ruth Rendell

Fame comes at a price

When the body of a brutally beaten girl is found in a quarry during a hedonistic hippy festival at Sundays near Kingsmarkham, Wexford is first on the scene. The victim's face has been pulped by the back end of a bottle, but who, in this atmosphere of peace and love, could be capable of such violence?

The body is that of local girl turned stripper Dawn Stonor, but it is the unlikely link between this ill-fated woman and the mysterious folk singer Zeno Vedast that piques Wexford's interest.

Through a web of lies and deceit Wexford uncovers a history of love and hate that began years earlier, and he realises that never has he witnessed a murder of such desperate passion . . .

'Ruth Rendell is streets ahead'
Sunday Telegraph

arrow books

A WEXFORD CASE NOVEL

Shake Hands For Ever

Ruth Rendell

Play with death. Deal with the devil.

Angela Hathall is found strangled in her bed but, shockingly, the death of this meek and solitary woman sparks little emotion from her husband. Called in to investigate, Wexford's curiosity only deepens when he discovers that the Hathall household has been meticulously cleaned but for a single distinctive palm print.

As the case develops Wexford is increasingly frustrated by the seemingly pointless nature of the murder. There is no motive, no weapon and no suspect. Nothing except the unidentified print.

But despite the sparse evidence, Wexford is convinced Hathall is hiding something. So when Wexford is taken off the case he decides to take matters into his own hands . . .

'Rendell gets into the mind not only of the hero, she gets into the mind of the villain'
Jeffrey Deaver

arrow books

A WEXFORD CASE NOVEL

A Sleeping Life

Ruth Rendell

Death is always solitary. For some, so is life . . .

On a sultry August evening, the bloody body of a middle-aged woman is discovered beneath a hedge by a small boy.

There are two things that surprise Wexford about the murder scene. One, that the only contents of the woman's handbag are some keys and a wallet containing nothing but some money. And two, how even in death, her deathly grey eyes possess a scornful glare.

The woman turns out to be Rhoda Comfrey, but there's no murder weapon, no apparent motive, and no one who actually cares she's died. Wexford's only hunch is that the clues to her murder must lie in her solitary London life. But her existence there becomes frustratingly impossible to trace.

'Intelligent, well-written, and with a surprising twist at the end'
Times Literary Supplement

arrow books

A WEXFORD CASE NOVEL

Means of Evil and Other Stories

Ruth Rendell

Innocence is in the eye of the beholder

What connects a kidnapped baby, a woman's body left to rot in a cove in Yugoslavia, a suspicious suicide and the century-old case of a wife who poisons her husband? The answer: Wexford.

In the first of five cases, Wexford is brought in to deal with a distraught mother whose baby girl has been swapped with an unknown baby boy. When a local priest discovers the missing baby, safe and sound, on the church steps, the hunt for the missing girl is quickly over.

Mother and daughter are happily reunited, but the mystery of the baby boy remains unsolved. Then Wexford discovers Paddy Jasper has returned to Kingsmarkham, a man previously investigated by Wexford for violently abusing a child. Now Wexford fears this reunion may not be as happy as the last . . .

'Full of ideas . . . as a page-turner there are few who can match Ruth'
Colin Dexter

arrow books

A WEXFORD CASE NOVEL

Not in the Flesh

Ruth Rendell

The past is a shallow grave

Searching for truffles in the woods, a man and his dog unearth something less savoury. The body has lain buried for ten years or so, and the post-mortem can not reveal the precise cause of death.

Wexford knows it will be a difficult job to identify the corpse. Although it covers a relatively short period of time, the police computer stores a long list of missing persons. People disappear at an alarming rate – hundreds each day.

When another body is found nearby, the detection skills of Wexford, Burden and the other investigating officers of the Kingsmarkham Police Force are tested to the utmost to discover whether the deaths are connected and to track down whoever is responsible.

'Gripping and memorable'
Sunday Times

arrow books

ALSO AVAILABLE IN ARROW

Portobello

Ruth Rendell

'Found in Chepstow Villas, a sum of money between eighty and a hundred and sixty pounds. Anyone who has lost such a sum of money should apply to the phone number below.'

The chance discovery by Eugene Wren of an envelope filled with banknotes would link the lives of a number of very different people – each with their own obsessions, problems, dreams and despairs. It would also set in motion a chain of events that lead to arson and murder.

'It is Rendell's superb sense of place that counts. She makes you smell the excitement and the desperation. *Portobello* is as brilliant as anything she has ever written' *Evening Standard*

'Rendell has a Dickensian empathy, informed by a prodigious love of London life. Her account, bursting with colour and vitality, is a treat to read'
Independent

arrow books